Detective Parker Bell Series

A SECRET TO THE GRAVE
WINTER WONDERLAND
DEAD OR ALIVE
LITTLE GIRL LOST
FORGOTTEN

Count to Ten Series

ONE
TWO
THREE
FOUR
FIVE
SIX
BURNING SECRETS
SEVEN
EIGHT

Christmas Romantic Suspense Series

CHRISTMAS HOSTAGE
CHRISTMAS CAPTIVE

I'd like to thank everyone who played a part in bringing this story to life. Particularly my mom who is always there to share her thoughts and opinions with me. My wonderful beta readers for giving me their insight. My awesome cover designer, Amy, who whips up covers for me so quickly and who patiently makes every change I ask for, and there are usually lots of them! And my lovely editor Mitzi Carroll, and proofreader Marisa Nichols, for all their encouragement and for all the hard work they put into polishing my work.

Eight

Jane Blythe

Bear Spots Publications
Melbourne Australia

bearspotspublications@gmail.com

Paperback
ISBN: 0-6484033-4-3
ISBN-13: 978-0-6484033-4-0

Cover designed by QDesigns

AUGUST 14TH

He was getting his family back.

Nothing was going to stop him.

He would kill anyone who got in his way.

Deacon Staines hid his car in the bushes. He wasn't sure what kind of security system they had here; for all he knew, there were cameras aimed at the extensive wooded area surrounding the house, but he couldn't worry about that. Even if the cameras did spot his car, he just needed enough time to get in there, get his wife and daughter, and then get back to the car. As long as he got back to the car with his family, then he didn't care if he got caught on camera.

He'd never been here before, so he wasn't entirely sure where he should be going. The place was big. Enormous. It was by far the fanciest hotel he'd ever seen, and he wondered how his broke wife could afford to stay here. She wasn't smart enough to get a job and support herself, and she had left with only the clothes on her back. How had she landed here?

And where exactly was here?

The Matilda Rose Women's and Children's Center; that was the sign he'd seen when he drove past. Center for what? Stupidity? Uselessness? Maybe this place wasn't a hotel. But what was it? Why would she come here? Why had she left in the first place? Deacon didn't understand. He had always provided for his family. He made sure they had a roof over their heads, clothes on their backs, and food on the table. What more did his ungrateful wife want?

She thought she could walk away; well, she was wrong.

If she hadn't taken his kid, then he might have let it go.

But *no one* took his kid from him.

His daughter was his. She belonged to him. She was his property, and no one was permitted to take his property. He *would* get her back. Both of them. And then he'd teach his wife a lesson for messing with what was his.

He loved his daughter, and he loved his wife. He didn't understand why she didn't see things the same way he did. Why would she leave him?

Why?

Why?

It was killing him that he didn't have an answer to that.

How was he supposed to put his family back together when he didn't even know what it was that had torn them apart?

All Deacon wanted was for things to go back to the way they had been before.

So how could he make it happen?

There had to be a way, and he had to figure out what it was because if his wife ran again, he doubted he'd be able to find her. It had taken him almost seven months to find her this time. It hadn't been easy. She hadn't taken her cell phone with her or any of her bank cards, so finding where she had squirreled herself away had been nearly impossible. It was only by pure luck that he'd found her. For the last seven months he'd been stalking all of her favorite places, hoping that eventually, habit would get the best of her, and she'd turn up at one of them.

And then, this afternoon, she had.

He had been sitting in his car outside her favorite bakery when he'd spotted her. He'd resisted the urge to go storming off in there and drag her back home because she hadn't had his daughter with her. Instead, he'd watched and waited. Then when she'd left, he had followed her all the way back here to this mansion.

Again, he had to enact an inordinate amount of self-control not to ram his car through the gates and then into the house to get her.

But now wasn't the time to be impulsive.

Now was the time to be smart.

So, he had studied the property, looking for a way to get in without being stopped. While he would kill anyone who got in his way, he didn't really want a string of dead bodies on his conscience.

The house was surrounded by thick woods, so he'd driven his car back here, parked it under the cover of the trees and was now hurrying toward the house. Deacon had no idea how he was going to find his family once he got inside; there had to be over a hundred rooms in there. Maybe he could use his gun, get a hostage, and demand to be taken to his family. Then, if he had no other choice, he'd kill whoever helped him find them and anyone else who got in his way.

The trees were starting to thin out; through them, he could make out the large building. With a place this big he was sure there were security cameras everywhere. They would, no doubt, spot him as soon as he got out of the woods.

This was going to have to be quick.

Every second that he was in the house he was at risk.

In and out.

As quick as he could.

That was the only way he was going to get away with what he wanted.

"Deacon Staines?"

The voice caught him by surprise, and he skidded to a stop.

A woman was standing just a couple of yards away. She was stunning, with long, silky black hair that tumbled over her shoulders and large violet eyes. As beautiful as the woman was, it wasn't her looks that left him staring at her in shock. It was the fact that she knew his name.

3

He didn't know her.

But she knew him.

A friend of his wife's?

Was she partly responsible for keeping his family from him?

He saw red.

Apparently, the woman saw it happening. "Don't do anything stupid, Deacon. Being here isn't a good idea. You're only going to make things worse. Please. I don't want to see anyone get hurt. Macey and Elle are finally doing well; don't mess things up for them."

Mess things up for his family?

How dare this woman say that!

Macey was *his* wife, and Elle was *his* daughter. *He* was what was best for them.

The woman seemed to sense that, too, because she pulled out a phone.

Deacon didn't think. He just acted.

The knife plunged deep into her belly.

She dropped.

He ran.

Time was not on his side.

He had to get his family.

Nothing and no one was going to stop him.

* * * * *

3:42 P.M.

Sofia Xander had a million things running through her mind.

As she walked into the living room at the women's and children's center that she had started with the money she inherited after her family was murdered, she took note of who was in there. It was something she always did. With so many women and children living here who'd fled violent situations, she made sure that she was always aware of what was going on.

The living room was the area where most of the people living here hung out. Teagan Vonce was over by one of the windows staring out it. She was in her sixties and had finally fled an abusive marriage after almost forty years. She'd been here only a week or so and hadn't really settled in yet. Sofia made a mental note to check in with her.

Amy Frankstone, a twenty-seven-year-old who had also fled an abusive relationship and who was struggling to kick an addiction to painkillers, was watching TV. Well, she was sitting in front of the TV, but it looked like she wasn't really paying attention to it. She had a blank, faraway look on her face that suggested she was lost in thought.

Nineteen-year-old Tara May who'd fled an abusive family only to wind up in an abusive relationship was curled up in a chair in the corner, a book in her hands. Tara was doing so well, Sofia was hoping that soon she would be ready to move out on her own and start her life.

And thirty-three-year-old Macey Staines was moving restlessly about the room. The woman had been here for around six months, and although she was doing well, her fifteen-year-old daughter Elle was struggling. Kimberly Ute was walking with Macey; the two had been friends before either of them got here. Kimberly was the one who had brought Macey and Elle here when they'd fled their abusive home. She was a nurse and had heard about this place from a colleague. Now she worked here; they liked to have an in-house nurse since a lot of the women and children arrived with injuries, or addictions. Because some were in hiding and didn't like to leave, it helped to have a nurse on site who could tend to anyone who was sick.

They were really making a difference in the lives of so many people. In the decade since this place was built, there had been hundreds of people to come through here—teenage runaways fleeing abusive homes, and women fleeing abusive relationships with their children. Here they found a safe place where they could get counseling, where they could learn new skills to help them become independent and be able to take care of themselves and their families, where they could start over.

She was living her dreams.

She was married to a man she adored, mother to two amazing children, and making a difference in people's lives. Even if she could, she wouldn't change a single thing about her life.

Well, maybe she'd change just one, teeny tiny little thing.

If it were possible, she would add in a few extra hours to her day.

There was just so much to do.

She had a huge charity event coming up in less than a month now. Yes, she had inherited a lot of money, as well as a lot of businesses. A lot of the money had been well invested and continued to bring in income, but running the center was expensive, so she supplemented it with donations.

This charity ball was the first one that her daughter was going to be helping with. She'd been surprised when her ten-year-old daughter Sophie had approached her and asked if she could help. Surprised, but in a good way. Sofia couldn't be prouder that her daughter wanted to step up and do what she could to help people.

Although she had grown up in a very wealthy family, Sofia had always known that something was missing. Her family was the very epitome of dysfunctional, and she had never really known what family meant until she'd met Ryan. Now she had a real family, one who loved her and cared about her, who supported her no matter what and who were there for her when she needed them.

Sofia checked her watch; it was approaching four. It was her evening to stay here and have dinner with whoever decided to eat in the large communal dining hall. She ran this place with three of her friends. She worked here full time as the main administrator; her friend Annabelle Montague ran the children's programs and the day care, and her friend and sister-in-law Laura Xander was the psychiatrist. Her friend Paige Hood worked full time as a cop and also taught self-defense classes for anyone who wanted to take one. They all took turns working a night a week and weekends. They wanted the women and children who came to stay here to know that they genuinely cared about every single one of them.

This wasn't just a job to any of them.

Each one of them had gone through their own struggles. They knew in part what these women and children were going through. They knew what it was like to fear for your life, to have to fight to get through each day, to feel lost with nowhere to turn. They all wanted to give the people who came through here that safe place to turn.

She set the stack of books that had been donated by a local library on the closest table and headed straight for Teagan Vonce. Sofia really liked the older woman and wanted to find a way to connect with her, help her settle in here. She was thirty-eight. Teagan was around the age her mother would have been had she still been alive. Sofia had never had a real mother and Teagan Vonce was exactly the kind of woman she would have wanted her mother to be like. Teagan thought she was weak, but the strength and courage it took her to walk away from an abusive marriage after so many years was more than Sofia thought she would have had.

"I waited too long," Teagan said softly as she approached, not taking her eyes off the view out the window.

"Too long for what?" she asked, joining the older woman at the window. It was a gorgeous summer's day. The sky was bluer than blue and reminded her of her husband's eyes, and the sunshine was warm without being too hot. Maybe once she got home tonight, if it wasn't too late, she and Ryan would take Sophie and Ned out to the park. She loved hanging at the park with her family. Especially after dark. Then walking back home with the stars twinkling overhead was priceless. Those moments with her family were what life was all about.

"Forty years I let him do that to me," Teagan said.

"But then you left," she reminded the woman.

"To do what?"

The hopelessness in the woman's voice told her what Teagan was thinking. After doing this for so long, she found it easier to understand where these women and their children were coming from. Carefully she laid a hand on Teagan's shoulder, she had learned from experience that a lot of the women who came here didn't like to be touched. "You can do whatever you want."

Teagan turned large brown eyes in her direction; those eyes were filled with so many emotions. There was the hopelessness, and the loss of identity that came with so many decades of being told that you were worthless, of not being able to figure out who you were. Teagan had married her high school sweetheart when she was only eighteen, she'd never had a chance to be Teagan Vonce. "It's never too late to live your life."

"I don't know what to do," Teagan said helplessly, tears brimming in her eyes.

"There are no right or wrong answers to that. You can do anything that will make you happy. It's never too late to make a difference in the world."

"Do you think ... that maybe I could ... that I could work here?" Teagan asked tentatively.

Teagan wasn't the first person who'd lived here to ask that. This had become a safe place, and a lot of the women and their children who stayed here became reluctant to leave. But Sofia felt that Teagan was different. She believed the woman might really be able to become an asset to their team and make a difference here. She was about to tell the woman as much when she heard a commotion behind her.

An ear-piercing scream had her turning toward the door.

Her heart was already picking up speed, her stomach already

plummeting. She knew that kind of scream; she'd heard it before, she had even given one of those screams before.

With two children she'd heard all kinds of screams from stop tickling me, to joy, to excitement, to pain, to abject terror.

This scream fell into the abject terror category.

As much as she didn't want to, she had to know what was going on, and as she turned, she caught sight of something that ramped her fear up several notches.

A gun.

There was a huge man storming through the room, gun in hand.

He was heading straight for Macey Staines—the one who'd screamed.

This had to be Macey's husband.

The man who had beaten her and her fifteen-year-old daughter so badly they had been hospitalized.

Somehow, he had tracked them down.

Somehow, he had gotten past the security guard.

Now he was here.

With a gun and a look in his eye that said he was out to kill anyone who tried to stop him from getting his wife and daughter back.

* * * * *

3:58 P.M.

Ten-year-old Sophie Xander danced down the halls.

She was so excited for the charity ball.

It was still three weeks away, but she and her mom had already started shopping for a dress. There was one she wanted but her mom had said it was more than she wanted to pay for a dress that Sophie was probably only going to wear once. She and her best friend Hayley had been brainstorming ways to convince her mom to buy it for her. It was so beautiful—blue satin—and she felt like a princess when she wore it.

Sophie didn't understand why her mom didn't just buy the dress. Her mom was rich even though she pretended she wasn't. They lived in a regular, three-bedroom house. She didn't go to private school, and her dad was a police detective. She knew her mom didn't pay herself much for all the work she put into running this place.

But she had a bad habit of listening in when grown-ups were talking, and she knew that her mother had more money than she could count. Why shouldn't she have the dress she wanted? She wanted to look beautiful for the charity ball; she wanted to help her mom raise money for the boys and girls and their mothers who came to live here. She knew she was lucky to have parents who loved each other and who loved her and her brother, and she wished that every kid in the world could have that too.

Sophie spun in circles just like she'd learned to do in her ballroom dancing classes. Her mom had said that if she wanted to help with the ball, then she had to learn how to dance like people did at balls.

She wasn't usually a girly girl. She much preferred to play in the mud and climb trees. She loved being a tomboy, but more than that, she loved being her. She could be a tomboy and still love dancing and getting all dressed up in a ball gown and have her hair done and wear makeup.

Her parents always told her to be herself; some people weren't going to like you because of it, but you can't control what other people thought. All you could control was you, so be the best, kindest, most thoughtful you, you could be. *You be you* was her mom's favorite saying, and it was something that even at ten Sophie was comfortable doing. She didn't care what other people thought. She didn't care if the other kids at her school liked her or not. She had lots of friends, and the kids who didn't like her probably weren't kids she wanted to be friends with anyway.

She paused at the door to the library and looked inside hoping to find her mom, but the room was empty.

Where was she?

Sophie really wanted to convince her mom to let her get the blue dress. Sure, she might only wear it once or twice, but this was the first time that she was going to really help with this place besides just playing with some of the kids who stayed here. She wanted to do so much more. She wanted to run this center with her friends when her mom retired just like mom ran it with her friends.

This was her legacy.

She was so proud of her mom for building this place. They were saving so many people's lives and giving them a second chance they wouldn't have if they'd not come to live here and be safe. Figure out what they wanted to do with their lives.

Maybe Mom was in the living room. Sophie was sure that if she told Mom how proud she was of her and how she wanted to run this place when she was grown up, she could persuade her to buy the dress.

Not that it wasn't true, because it was, but telling her would make her happy, and happy people were more likely to do things that they usually wouldn't.

She skipped down the hall and turned right, heading for the living room where her mom probably was. She was so excited, and she couldn't wait to get all dressed up and then stand up in front of everyone to give her speech at the ball. She wanted everyone to know how important this place was. Since her dad was a cop, she knew better than most kids her age that most people who got themselves into a bad situation never got out of it. But here, they could. Here, they could get their second chance, and she didn't want that to change. She wanted this place to be around forever, to get bigger so they could help save even more people, and she was so thrilled that she got to be a part of this.

Sophie was just about to open the living room door when she

got a feeling in her stomach.

It was something she'd never felt before.

It was a swirling sort of feeling that kind of made her feel sick, and she started to tremble.

Something was wrong.

She knew it.

She just didn't know what.

She had been told lots of times before that, although this was a safe place, there was always a chance that one of the husbands or fathers might track down the women or children who ran from them.

Was that what had happened?

What should she do?

Should she go try and get help?

But what if she was wrong?

What if her weird feeling was just because she was trying to convince her mom to get her something she'd already been told she couldn't have?

Or what if she was just imagining things?

She was just a kid—not a cop, like her dad. She didn't know anything about trusting her instincts.

She had to know what was going on.

Cautiously, she curled her fingers around the door and inched it open.

Inside was a man with a gun.

And her mom.

Her mom was in there.

Sophie knew she should close the door and run before the man with the gun realized she was there, but she couldn't move.

She was frozen in place, her eyes riveted on the gun.

She'd seen guns before, of course, her dad was a cop and he'd taught her mom to shoot, she even knew where the gun safe was at their house. This was different. This was a stranger, probably one of the men who had beaten his family until they'd had no choice but to leave everything behind and flee, holding a gun on her mom and a room full of innocent people.

She had to get help.

She had to stop him.

She wished her dad were here.

Tears burned the backs of her eyes, and she hoped she wasn't going to start crying. If she made a sound, he would see her; it was only by some miracle he hadn't already.

The man was shouting something at everyone when suddenly her mom looked right her way.

Their eyes met.

For a moment, panic coursed through her mom's silvery gray eyes, and Sophie knew it was fear that the man with the gun would notice her.

She and her mom had the same eyes.

It struck her that she could lose her mom. That man could kill her mother. She might never walk out of that room alive.

What would life be like without her mom?

Sophie couldn't imagine it.

Her mom held their family together.

She was … *Mom.*

Then her mother's eyes cleared, and instead of broadcasting fear, they clearly said *run, get help.*

She heard it as clearly as if her mom had spoken the words out loud.

Sophie blew her mom a kiss, knowing it could be the last one she ever gave her, then carefully eased the door closed and ran.

Without really thinking about it, she headed for the daycare room. It was just a little farther down the hall, and she didn't know if the man had hurt anyone else along the way, so it was probably safer to go there. Annabelle would be there, and as confident and mature as she had always thought herself to be, she knew she needed grown-up help right now.

"Annabelle!" She rushed to the woman as soon as she entered

the daycare room.

Reading the panic on her face, Annabelle came toward her and wrapped her in a hug when she reached her. "What's wrong, honey?"

"There's a man with a gun in the living room," Sophie said in a rush. Then her voice started to tremble. "My mom is in there."

For a moment, Annabelle just looked at her in shock, then she sprang into action. Grabbing one of her babies, Annabelle shoved it into Sophie's arms. "Take the babies and go to the safe room. Lock yourself in there and don't come out until your dad or your uncle or Xavier comes to get you, okay?"

Just like that, it was so good to hand over control to someone else, someone who knew what to do. "Okay," Sophie agreed, taking Annabelle's other baby and balancing the twins in her arms.

Annabelle kissed both of her four-month-old babies' heads and then kissed her head too, shoving her gently in the direction of the safe room.

With her ears straining to hear for any gunshots, she took JP and Katie with her and went and locked them all inside the safe room. They were safe now, but her mom wasn't and the twins' mom wasn't and neither was anyone else who was in that room with the man with the gun.

Sophie began to cry.

* * * * *

4:04 P.M.

The world kept fading in and out.

Laura Xander knew she was badly hurt.

Very badly.

So badly she wasn't sure that she was going to live.

She couldn't think of that right now though. She had to get help. She had been taking her daily walk through the woods surrounding the women's and children's center where she worked. If she didn't make it a point of forcing herself to spend time outdoors each day then her agoraphobia started to strangle her, crushing the life out of her. She had been just about to head back inside when she'd seen the car. There shouldn't be any cars back here, so she'd immediately gone to see what was going on.

When she had seen Deacon Staines she knew exactly what was going on; she just hadn't known how to stop it.

Deacon had run off after he'd stabbed her. That he was here to get his family was obvious. That he would hurt anyone else who got in his way was also pretty evident.

She had to stop him before anyone else got hurt, or worse.

Her sister-in-law Sofia was still in there, as well as her ten-year-old niece, and one of her closest friends Annabelle, and Annabelle's four-month-old twins, plus at least a dozen of the nearly one hundred people who were currently living at the Matilda Rose Women's and Children's Center.

She had to save them.

She had to.

Only the world was fading away into nothingness again.

Sometime later she slowly emerged from the darkness into a world so full of pain she almost wished she would pass out again.

Pain wasn't something that was new to her. She had lived through a four-day-long ordeal where her attackers had tortured and raped her, but this was something on a whole different level.

This was the kind of pain that said that death was coming for her.

If she stayed here, she was facing certain death.

She had to move.

Laura believed she was too far away from the house to be able to get to it, but she had to try.

She couldn't just lie here and die.

She could never do that to her family.

Her husband Jack and their two children, seven-year-old Zach and five-year-old Rosie were her life. She loved them with every fiber of her being. They had saved her. After her ordeal, she had locked herself away, no longer able to face the world. But slowly they'd taught her to live again. They gave her confidence and strength when she didn't have any of her own. They were her reason for living, and she couldn't leave them.

The knife Deacon Staines had used to stab her was still embedded in her stomach. As much as she wanted to yank it out, it was probably the only thing keeping her alive right now. It was like a plug preventing her from bleeding out, and if she took it away, she was as good as dead—probably within minutes.

Already she was feeling the effects of blood loss, but she had to ignore it.

Move.

That was all she had to focus on.

Standing was out of the question; she was too weak, and if she attempted it and fell, she could push the knife in deeper, hastening her death.

Laura wasn't even sure that crawling was an option.

That only left dragging herself along the rough ground.

She'd been right here before.

Different location, same struggle.

Out in the woods, alone and hurting, fighting with everything she had for her life.

Last time she had lived—just—but, she had survived.

She prayed this time she would too.

Balancing on her side, Laura dug her fingernails into the dirt, and using all the strength she still possessed, she pulled herself forward.

Pain tore through her like there was something inside her trying to claw its way out.

Tears streamed down her face, and she screamed—the only outlet she had for her pain right now.

Her voice was weak, and the sound wouldn't have carried far.

No one would have heard it unless they had already been close enough to see her anyway.

Her eyes wanted to close; her body wanted to give in to the pain and fade away, but she fought against it.

She had to clear her mind.

Just like she had done when the Garrett brothers were torturing her.

Clear her mind.

Think of nothing but keeping moving.

No pain.

No fear.

Nothing.

Move.

Just move.

Time blurred … the world blurred … she didn't see anything … she didn't hear anything … she didn't even feel anything. She knew besides the stab wound she was causing herself other injuries by dragging herself over rocks and sticks and tree roots, but she didn't care. She didn't have time to care.

Laura was only moving an inch or so at a time, and with every inch of ground she covered, she got closer and closer to the end of her rope.

The world was graying around the edges.

She wasn't even halfway to the tree line, and she'd only been no more than ten yards in when Deacon had stabbed her.

She was quickly losing hope.

As her hope faded, so did her strength.

She couldn't do this.

Despite her best efforts to keep up a wall around everything but moving, it was starting to crumble.

She hurt so bad, and knowing that her husband was soon going to be a widower, that her children would grow up without a mother, was too much to bear.

She didn't want to die.

She didn't want to leave her family.

She wanted to watch her children grow into the strong, compassionate adults she knew they would be and grow old with the man she loved at her side.

She had fought so hard to get her life back, and now, she was going to lose it because of one angry, violent, abusive man who wanted to regain control over the family he had lost.

"I'm sorry, Jack," she whispered aloud as she sank down against the dirt.

It was over.

She couldn't keep moving, and down here in the woods no one would find her until it was too late.

Laura could no longer hold her eyes open.

Her whole body was shaking, and she was cold—so cold.

Every shiver sent pain slicing through her from top to bottom.

She began to feel like she was floating.

It was like someone had tied a bunch of helium balloons to her limbs, and they were slowly lifting her up toward the sky. But she didn't want to go because going to the sky meant going to death.

Her ability to think was fading.

Now she just felt.

So much love for her family, almost more than she could hold inside her. She prayed that they would be okay without her.

"I love you," she murmured as she finally floated away.

* * * * *

4:14 P.M.

"Ryan, do you see that?" Jack Xander asked as they headed toward the car they'd seen partially hidden in the woods surrounding the center where his wife worked.

As much as Jack respected his wife's job and what she did to help people save themselves, he hated that it kept her in a perpetual state of danger. He knew that Laura didn't always like or appreciate his sometimes over-the-top protectiveness, but it was who he was. Nothing was more important to him than his wife and his children, and no one messed with them and got away with it.

Both he and Ryan had the center's security system linked to their phones, so when they got an alert to say that one of the sensors had picked up a car coming through one of the back gates, they'd dropped what they were doing and come straight here. The property his sister-in-law had inherited was over fifty acres and a lot of that was woodland. If one of the abusive husbands or fathers of the women seeking refuge here had somehow managed to track them down, then that's where they would likely try to break in, so they had set up security at all the gates.

"There?" his younger brother asked, pointing to something lying on the ground just up near the tree line.

As they got a little closer, he saw what it was. "Ryan, it's a body."

They both started running, and when they got even closer Jack skidded to a stop.

The bottom fell out of his world.

He had expected the body to be the wife or child of the man who had broken in here, but it wasn't.

The body was his wife.

"Laura!" he yelled as he ran to her and dropped to his knees at her side.

Without even thinking, his hands went straight to her neck to search for a pulse.

She had one, but it was so weak that it didn't really reassure him.

Her entire front was drenched in blood.

The wooden handle of a knife protruded from her stomach.

She must have stumbled upon whoever had broken in, and

he'd stabbed her to get away.

"Jack?" Ryan sounded panicked.

"Call an ambulance," he ordered his brother.

"Is she …"

"She's still alive. Just."

He was shrugging out of his shirt to cover her icy cold body with when his wife began to stir.

"Laura?" He cupped her face in his hand and gently traced his fingertips across her dirty, tearstained face. In his mind, he knew that this was what she must have looked like when she'd been saved from the four-day-long ordeal that had almost claimed her life while she was in college. Although they had known each other all their lives and dated all through high school, they'd broken up before they graduated. It was during that time that Laura had been abducted and nearly killed.

"Jack?" The sound was the merest hint of a whisper and was absolute music to his ears.

"Right here, angel," he assured her. "Just hold on, an ambulance will be here soon." He just prayed it would be here soon enough. She might be awake for the moment and talking to him, but he knew her injuries were serious. Serious enough that she might not recover from them.

"This knife," she murmured, and before he could stop her, her hands went to grab it, presumably to pull it out.

"Laura, no." Jack wrapped his hands around hers and stilled them. If she pulled the knife out, she'd bleed out before help could arrive. That knife was the only thing keeping her alive right now. "Don't touch it, sweetheart," he said, brushing her hair off her clammy forehead and tucking it behind her ear.

"It hurts," she whimpered, her large violet eyes fluttered open and met his for a moment before falling closed again.

His wife was the toughest, strongest person he knew; evidence of that was right before him. There were drag marks leading from the direction they'd come to here. She'd tried to get to help. If he knew her, and he did, then she didn't just want help for herself but also for everyone who was inside the center and no doubt in danger from whoever had broken in here.

Ryan's wife and daughter were in there.

Along with at least a dozen other innocent people.

If it weren't for the fact that his kids were on summer vacation and had planned a trip to the local water park, then they would be in there, as well.

"Jack, get it out, please," Laura begged, her hands trying to break free of his grip to get to the knife and wincing at every movement, which he was sure tugged on the blade lodged inside her belly.

"I can't, sweetheart. I'm sorry." He hated to see his wife in pain. He would much rather throw himself into a vat of burning acid than see his wife or his children suffer. He rolled up his shirt and circled it around the knife. Then he ripped at the hem of Laura's purple dress so he had something to use to secure the donut bandage and limit how much the knife could move as well as helping to keep pressure on the wound to stem the blood flow as much as they could.

Ryan joined them, using his own shirt to drape over Laura to try to keep her warm. His gaze darted constantly from Laura to the house where his wife and ten-year-old daughter were. His brother wanted to go running in there, but they couldn't, not until they knew what they were dealing with.

"Angel, did you see who hurt you?" he asked, taking hold of Laura's blood-coated hands again, partly to make sure she didn't attempt to pull out the knife and partly because he just needed to maintain physical contact with her right now.

"H'gn, gt C L. Kl'm." Her words slurred to the point that he couldn't even understand what she was trying to say. She was so cold, so close to death. If he didn't have to remain calm to keep Laura as calm as possible, then he would be in a blind panic right now. He wanted to fix his wife. He wanted to track down the man who had hurt her and tear him limb from limb. He wanted to do *something*, anything; he hated feeling impotent, and right now he felt like the most useless person on the planet.

"Honey, what does that mean?" Ryan asked, sounding every bit as helpless as he felt.

They didn't get an answer.

Laura made a gurgling sound and went still.

Panicked, Jack felt for her pulse again, found it bumping weakly and erratically against his fingers.

Where was the ambulance?

"Jack, I have to go in there." Ryan was already standing and reaching for his gun.

"You can't. We have no idea who hurt her, what they're after, or what's going on in there." He would go with his brother, but he couldn't leave Laura alone. If she didn't make it, he couldn't live with himself knowing that she died alone.

Before he had to make a choice, they heard footsteps approaching.

Jack angled his body protectively over Laura's, and Ryan put himself between them and whoever was approaching.

"Annabelle?" Ryan asked.

"Ryan? Thank goodness. Oh," Annabelle broke off when she got closer and saw Laura. "Did Deacon hurt her?"

"Deacon?" Ryan asked.

"Deacon Staines. He's the abusive husband two of our residents ran from. He's in there … He has a gun … I saw him on the surveillance system—he's in the living room. He killed the security guard," Annabelle said in a rush, joining him at Laura's side.

"Sofia and Sophie?" Ryan asked tightly.

"Sophie's okay. She's the one who told me what happened. She's in the safe room with the twins." Annabelle sounded conflicted about having left her infant children inside there, but she'd done the right thing. They were safe. There was no way to get inside the safe room unless the person inside there opened the door and let you in. His niece was a smart kid. She knew what to do and she would make sure that she kept herself and the babies safe.

"Is Sofia in the living room with Deacon Staines?" Ryan asked, his tone saying he already knew the answer.

Annabelle nodded. "I don't know how he found them, but he obviously knows his wife and daughter are here and he wants them. I don't think he's leaving without them, only Elle isn't here. She went to the water park with the other kids. When he finds out that he can't get what he wants …" Annabelle trailed off.

She didn't have to finish her sentence.

They already knew what would happen.

When Deacon Staines realized he couldn't walk out of there with his family, then he was going to start killing people.

* * * * *

4:19 P.M.

"Where is she?" Deacon screamed, shaking his wife.

Macey just stood there and trembled, staring up at him with those big brown eyes. Her eyes had been the first thing he had ever noticed about her.

They'd met for the first time when they were in middle school. They'd fought likes cats and dogs but secretly he had liked Macey. There was something so engaging about her—she was effervescent and charismatic, and even at eleven she had been drop-dead gorgeous. Macey had been his first kiss, a quick peck on the lips under the bleachers in the school auditorium.

After the kiss, his family had moved for his mom's new job and things with Macey had been over before they ever had a chance to go anywhere. Over time, she had moved to the far recesses of his mind, but she was always there.

Deacon had always known that Macey was his. There had never been any question about that. When they had met again after graduating high school they had immediately reconnected, picked things up like they hadn't spent five years apart. They'd married while still in college. They'd had their daughter, bought a house, lived their lives, and then it was all just over. Macey had taken Elle and left.

Where had things gone wrong?

How had they gotten to this point?

Deacon's attention was drawn to the other end of the room where people were trying to get to the door.

No.

He wasn't having any of that.

If people got out, they would tell someone he was here. The cops would come, they'd arrest him, and he would lose his wife and daughter forever.

"Nobody move!" he screamed.

Everyone froze, but several of them still looked like they were prepared to make a run for it.

Without hesitation, he aimed the gun at the ceiling and fired off several shots.

One of the women began to sob, while a pretty redhead herded them all into the far corner.

That was fine.

They could stay as far away from him as they could get. He couldn't care less about any of them, but if they tried to stop him, he wouldn't hesitate to kill them just like he'd killed the lady in the woods and the security guard who had accosted him at the door.

He was wasting time, reminiscing about better times with Macey, worrying about the others. None of that mattered. He had to find out where his daughter was and then take his family and leave.

"Where is she, Macey? I'm not asking you again," he threatened. If it came down to it, a choice between his wife and his child, then his daughter would win. He wanted to walk out of here with both, as the family they were meant to be, but he would sacrifice Macey if she gave him no choice.

"Elle isn't here," the redhead said, tentatively inching closer.

Not here?

Macey had not only left him but abandoned his daughter as well?

"What did you do with her?" He screamed so loudly the sound hurt his ears. He shook Macey so hard she moaned in pain but didn't try to get out of his grip.

"It's okay," the redhead piped up. "She just went out with the other kids to the water park."

The water park?

So, she had been here, but she wasn't right now. She'd obviously be back soon, but would it already be too late by then? His timing couldn't have been worse. After six months of trying to track down his family, he finally did, but when he came to claim them, only one of them was here.

"You're Deacon, right?" The redhead again, and she was still inching closer. Apparently, she was the only person in the room who wasn't afraid of him.

How did she know him?

Who was she?

His head was pounding, making it difficult for him to concentrate. He had a lot of headaches these days. They made functioning difficult. Sometimes he couldn't remember things properly. Sometimes people said and did things and he had no idea why; it was like a large piece of his day just vanished into oblivion.

"Deacon? Maybe you could put the gun down and we could talk," the woman suggested.

That snapped him back to reality.

Maybe this woman was a shrink.

Was this place some kind of hospital?

He couldn't let his guard down.

Shrinks were always trying to trick you.

He had one focus, one reason for being here, to get his family. That was all that mattered to him.

"No talking," he growled. "I want Elle."

"I'm really sorry, but she's not here. They won't be back for at least another hour or so. If you put the gun down, we can sit down and wait for them. I'm sure your daughter misses you."

Of course, she did.

Elle was his flesh and blood.

Blood was thicker than water.

Blood conquered all.

He would get his daughter, but putting his gun down wasn't the way to do it. As soon as he was unarmed, they would pounce on him.

Trust no one.

That was his new motto.

Once you'd been betrayed by the woman who had pledged to love and support you for better or worse, for richer or poorer, in sickness and in health, until death do they part, then you no longer had faith in anyone.

"Macey, come over here," the redhead said.

His wife attempted to wiggle free from his grip.

If he let her go, it was over.

He could never get his family back.

Deacon grabbed a handful of Macey's long brown locks as she tried to flee and yanked her backward and up against his chest, jerking a pained squawk from her lips.

He wasn't a monster; he didn't like hearing the woman he loved in pain. Knowing that he had caused it took a little piece of his heart and burned it up.

But Macey obviously didn't care about hurting him.

If she did, she would never have taken his daughter away from him.

With an angry growl he shoved his gun to her temple and wrapped his arm across her neck, taking a small amount of pleasure in the fact that she clawed at his forearm as it crushed her neck, cutting off her air supply. When he felt her start to go limp in his arms, he loosened his hold. He didn't want to kill her; he just wanted her to understand how badly she had hurt him.

"There's no need to hold the gun against your wife's head, Deacon. You're scaring her. If you feel like you need to hold on to her, okay, but put the gun down," the redhead ordered.

Who was this woman?

She seemed to have no fear.

He had a gun and yet she spoke to him as if she were the one with all the power.

Well, she was wrong.

He had the power, and he wasn't afraid to use it.

"Stop telling me what to do," he yelled.

She held up her hands, palms out. "I'm sorry, Deacon. I don't mean to try to tell you what to do. I just want to make sure we all walk out of here alive."

"Stop using my name; you don't even know me." It unnerved him every time this stranger called him by name. She was doing it to try to confuse him, and it was working.

"You're right, I don't know you, but I've gotten to know Macey and Elle over the last six months, so I've heard a lot about you."

She had heard a lot about him?

Why?

What had his wife and daughter been saying about him behind his back?

"You've made mistakes, Deacon, but it's not too late to fix them."

Made mistakes?

What mistakes had *he* made?

The only thing he had done wrong was trusting that his wife

would remain faithful and loyal.

"I haven't made any mistakes," he snapped. This woman was really grating on his nerves. If she didn't stop, he'd just fire a bullet through her head, drag his wife out of here, track down his daughter, and take them both home.

"Laying your hands on your wife was a mistake, but it's one you can fix."

Lay his hands on his wife?

He would never do that.

Ever.

Okay, he had his hands on her right now, but this was just self-preservation, so the three of them could go back home together.

How dare this woman even suggest such a thing.

"Take. That. Back." He bit out each word.

"I saw the bruises she had when she got here, Deacon," the woman said quietly. "Macey had a lot of them. All over her body. Some of the worst I'd seen, and I've been working with women and children who were abused for the last ten years."

Abused?

Women and children who were abused.

That's what this place was.

A place where abused wives fled with their children to get away from the men who beat them.

His wife had told these people that *he* beat *her*.

That was the most insane thing he'd ever heard in his life.

He had worked hard, long fourteen and fifteen-hour days so that Macey could stay home with Elle before she started school. He worked weekends so he could take his family on vacations around the world. He had gone to every single one of Elle's parent teacher conferences, every dance recital, every baseball game. He'd helped her with her homework and taken care of her when she was sick. He took his wife out for surprise dates; he bought her jewelry and flowers; he held her hand; he listened to her when she wanted to talk, and he'd never even so much as looked at another woman since they'd gotten together.

And this was how he was repaid.

"I never hit my wife," he screamed.

Why had Macey lied?

Why had she come here?

He'd seen her the morning she'd left, and there hadn't been a bruise on any inch of that perfect, smooth skin.

Whatever his wife had told these people wasn't true.

"Tell them," he raged, slamming the barrel of the gun into Macey's temple. "Tell them I never hurt you. Tell them I never laid a hand on you. Tell them I never left any bruises on your body." Deacon shook her as he spoke. He had never been this angry in his entire life. It felt like there was a volcano in his belly that was erupting and spewing red hot angry lava all over the place, filling him up until he had no choice but to let it burst out.

"It's okay, Deacon, it's okay," the redhead soothed. "We can figure this out, we can. We can do whatever we have to, to make sure you get to see your daughter. We can get you the help you need so you don't hurt the people you love again."

Help.

He didn't need help.

He didn't want help.

All he needed and wanted was his family back and this woman was getting in the way of that happening.

Pointing the gun in the redhead's direction, he fired.

* * * * *

4:26 P.M.

Gunshots.

As Ryan Xander and his partner—who he had called as soon as he heard what Annabelle said was happening inside the center—made their way to the living room at the women's and

29

children's center that his wife ran, he heard the unmistakable sound of gunshots.

"Ryan, don't," his partner warned. They had been partners for a decade now and were good friends as well as working together, and they usually knew what the other was going to do before they did it. And right now, his partner knew that all he wanted to do was go running in there, regardless of the consequences, to make sure that his wife had not been the recipient of the bullet fired.

It was killing him that his wife and his daughter were in danger. He wanted to go and see Sophie, convince himself that she was, in fact, all right. But Annabelle had said that she was safe, and the safe room was probably the safest place she could be right now. It didn't open from the outside once someone had gone in there so there was no way anyone could get to his daughter.

This place might be a shelter for women and children who had experienced violence in their home, but that didn't mean that the center was a secret, a place for people to hide out in anonymity. Everyone knew about this place. The attackers of some of the people who came to live here were already in prison, or the break had already been made and they just needed help starting over. Some of them had moved hundreds of miles to finally break free of their tormentors. But some had recently run, and their husbands were still out there. They posed the most risk to everyone. Because everyone here had fled for their lives, there had always been a chance that one of the people they were running from would come looking for them, so they had built the safe rooms. Twelve, in fact, spread throughout the building.

Sophie was safe, but Sofia wasn't.

So right now, his focus had to be his wife.

She was the one being held hostage in a room with a violent, abusive man hell-bent on getting back the family he had abused.

"We have no idea what we're going to walk into," Paige reminded him.

His partner was right.

Annabelle had told them who the man was who currently had six women held hostage at gunpoint. And they knew how dangerous Deacon Staines was. Ryan's sister-in-law Laura was being rushed to the hospital in critical condition, and Colton Vires, the security guard who had the misfortune of working today, had been shot once through the head, killing him instantly. Ryan knew that Deacon would shoot Sofia or anyone else who got in the way without a second thought.

"Okay." He tried to calm his racing heart and drew in a long, slow breath in an effort to calm himself. "We go in slowly, see if we can talk him down." It was risky for them to go in there because they'd essentially be giving Deacon Staines two more hostages, but Ryan wasn't waiting for a hostage negotiator to arrive. He didn't care about protocol or anything but getting his wife out of there alive.

"I should go in. You stay out here; you're too emotionally invested," Paige said.

"No," he replied simply. He got what she was saying but nothing was stopping him from going in there. Besides, Paige and Sofia were very close friends, so she wasn't really much less emotionally invested than he was.

Paige sighed but didn't offer any more protests. Instead, the two of them hurried down the last couple of yards of the corridor to reach the living room.

As he pushed open the door, he saw Sofia huddled on the ground.

His bubbling hysteria was quickly calmed when he heard Deacon Staines snarl, "Next time you can't keep your mouth shut, that bullet goes right through your brain."

Sofia was alive.

And if he knew his wife, which he did, she had been trying to talk Deacon down. Sometimes Ryan both loved and hated his wife's confidence and compassion. It made her both an amazing wife and mother as well as amazing at her job. But it also sometimes got her into risky situations, like this one. She should be hanging back, not drawing any attention to herself. She was all but shoving herself front and center into Deacon Staines' dangerous game.

The man's attention was—for the moment—focused on both Sofia and Macey, who he held pinned to his chest. Ryan took advantage of that and took a moment to scan the room and see where everyone else was. He made it a point of knowing every single one of the hundred or so people who lived here at any one time. He saw Tara May, Amy Frankstone, Kimberly Ute, and Teagan Vonce. Of the four women, he thought the oldest, Teagan Vonce, was the most likely to panic and do something that would get her hurt or killed. He knew that she was struggling to settle in and hadn't yet bonded with anyone because she hadn't been here very long.

Apparently deciding he had taken care of Sofia for the moment, Deacon had returned his attention to his wife and was shaking her violently.

"Tell me where my daughter is," Deacon screamed.

It was time to make their move.

Guns drawn, he and Paige entered the room, Paige went to stand between Deacon and where the rest of the women minus Sofia and Macey were huddled down one end of the room. He slowly made his way down to the other end of the room; if he could, he wanted to get himself between Sofia and Deacon.

"Put your weapon down, Deacon," Ryan ordered, aiming his own weapon directly at Deacon's forehead.

Deacon started. He'd obviously been distracted and never even noticed them entering the room. Now that he was up close, he could see that the man's green eyes were wild. Off the charts wild. Ryan had seen a lot of angry criminals, a lot of high or drunk ones, and a lot of mentally disturbed ones, and Deacon appeared to be a mix of all three.

"Go away," Deacon screamed at him, seemingly undeterred by

having a gun pointed at his head. It was like the fact that he was armed never even registered.

"I can't do that, Deacon," Ryan said.

"This doesn't concern you."

"My wife is in this room; this concerns me."

Deacon's gaze darted to Sofia, who had climbed to her feet and moved a little closer to him. "You should teach your wife to keep her mouth shut," he growled. "She's full of lies. She said I beat my wife. I never laid a hand on her."

Ryan knew that wasn't true. He had been here the day Macey and her fifteen-year-old daughter Elle had arrived and both had been covered in bruises. But Deacon seemed so earnest, like he honestly believed he'd never laid a hand on his wife. He was trying to figure out just what he was dealing with here. Maybe Deacon suffered from some sort of mental illness. It could certainly account for the differing stories and the seemingly disassociation Deacon was displaying.

He decided it was best to play along with Deacon right now; try to calm the man down and get him to relinquish his weapon and let them walk him out of here without anyone getting hurt. "Then let's figure this out, let's prove that you're right."

"We can do that right now, if Macey would just tell the truth," Deacon retorted, giving his wife another sharp shake.

"Don't tell him you can get him help," Sofia whispered behind him.

He didn't need to ask more. If Sofia told him not to say that, then he wouldn't; no doubt she'd already said it to Deacon without good results.

"Tell them, Macey! Tell them! Tell them now."

Deacon was devolving before his eyes. It wasn't going to be long before he did something they would all regret, but with Macey in between them, it made taking a shot risky.

"Just calm down, Deacon; this isn't the way to do this," Ryan said, sensing that Macey was losing control just as quickly as her husband was. If she started to freak out, then Deacon was likely to shoot her and then as many of the rest of them as he could before either he or Paige could kill him.

"No. I just want Macey and my daughter. They're mine. You can't stop me from taking them home." Deacon eyed him defiantly, like a child demanding to have his way.

"Elle's not here right now," he said. "Maybe we could go and wait for her downstairs." It looked like it was working, like Deacon was finally considering giving up.

"No." Fire suddenly flashed through Macey's brown eyes and she began to struggle in her husband's grip. "You stay away from my daughter. I won't ever let you lay a hand on her again."

* * * * *

4:32 P.M.

Detective Xavier Montague jumped out of his car and scanned the crowd that had gathered outside the Matilda Rose Women's and Children's Center where his wife worked.

The last seven months he'd been working virtually night and day on a cold case, using every spare second he had between his current heavy caseload, and helping his wife with their four-month-old twins. He and his partner, Jack Xander, had wrapped up a case this morning, and once he'd finished his paperwork, he had put a couple of hours into tracking down a dangerous man who abducted teenage runaways and forced them to provide him with babies he could sell on the black market.

He'd been following down the best lead he'd had so far when he'd received a phone call.

The kind of phone call everyone dreaded.

A phone call to say that there was an active shooter at the place where his wife worked. Not only was it where his wife worked but it was where his children attended day care. Since his wife ran the children's program here at the center, it just made sense financially and because they would both rather look after their kids themselves than pay someone else to do it.

Now he was wishing his kids and his wife were anywhere but here.

He had always known there was the possibility that one of the abusive husbands might track their runaway wife down here and come for them, but he had never really thought it would happen.

Where was Annabelle?

There were people everywhere.

Most of the residents of the center were out today, taking the kids on a trip to the local water park since the weather had been so hot lately. It seemed that the buses that had driven them there had returned and now everyone had spilled out into the street. There were several cop cars parked here as well, and the cops were milling about making sure no one got too close to the building. They weren't exactly sure what was going on in there yet beyond the fact that a man named Deacon Staines had tracked down his wife and daughter to get them back. He'd killed a security guard in the process and critically injured Jack's wife Laura.

Xavier knew that Annabelle wasn't still inside the house but knowing that didn't negate his need to see her.

He was a hairsbreadth away from just starting to scream her name until she heard and came to him when he spotted her. She was over to the side, a little away from everyone else, standing under a tree, leaning against the trunk with her eyes closed.

It was like somehow the connection they shared alerted her to his presence and she straightened and scanned the crowd until she found him.

Their eyes met and for a moment neither of them moved.

They just stood there and stared at one another.

She was alive and unhurt. She was lucky. If Deacon Staines had found her she would either be dead like the security guard, fighting for her life like Laura, or trapped inside as a hostage like Sofia and the others.

Instead, she was out here safe and sound and whole.

Xavier didn't remember moving. The next thing he knew, he was at Annabelle's side, snatching her up into his arms and crushing her against his chest.

He held her tightly and let the feel of her soak through his skin and inside him. Annabelle was his heart, and sometimes it was hard to let your heart, the very essence of your being, walk around outside your body. He tried not to play the overprotective husband too often. His wife was strong—the strongest person he'd ever met—even if it had taken her a while to learn that. He didn't need to worry about her. She was smart and tough and resourceful, and she knew how to keep herself safe. If she couldn't, then she knew how to minimize the danger until she could find a way to escape or help arrived.

But this time, disaster had been averted. She had been able to get out before Deacon even knew she was in there.

"Where are JP and Katie?" he asked, looking around but keeping his wife close. It was unlikely that given what had just happened Annabelle would let them out of her sight, so they must be close by.

Annabelle shuddered against him, and Xavier felt his heart rate pick up. Something was wrong.

"What?" he asked.

"They're still in there," she said in a small voice. There was self-deprecation in her tone as well as fear as though he was going to be angry with her, and it reminded him of when they'd first met. Back then Annabelle hadn't had any self-confidence and had always been scared of saying or doing the wrong thing. They'd worked through those issues together, but sometimes when she was under extreme stress or pressure, she reverted to old patterns of behavior and thinking.

"Why?" he asked, probably a little harsher than he should

have. He didn't blame his wife, but the thought of his infant children in there with a dangerous man in possession of a gun was beyond terrifying.

"Sophie came running into the day care room saying there was a man with a gun holding her mom and some of the others hostage. I didn't know if he was going to stay in there. I didn't know who it was or what he wanted. I couldn't risk carrying them through the center to get out. If he found us, I'd be unable to protect us carrying two babies. I told Sophie to take the twins and go into the safe room off the day care room. I told her not to come out unless someone she knew came for her." Annabelle looked up at him anxiously, expecting the worst and trying to prepare herself for it.

There was nothing he could say to ease her fears right now. She was a mother who knew she had left her children in a dangerous situation even if it had been the best and safest option at the time. There might not be anything he could say to make her feel better, but maybe there was something he could do.

Xavier took Annabelle's chin between his thumb and forefinger and tilted her face up, brushing his lips across hers. "You did the right thing," he whispered.

"Are you sure?" Annabelle's pale blue eyes—so pale they appeared white—searched his, seeking reassurance.

"I'm sure," he promised, and gave her another kiss. "I'll go in and get JP, Katie, and Sophie."

"No, Xavier," Annabelle exclaimed, her fingers curling into his shirt and clawing convulsively at him. "It's too dangerous. Ryan and Paige went in, and I heard gunshots. I don't want anything to happen to you."

"It won't," he promised and prayed he wasn't lying.

"Then if you're going in, I'm going with you," Annabelle said, resolutely straightening and tugging herself from his arms.

"No," he said simply. That wasn't happening. He was a trained police detective; he knew what he was doing. Annabelle knew how to shoot a gun because he'd insisted on teaching her, and she knew a little self-defense, but that was it. He wasn't risking her safety by bringing her into a dangerous situation with him.

"It's not up for discussion. Let's go." She held out her hand. "Give me your backup, and I can cover you."

This was crazy.

He should tell her no, handcuff her to this tree, and take one of the cops here in with him. But Xavier didn't. Instead, he pulled out his backup and handed it over.

"You stay behind me at all times," he warned as they headed for the house. They circled around and went in the back. The place was huge, well over a hundred rooms, and right now it was deadly quiet in here. As much as the cop part of him wanted to go and see if there was anything he could do to help Ryan and Paige, the dad part of him needed to get his children to safety.

Being a father was still new to him. He was forty-two, and he and Annabelle had been together for a decade, but before he met Annabelle he'd been married. His ex-wife Julia had delivered a stillborn baby girl and that loss had left with both a hole in his heart and a longing to have children of his own one day. The day his son and daughter had been born was one of the best of his life, equaled only by the day he married the woman he loved.

Now he led that woman into the fire. They didn't really know what was going on in here besides Deacon Staines had a gun and wasn't afraid to use it.

On hyper alert, Xavier crept along, taking more time than was strictly necessary to reach the day care room but going on the *better safe than sorry* philosophy.

Eventually, they were at the nursery door and his restraint vanished. Annabelle's too.

They both ran for the door to the safe room that was hidden behind the storeroom. There was no way for them to open it, assuming Sophie had closed it properly, and knowing what a smart kid she was, Xavier knew she would have.

Pressing the intercom, he said, "Sophie, it's Xavier and Annabelle. Open up, honey."

He and Annabelle both waited anxiously to see if Sophie was going to comply, and after possibly the longest eight seconds of his life, the door swung open and Sophie's tearstained face peeked out.

"Where's my mom and dad?" the little girl asked.

"Your dad is working on getting your mom and the others out safely," he assured her as Annabelle ducked past them and scooped the babies off the couch.

Bringing Sophie with him, Xavier joined his wife and children, wrapped his arm around Annabelle, and kissed his son and daughter's soft little heads. JP opened his big brown eyes, then beamed and gave a gurgley laugh when he saw his daddy. His son was such a smiley, happy baby. He had smiled early around a month old and started laughing by two and half months and hadn't stopped yet. Katie also opened her eyes and reached out her little hands toward him. His daughter wasn't as smiley and laughy as her twin brother, but she was a cuddler and loved nothing more than being cradled in her mommy or daddy's arms.

His family meant the world to him. They were his everything—his life, his heart, his soul—there wasn't anything he wouldn't do for them. Now they were safe and together again. They just had to make sure Sophie got the same outcome.

* * * * *

4:41 P.M.

Jack Xander sat on the floor outside his wife's hospital room clutching the photograph of his family that he kept in his wallet.

It was a recent photo, taken just over a month ago at his family's big annual Fourth of July picnic. His kids were growing so fast that even in the last month they had changed a lot.

His five-year-old daughter had lost her first tooth, an event that had been almost earth shattering in her little world. Rosie had been convinced that all her teeth were going to fall out and she would never get new ones, and that the rest of her would start falling apart as well. It didn't matter how many times they told her that the tooth would grow back and that she wasn't going to fall apart. It didn't matter that they told her that her big brother, her older cousins, he and Laura, and every other adult on the planet had all had their baby teeth fall out, she wasn't to be comforted. It wasn't until the new tooth had started to grow in that she had finally believed them.

His seven-year-old son was going to be starting second grade in just a couple of weeks. Zach was already so excited. He loved learning and practically inhaled books; they downloaded a new one onto his Kindle every second day. To Zach, books were a special kind of magic that transported him to other worlds and let him do things he could never otherwise do. Jack wouldn't be surprised if he became an author when he was older.

Every second he spent with his wife and his kids was precious, but it was so easy to take things for granted. If he had known what was going to happen today, he wouldn't have rushed out of the house this morning without kissing his wife goodbye just because he was in a hurry to get to work because he and Xavier had been on the brink of closing one of their cases.

Now he might never get to kiss her again.

Laura was in critical condition.

By the time the paramedics had shown up, she'd been barely breathing. She had lost so much blood—more than a person should lose and still live.

He and Laura had the same blood type, and he'd donated in the ambulance on the ride here, but even he could see it wasn't enough.

How was he going to tell the kids what had happened to their mother? How was he going to raise them on his own if Laura

40

didn't survive? Zach and Rosie were strong. Zach had battled pneumonia as a young baby, spent almost two months in the hospital, but his little fighter had survived. And his little girl was every bit as tough as her namesake. Rosie had been named after his old partner who had died protecting Laura. Laura had gone into premature labor and delivered their daughter over a month early, but Rosie had been amazing, surprising even the doctors with how well she had done and how quickly she'd been able to go home. His kids were amazing; every day they surprised him.

Raising their kids was something they were supposed to do together. Every step of the way they'd been a team. He didn't want to have to do this alone.

"Jack."

He started at his name. He'd zoned out, blocking out everything that was happening around him.

His youngest brother Mark—a trauma surgeon—stood above him.

His brother's face said the news wasn't good.

He shoved the picture back into his pocket and scrambled to his feet.

Although he hadn't wanted to leave Laura's side, he'd been dragged away from her once they reached the ER. Not being able to see her and touch her was hell. Not knowing what was happening made him feel so helpless. Laura was his wife. It was his job to take care of her, protect her, keep her safe, and now she'd been stabbed and was fighting for her life.

"Jack."

He blinked. He'd zoned out again. Now Mark was watching him with a worried expression. His brother's expression only added to his fears. If Mark was looking at him that way, then something was wrong. "Did you see Laura?" he asked.

"Yes."

"And?"

"And they're about to take her up for surgery."

"And?" Why was his brother suddenly so reluctant to share information? "How bad is she, Mark?"

His brother's gaze dipped to the floor, a sure sign he didn't want to answer that question. Which in and of itself was an answer. But he needed more. He needed to know every single detail, no matter how bad things were. The less he knew, the more he panicked. Reality surely couldn't be any worse than what his over-burdened mind was conjuring up.

"Why don't you head up to the surgical waiting room," Mark said, blatantly avoiding his questions.

"Aren't you operating on her?" There was no other doctor he would trust more with his wife than his brother.

"You know I can't. No operating on relatives is the hospital's policy."

As well as Laura's brother-in-law, Mark and Laura were also very good friends. He and his family had lived across the street from Laura and hers when they'd been kids, so they had all known each other their entire lives. They had gone to school together, spent their summers playing together, celebrated holidays together. Laura had been a part of his life for as long as he could remember, and he couldn't—nor did he want to— imagine his life without her in it.

"Can't you make an exception this one time?" he asked his brother. "I need you in there, Mark."

Mark looked undecided, but then nodded. "I'll see what I can do. Maybe I can assist."

Jack nodded. His attention was now riveted on the blood staining Mark's hospital scrubs.

Laura's blood.

It was all over him as well. In addition to his clothes, his shoes, and his hands, it was smeared over his face.

He knew he should wash it off. One of the nurses had brought him a wet towel at one point but strange as it was, he couldn't bring himself to clean up. This could be all he had left of Laura, and for some reason, he couldn't make himself wash it away.

"Mark, is she going to make it?" His voice wobbled on the last word.

"She's hanging in there," Mark said vaguely.

"I need to know. No sugarcoating things. Is Laura going to survive?" he demanded, more forcefully than he should have since he knew his brother was only trying to protect him, but he didn't need protecting right now. He needed answers. He needed to start preparing himself for the worst if the worst was what he should be expecting. Hanging in limbo wasn't helping him.

His brother sighed, long and hard, and when Mark spoke, his voice was rough with emotion. "I don't know, Jack. Right now, it's very touch and go. She's hanging in there, and we all know how tough she is, but it doesn't look good. She's lost a lot of blood, and she's already coded once."

His own heart stopped beating when he heard that.

Laura had been dead.

His wife had been dead.

Dead.

If she hadn't been revived, it would already be over; he would already have lost her.

"Is she going to make it through surgery?"

"There's no way to know for—"

"Mark."

"The odds aren't in her favor. I'm sorry, Jack." Mark looked devastated.

"What are her chances?" He wished he didn't have to torture himself, but he had to know. Every single horrible detail.

"I'd give her a twenty or thirty percent chance of making it through. I'm sorry, Jack," Mark said again.

Twenty or thirty percent.

That meant there was a seventy or eighty percent chance that she was going to die.

"Can I see her?"

"I don't think that's a good idea. They're taking her up for surgery any minute now."

"I need to say goodbye, Mark. This might be my only chance to tell her I love her one last time while she's still alive."

"She might not even be conscious, she's been in and out. And even if she is awake, she's doped up on drugs and she's lost a lot of blood. She might not even be aware that you're there let alone able to hold a conversation."

"I don't care. I just need to tell her."

"Okay." Mark nodded and stepped to the side so Jack could get to the door.

He had seen his wife in a hospital bed before, but still, he was unprepared for what he saw when he walked into her room. Laura was wearing a blood-soaked hospital gown and the floor around the bed she lay on was stained with her blood. She was hooked up to various machines, and she was wearing an oxygen mask, which he took to be a good thing. At least she was still breathing on her own.

Despite that, her eyelashes fluttered on her cheeks as the door whooshed closed, and then a moment later, he was looking into her big violet eyes.

"Hey, angel." He pasted on a smile as he went to the bed and took her hand.

"Jack." Her voice was so soft, so weak. He wished there was a way to infuse her with his strength, his life.

"I'm right here. I love you, Laura." His heart broke as he said the words, and he prayed it wasn't for the last time.

Her expression grew focused, and she squeezed his hand. "Deacon."

"We know, sweetheart. We know it was Deacon who stabbed you." He wasn't going to tell her that Deacon was now holding eight people, including Sofia, hostage, and that Ryan and Paige were trying to talk him down before anyone else got hurt.

She shook her head, but before she could say more, her eyes

began to droop closed. Her grip on his hand tightened. "Daughter. Deacon's daughter," she murmured.

Jack had no idea what she was trying to tell him, but it didn't really matter. Deacon Staines would be stopped one way or another, and then his wife and daughter would be safe.

Laura's eyes suddenly opened again, and they locked onto his. "I love you, Jack," she said, and then she was gone.

* * * * *

4:49 P.M.

Deacon was never going to give up his weapon and walk out of here.

Sofia was positive about that.

She just prayed that Sophie had gotten to safety. Her heart had stopped when she'd seen the door open and her ten-year-old daughter standing there. If Deacon had seen her, he wouldn't have let her go, and the thought of one of her children in danger made her blood turn to ice.

She wished Ryan hadn't come in here. She knew he couldn't stand back and do nothing with her in danger, but now if something happened, they could both wind up dead leaving their children to grow up as orphans.

It was only by a fluke that the place was this empty today. If this were any other day, there would have been dozens of innocent people here. Usually, they had around a hundred residents at any one time. A large portion of those were children, so most of them attended school during the day. Some of the adults worked various jobs that they were able to procure for them, but others weren't at that stage yet and spent their days here, studying or attending therapy sessions with Laura, or just recovering from the hell they had lived through. Sofia thanked God that all but a handful of the women and children who lived here were out today at the planned excursion to the water park.

Otherwise, Deacon would have had so many more victims.

Since there was no way he was going to walk calmly out of here, the only way he'd be leaving was in a body bag.

Paige was down at the other end of the room, between the other women and Deacon.

Ryan was trying—unsuccessfully—to calm Deacon down and convince him to give himself up.

One or the other of them was going to have to end up shooting Deacon when he lost it enough to turn his gun on one of them.

"I never laid a hand on Elle!" Deacon screamed in response to Macey's accusation that he had hurt their daughter and that she would never allow him to do it again.

"You hurt me, and you hurt our child!" Macey screamed back. Although she'd been in shock at first, lolling like a ragdoll in her husband's grip as he shook her and screamed at her, now it seemed like she had sprung back to life with a vengeance and had obviously adopted the attitude that if she was going down, she was going to go down in flames.

"I never touched her," Deacon growled, ramming his gun repeatedly into Macey's temple.

Sofia didn't know if Deacon had been abusing Elle or if it had been a one-off. The girl had had some bruises when she and her mother arrived, but Elle had never mentioned anything about her father hurting her—not that that meant it hadn't happened. Macey had been very protective of her daughter ever since they came here, not really letting anyone get close to her. She had been reluctant to let the teenager attend the local school, and Sofia had been surprised when Macey had allowed Elle to go to the water park today with the other kids and that she hadn't insisted on tagging along to keep an eye on her daughter.

"You left bruises on her that took weeks to heal," Macey returned.

"Stop saying that." Deacon looked like a wild man, his eyes were manic like he'd already lost touch with reality. Maybe that was what had led him to be violent with the family he claimed to love.

It didn't matter how many times Deacon claimed he'd never laid a finger on his wife, it didn't make it true. She knew Deacon had beaten Macey. She *knew* it. She had seen the bruises.

This was going nowhere.

Macey was going to keep insisting that Deacon had hurt them, and that's why she had fled with their daughter, and Deacon was going to keep denying it.

"You had no right to take my daughter from me," Deacon yelled. "She's mine. She belongs to me."

Sofia couldn't count the number of times she'd seen or heard violent abusive men talk about their families like they were nothing more than possessions. She supposed in some way it made it easier to hurt them if you just viewed them as things.

"Put the gun down, Deacon, and we can sort this out," Ryan inserted, trying to diffuse the situation.

"I'm not going anywhere until she admits she's nothing but a liar," was Deacon's response.

"Then at least let everyone else go, then you and Macey and I can talk this through," Ryan suggested.

Sofia felt her heart clench at that.

She didn't want to walk out of this room without her husband. She knew that Ryan was a cop, and this was his job and that he was perfectly capable of protecting himself, but that didn't mean she didn't worry about him. Particularly in situations like this. Deacon was so dangerous because he was so irrational and unpredictable. But Ryan wasn't thinking about himself and his personal safety right now. It was his job to ensure that no one else got hurt, and his focus was getting her and the other women out of this room.

"No," Deacon said. "No one leaves. No one moves. I need to

think, and I can't think when you're distracting me." He scrunched his eyes closed and then shook his head as though he was trying to dislodge something from his brain. Sofia was convinced that the man was unbalanced, whether from mental illness, drugs, or alcohol she had no idea, but she didn't see an end in sight to this standoff.

With Macey in between him and Deacon, the chances of Ryan being able to get a shot off were slim, and Deacon pretty much kept his gun shoved against Macey's head, except for when he shook her in anger. Even if he could get a clean shot, Ryan would only take it if there were no other options.

But, by then, it would be too late.

If Deacon realized that he wasn't getting his wife and daughter back, then he was going to try to take out as many of them as he could before the cops shot him.

There had to be something she could do.

Right now, Deacon had forgotten about her. She was partially hidden behind Ryan, and although he clearly didn't like her since she had made the mistake of suggesting he needed help—he liked his wife a whole lot less, and Macey was the focus of all his attention and rage.

All of a sudden, she knew what she should do.

Given that she had been harassed by a relentless stalker for over five years, she was extremely safety conscious. Her stalker had still been at large while this place was being built, and she and Ryan had thought it was a good idea to not only build several safe rooms but also several secret cavities where weapons could be stowed. There was one in each of the common rooms but not in the bedrooms. No one knew about them except for her and Ryan, Paige, Annabelle and Xavier, and Laura and Jack. So long as Deacon's attention remained riveted on Macey and Ryan, he shouldn't notice her making her way to the secret safe or know what she was doing should he notice her crossing the room.

As surreptitiously as she could, she started to move toward the

TV which hung on the wall behind Deacon. Underneath the TV was a cabinet with an array of DVDs, and hidden in a compartment just behind it, was a gun.

Ryan noticed the second she moved out from the relative safety of being blocked behind his body. Paige, too, stiffened and watched her every move, but luckily, Deacon was too busy bickering with his wife to pay her any attention.

With every passing second, Deacon was growing more and more unhinged. It wouldn't be long before he turned his weapon on Macey, himself, or one of them.

She had to make it to the gun.

Unless he moved out from behind Macey's body, neither Ryan nor Paige were going to be able to take him out until it was already too late. But she didn't want anyone to die, and if she could stop it from happening, then she would.

Sofia knew how to shoot a gun. Ryan had taught her. He'd tried to anyway, but he'd made her too nervous, and in the end, it had been Paige who'd successfully taught her how to load, aim, and shoot to hit her target. She knew the theory and she went with her friends to the range to practice once a month, but she had never had to do anything like this before.

Could she do it?

Would she hit her target?

What if she got Macey by mistake?

If there was any way to avoid this, she would, but every single person who came to her center was her responsibility, and she wouldn't let anyone hurt them.

Aware of Ryan shooting daggers at her, clearly telling her to stop what she was doing and get herself someplace safe, she ignored him and knelt to retrieve the gun.

"Bring me my daughter right now," Deacon demanded.

"I can't do that," Ryan replied.

"Then I'm going to start shooting people," Deacon threatened. He didn't give anyone time to do anything. It was as though he believed they should conjure his daughter out of thin air and present her to him instantaneously. When no one could do that, he started firing.

Without hesitating, Sofia spun, aimed, and fired.

* * * * *

5:06 P.M.

The sound of the guns going off seemed unnaturally loud.

For a moment, Ryan wasn't sure who had fired and who had been hit and wildly scanned the room needing confirmation that Sofia was alive and uninjured.

When he saw that she was standing and not drenched in blood, his mind settled, and he was able to start assessing the scene.

Deacon lay unmoving in a heap on the ground in an ever-growing pool of blood.

Macey stood above him screaming.

Paige was kneeling on the ground above one of the other women who'd been held hostage. It looked like twenty-seven-year-old Amy Frankstone.

Some of the other women were crying, some were screaming, but Paige seemed to have that under control.

He ran to Deacon Staines, kicking the gun away from him then yanking the man's arms behind his back to handcuff him. Deacon was already dead, he could see that, but he was restraining the man nonetheless.

With Deacon taken care of, he turned his attention to Macey Staines who was still screaming. Grabbing hold of the woman's arms, he gave her one brisk shake. There was blood on her, and he needed to know if any of it was hers.

"Macey."

At her name, she slowly shifted her eyes from her dead husband to meet his. She was shaking badly, already going into shock.

"Are you hurt?"

His words didn't seem to register through the fog she was clearly swamped in. She just stared blankly back at him.

"Macey, there's blood on your clothes. Is it all Deacon's or are you hurt as well?" Ryan spoke slowly, carefully enunciating each word to try to make sure she understood what he was saying.

Her eyes cleared a little and she spoke softly, "I-I-I don't think so. Is-is Deacon d-dead?"

"Yes, he is," he replied gently. He was sure the woman had mixed feelings about her husband, but part of her probably still loved him and would feel his loss.

He had to get Macey out of here. She no doubt wanted to see her daughter. He had to check on Paige and the other hostages to see who was hurt, how badly, and how everyone else was doing. He had to let everyone know that the hostage situation was ended.

And he had to hug his wife.

He was simultaneously fiercely proud of her and furiously angry with her. She should have stayed behind him where she'd be relatively safe, not put herself in danger by sneaking across the room to retrieve a gun. It was a miracle Deacon hadn't noticed her. She had known that neither he nor Paige had a clear shot at Deacon, so she'd risked herself to get into a position where she could take him out if need be. If she hadn't, who knew how many of them Deacon would have shot before they were able to kill him.

Ryan put his arm around Macey to lead her away from her husband's dead body when his gaze landed on Sofia.

He had expected her to have put the gun down, gone to get help, or gone to see what she could do for Paige and the other women.

But she hadn't.

She was standing right where she'd been when she fired. The

gun was clutched so tightly in her hands that her knuckles had turned white, and her eyes stared unblinkingly at Deacon's dead body.

Sofia was in shock.

He should have expected that. She had just taken a life, and no matter how justified, of course, it would affect her. He needed to go to her, comfort her, but he also had to get Macey out of this room.

Torn, he was going to quickly get Macey into the hall, then go to his wife, when Paige appeared beside him.

"I'll take her," his partner said, slipping her arm around Macey. "You go to Sofia."

He didn't need to be told twice.

Ryan approached his wife slowly. She was in shock and still holding a weapon. He didn't want to startle her and wind up shot.

"Hey, cupcake." He used the cheesy nickname his dad used to call his mom when he was a kid and which he occasionally called Sofia. She said she liked it, but he always felt it was too corny for a man of forty to call his thirty-eight-year-old wife, so these days, it was usually the nickname he used with Sophie and Ned.

Sofia didn't respond.

She just stood there and stared blankly into space.

"Sweetheart, it's Ryan," he said as he put his hand over hers and gently pushed down, so the gun now pointed at the floor. Carefully, he extracted it from her grip and tucked it into his waistband. Then he took both of her icy hands between his and began to vigorously rub them.

His touch finally seemed to rouse her, and she murmured, "I killed him."

"You saved every person in this room," he corrected. "You knew we didn't have a shot; that's why you got to the gun." For the first time ever, he was thankful to Sofia's stalker for something. If she and Paige hadn't been stalked by the same man when they'd been building this place, they probably never would have put in the safe rooms and the secret compartments. If they hadn't, then his daughter wouldn't have had a safe place to hide, and Deacon could have shot and killed them all.

Abruptly, Sofia straightened and pulled her hands out of his grip. She began to yank her long red hair into a ponytail, compulsively combing her fingers through her hair, smoothing it repeatedly before finally securing it with the hair tie.

"Are you okay?" he asked, surprised by her sudden and unexpected attitude change.

"I'm fine," she said briskly. "What about everyone else?"

"It looks like Amy might have been hurt," he answered, still trying to figure out what was going on inside his wife's head.

She paled when she heard that. "I wasn't quick enough," she said quietly, more to herself than to him he suspected. "Did Deacon hurt anyone else?" she asked before he had a chance to try to offer her some comforting and encouraging words.

As much as Ryan didn't want to tell her about Laura and the security guard, it was inevitable that she was going to find out, so he may as well just tell her and get it over with. "He killed Frank," he told her gently.

"Oh no." Her hands flew to her mouth and her silvery gray eyes grew wide.

"And he hurt Laura."

Sofia gasped. "Hurt? How badly?"

Bad enough that he wasn't sure she was going to live. Apparently, that was clear on his face because Sofia paled further.

"Poor Jack. We have to go and see her."

She turned and started for the door, but he caught her wrist and turned her around to face him. "Are you sure you're okay?"

"Fine," she answered shortly.

"Sofia, I—"

"I said I was fine," she snapped irritably.

Okay, well, she clearly wasn't fine; that was plain for all to see. When they went to the hospital to check on Laura, he'd get one of the doctors to check her out. She was obviously in shock.

Ryan hated not being able to help the woman he loved.

"You did the right thing, Sofia." He brushed the back of his hand across her cheek, tucking a lock of hair she'd missed behind her ear. She stood completely still, and when he put his arms around her and tried to draw her into a hug, she pushed him away.

"Where's Sophie?" she asked.

Trying really hard not to be hurt that she was pushing him away, he answered, "She went to the nursery and Annabelle had her hide in the safe room there. I assume that Xavier went in and got her so she's probably waiting with him and Annabelle outside."

"I want to see her." With that she turned and hurried out of the room.

He followed her through the house that was quickly filling with cops and EMTs, wanting to see his daughter every bit as much as his wife did. Maybe that was what she needed, to reassure herself that Sophie was all right. Hopefully, once she saw that their little girl was okay, she'd realize that if she hadn't done what she did, then their children could have lost one or both of their parents.

Ryan wasn't used to seeing his wife this way. Sofia was the warmest, sweetest, nicest, most compassionate person he knew. Seeing her cold and distant was disconcerting. It was like the foundation his world was built on had suddenly shifted, and he felt like he had back when they'd first met. Back then, he'd felt inadequate when it came to saying and doing the right thing for the woman he loved because he had failed his first love and been unable to prevent her from committing suicide. Sofia had helped him gain his confidence back, but in one instant, everything had changed. Sofia was hurting, and he didn't know how to help her or if he even could.

"Mommy."

As soon as they got outside, Sophie must have seen them.

Obviously, everyone knew that the threat had been neutralized because no one tried to stop Sophie as she came running across the grass toward them.

When she reached them, she flung herself into her mother's arms, and Sofia dropped to her knees and clutched Sophie close, both of them crying.

Tears were good.

Tears meant that she was feeling, and feeling was what she needed to do right now. She couldn't lock her feelings away. She had to acknowledge them if she was going to work through them.

Feeling better, Ryan knelt beside his wife and daughter and pulled them both into his arms. They were all alive. Everything else, they could deal with together.

* * * * *

8:29 P.M.

Mark Xander lingered at the door.

Part of him wanted to go in there, check on his sister-in-law, make sure she was still alive, but part of him dreaded it. He didn't want to have to go out to the surgical waiting room and tell his oldest brother that the chances of his wife surviving were slim.

His family had been through enough. They didn't deserve any more misery. Both his older brothers had followed in their father's footsteps to become cops, and the women's and children's center that his sisters-in-law ran helped so many people. They all spent their lives helping others. It shouldn't end this way.

He knew what must be running through his brother's head right now. The fears, the what ifs, the wondering how he would raise his two young children as a single father if his wife didn't make it.

Mark had been there.

Seven months ago, he and his family had lived their own

personal hell. When his wife's past had come crashing into her present, she had withdrawn from him and their family believing it was the only way she could keep them safe. Daisy had been ready and willing to sacrifice herself to protect him and their children, and while he was in awe of her strength, he was so glad that things hadn't ended up that way. While he understood why she had made the choices that she had, the damage to their relationship had required them to work hard to get back what they'd had before.

Now everything was going so well. They were happy, wounds had healed, trust had been rebuilt, and he had believed that the worst of life was behind them.

Now his family was suffering again.

He would do anything to make things better.

But there was nothing he could do.

Laura had survived surgery, which in and of itself was a miracle. Now, the best he could do was pray along with the rest of his family that she would make it through the next few days.

It didn't seem like enough.

He didn't risk his life every day to keep people safe, and he didn't change lives by providing a safe place to live for people who hadn't had it before. He fixed people. That was his job, and he was failing at it.

His family was counting on him, and there was nothing he could do to make this better.

Mark pushed open the door to Laura's room in the intensive care unit, and for a moment, he just stood and watched her. With her long, jet-black hair, Laura's pale skin always appeared paler, but right now, it was a translucent white, colorless. She looked dead. He didn't want his brother seeing the woman he loved this way, but once Jack knew that Laura was out of surgery, there was nothing that would stop him coming to see her. Jack would sit by her side, holding her hand for as long as it took—until Laura slipped away or until she came back to them.

He probably wouldn't leave the hospital until then either.

How could he?

He had to be here in case Laura needed him, or in case his brother needed him.

"Come on, Laura." He went to the bed and began to check her vitals, not because he needed to—they were all displayed on the machines that stood guard around her comatose form—but because he had to do something.

Someone had washed most of the blood away, but there were a few specks left on her cheeks. Mark pulled some tissues from the box on the table beside the bed and wet them at the sink, then gently washed the blood off his sister-in-law's face.

"You can't die, Laura," he told her, taking her hand. "You're so strong ... you can do this ... you can win."

Mark knew that Laura didn't see herself as strong because of the abduction and assault that had left her suffering from severe agoraphobia, but she was the strongest person he knew next to his wife. It was exactly what she saw as her weaknesses that were what made her so strong. She battled her phobia every single day and had learned how not to let it control her. This wasn't fiction land where problems went away as soon as you acknowledged them. This was real life where you had to struggle to overcome the things that tried to hold you down and you had to deal with the hand you were dealt no matter how much it sucked.

And that was what Laura did.

"We need you, Laura," he reminded her. "Jack needs you, and Zach and Rosie need you. Our family needs you, and all those women and children you counsel need you too. You better not go and die on us."

He leaned over and kissed her forehead. He couldn't put it off any longer. He had to go and tell Jack how Laura's surgery had gone.

As though he were walking toward his own death, Mark headed to the waiting room. He had assisted with his sister-in-law's surgery since it was what Jack had wanted, and he had told his colleagues that he should be the one to break the news to his family. They had agreed because no one liked giving bad news, and just because it was something that went with the job and that you had to do on a regular basis, didn't make it any easier.

"Mark."

Jack must have been watching the door like a hawk because as soon as he pushed it open his brother stood and rushed over.

Not just Jack. Their entire family was there. His wife, his parents, Laura's parents, Laura's sister and her husband, Ryan and Sofia, Paige and Elias who, while not blood related, were considered family by all of them. The only ones who weren't there were Xavier and Annabelle Montague, and Mark assumed they had offered to babysit all the kids so everyone else could be here to support Jack and Laura.

The fear on his brother's face hit him hard, and he almost backed out and decided to let someone else break the news. He couldn't imagine what it would be like to find someone you loved injured and dying. Then have to wait for an ambulance to arrive, through the drive to the hospital, and the initial examination in the emergency room when all you wanted was for someone to make them better. All things considered, Jack was holding up amazingly well, and Mark hoped he could hold on to that strength because he was going to need it to make it through the next few days.

"Is she dead?" Jack asked bluntly.

At least that was an easy question to answer. "No, she's not dead. She made it through the surgery."

The relief on his brother's face was almost worse. Jack thought that making it through the surgery was the hard part, but it wasn't. Compared to the battle that Laura was going to have to fight to live, the surgery was the easy part.

"Can I go and see her?" Jack asked.

"Jack, we need to talk," he said gently.

"About what?" His brother looked confused. "You said she made it through surgery. I need to go and see her."

Giving bad news was like taking off a Band-Aid. Just rip it off—the faster, the better. The more you procrastinated, the worse it got, and he wanted to make this as easy as he could for Jack and the rest of his family. They needed to know the truth. Living with false hope wasn't going to help any of them.

"Laura made it through surgery, but ..."

"But?" Jack prompted when he didn't immediately continue.

"But that doesn't mean she's out of the woods. She's still unstable; there is still a chance that she'll get an infection. There's still the chance that she'll suffer long-term complications."

"But there's a chance she'll just wake up and be fine, right?" Jack demanded.

"There is always that chance, but, Jack, right now I want you to prepare for the worst, okay?"

"Okay," Jack quickly agreed. His brother wasn't hearing him. All he cared about right now was that Laura had survived surgery and was still alive. The need to see her was blocking out everything else.

"Jack, I need you to listen to me, okay? I'll take you to see Laura, but I need you to understand that she is still *very* sick." He tried to catch Jack's eye to ascertain whether his brother was hearing him, but Jack's gaze was bouncing about, trying to see behind him into the ICU.

"I hear you, Mark," his brother said. "Now will you please take me to see my wife?"

There was no use in pushing it. Jack wasn't in a place where he could listen right now, and if he didn't take Jack to Laura, his brother was likely to go storming off on his own to try and find her.

"Of course," he agreed. "I'll take Jack to see Laura now. The rest of you may as well go home and get some rest. Tomorrow you can all go and see her one at a time," he addressed the rest of his family.

Jack might not be hearing him right now, but from the looks on everyone else's faces, they'd heard him.

Laura might survive, but the odds were not in her favor.

AUGUST 15TH

2:21 A.M.

She was scrunched up so close to the edge of the bed that if she wasn't careful, she was going to roll right off.

Sofia kept wriggling over every time Ryan tried to put his arm around her. Even in sleep he couldn't leave her alone. She didn't want to hurt his feelings, but she just needed some space right now. There was so much going on inside her head, and every time her husband tried to console her it made her want to scream.

It wasn't fair but that look he kept giving her, all sympathetic and understanding was only making her feel worse because she didn't even know how she was feeling; so for him to presume he did, was so annoying.

Ryan rolled over again, his arm draping across her shoulders, and she couldn't take it a second longer.

Careful not to wake him, she eased out from underneath him and crept out of the room. Sofia closed the door behind her and prayed that Ryan wouldn't notice her absence and wake up. If he woke up and found that she wasn't there, he would come looking for her. And when he found her, he was going to want to talk, and she really didn't want to talk.

Sometimes she hated having a husband who wanted to discuss things.

Again, she knew she was being unfair. Ryan liked to discuss things because the woman he had been engaged to before they met had committed suicide. He knew how important it was not to bottle things up inside and to keep the lines of communication open, so he was always wanting to talk through any problems they were having. Most of the time she appreciated that quality in a man, but sometimes she just wanted to wallow in self-pity for a while—not dissect everything and work it out.

Now was one of those times.

Sofia didn't know why she was having such a hard time with this.

She knew she'd done the right thing.

The *only* thing she could have done under the circumstances.

Deacon Staines had started firing at them. He'd only managed to shoot Amy, and luckily, the bullet had just skimmed her arm, but he wasn't going to stop.

She had saved lives.

She knew that.

She *knew* it.

So why was she struggling to come to terms with what had happened?

Sofia stopped at the door to Sophie's bedroom and quietly inched the door open a crack. She hadn't wanted Sophie to sleep alone tonight. After what had happened today, she knew her daughter was shaken up, and she'd wanted to spend the night sleeping on the floor beside Sophie's bed in case she needed anything during the night. But her strong, tough, independent child had been adamant that she would be fine.

Sophie was growing up way too fast.

Already her bedroom was starting to look less little girly and more preteen. She was starting to make the transition from stuffed animals and dolls and toys toward an interest in boys and clothes and makeup. Just the other day she had overheard Sophie and her best friend, Paige's daughter Hayley, talking about some boys they liked from their class at school last year, and hoping those boys would be in their class again this year.

She wasn't ready for that.

Her daughter was sprawled on top of the covers, one leg hanging over the edge of the mattress, the other tangled in the sheets. She was fast asleep and snoring softly, so Sofia closed the door and went to Ned's room.

Her son was the opposite of her daughter. While Sophie was a whirlwind, Ned was a gentle soft breeze. Sophie was full-on, always on the go—never stopping—but Ned was laid-back and quiet, preferring to sit back and watch and take things in before acting. Even in sleep they were different. While Sophie had been sprawled on top of her covers, Ned was curled up in a little ball under two blankets.

Those kids were her life.

Which was why she did what she had to today.

There was no way she could stand by and do nothing and let Deacon shoot her or Ryan.

Tears pricked the backs of her eyes and she closed Ned's door and headed downstairs. In the living room she dropped down onto one of the couches and closed her eyes. She wished she could turn her brain off. She didn't want to think. She just wanted to go to sleep and then wake up tomorrow and have everything go back to normal.

Try as she might to clear her mind enough to go to sleep, she couldn't.

One thought kept shouting out at her.

She had killed someone.

Killed another human being.

Right or wrong, whether she had had a choice or not, whether she would do it again or not, the facts were that she had taken a life.

She couldn't stop thinking about it.

The events kept playing over and over in her mind.

In slow motion so she saw everything.

The sound of the gun, the way the bullet pierced Deacon's head, the look in his eyes, the spray of blood and brains, the way he fell, the look on his face as his life ended.

Every horrible second of that moment was now etched into

her consciousness; she didn't think it would ever go away. How could she live the rest of her life like this?

Sofia didn't know how long she tossed and turned and battled her guilt, but the next thing she knew Ryan was standing over her.

"Did you spend the night down here?" he asked.

She wasn't sure how to answer that. She knew that he wanted to hear something like she couldn't sleep and didn't want to wake him because he needed the rest. It was true that he had needed rest. It had been late by the time they finally left the hospital, picked up the kids from Xavier and Annabelle's house, got home, got them into bed, and went to bed themselves. But it wasn't the reason she had spent the night on the couch. She just didn't want to be around Ryan right now. She wasn't quite sure why. It just was what it was.

Instead of giving any answer because whatever she said he was going to dissect and examine, she asked, "What time is it?"

"A little after six." His blue eyes were full of disappointment that she wouldn't open up to him. "I woke up, and you weren't there. I was worried. How long have you been down here?"

Sofia just shrugged restlessly.

"I wish you'd talk to me, tell me what's wrong. You should have let one of the doctors examine you last night. It might have helped."

How would it have helped? she wanted to ask. She wasn't hurt, and they'd been at the hospital to support Jack as they waited for news on Laura. Having a doctor look at her wouldn't have changed anything. She still would have killed someone and she still would have all these thoughts running through her head.

"Sofia—"

"Don't," she cut him off. "I don't want to talk about it."

"I can see that, but if you don't, then it's going to eat you up inside until it destroys you."

She hated that he was right. "There's nothing to talk about," she said as she stood and started tidying up the room because she needed something to do.

"Did you sleep at all? Did you have any nightmares?" he asked. She knew he was asking because he cared and because he was worried about her, but his interrogation made her feel like a child.

"Stop quizzing me; I don't need this right now," she snapped. She felt so bad taking her frustrations out on her husband. He didn't deserve it, but she felt so mixed up inside, and she didn't know how to sort herself out.

"What you *need* is to work through what happened. You killed someone. Even though it was justified, it's still going to have an impact on you. If you can't talk to me then find someone you can talk to."

"Would you please just stop being so—"

"Mommy?"

Sofia spun around to see Sophie standing in the doorway. Immediately, she pasted on a smile. "How did you sleep, sweetheart?"

"Okay. Are you and Daddy fighting?"

Despite her daughter's claims she was doing okay, she had called them Mommy and Daddy. She hadn't called them that since she was eight. It was time to stop worrying about herself and how what had happened had affected her. She had to make her daughter her priority.

"What do you want to do today, honey?" she asked, going to her daughter and giving her a hug.

"Can we go and visit Aunt Laura?"

She felt Ryan tense and knew he was going to tell Sophie no, but if their daughter wanted to go and see her aunt, then she should. From what Mark had said last night, it sounded like there was a good chance that Laura wasn't going to survive, so Sophie should get the chance to say goodbye to the aunt she adored if that was what she wanted to do.

"Of course, we can, sweetheart. Let's go and make blueberry pancakes for breakfast and then maybe we can pick some flowers to take to the hospital."

As they left the room, Sofia could feel her husband's worried eyes on her. He was probably right to worry. For the first time ever, she didn't feel like herself.

* * * * *

9:06 A.M.

"I don't understand why I'm here," Macey Staines said for probably the tenth time since he and Paige had arrived here about five minutes ago to interview her.

Ryan was finding it difficult not to snap at the woman and had to keep reminding himself that she was probably still in shock over yesterday's events.

It wasn't really Macey Staines that he was frustrated with; it was his wife.

He didn't understand what was wrong with her.

Well, that wasn't quite true. He knew what was wrong with her. She'd killed someone, and it was understandably having an impact on her. What he didn't understand was why she was pushing him away. She had to know that she had done the right thing. Deacon had started firing his gun at Paige and the other four hostages. The only shot he had was one that would have sent the bullet plowing through Macey on its way to Deacon.

Sofia had saved lives, and not just those of the other hostages, but Macey and Elle's as well. Presumably, when he realized that he was never going to be allowed to just walk out the door, Deacon had decided to use his wife as a human shield to try to find his daughter and then leave with both. The man had clearly been unbalanced so that had probably seemed like a workable plan to him.

So why was Sofia shutting him out?

She hadn't gotten out of their bed last night because she

66

couldn't sleep and hadn't wanted to disturb him. She'd left their bed because she didn't want to be near him. Every time he tried to touch her or to kiss her, she shied away from him as though the very thought of touching him was repulsive to her. He was hoping that getting out today, spending time with the kids, doing regular everyday life things, would help to clear her head, and she would start to feel better.

"Deacon is dead," Macey was saying. "Sofia shot him. I don't understand what you need to talk to me about."

"We need to understand why Deacon did what he did so that the shooting can be deemed justified," Paige replied with much more patience than he felt.

"Of course, it was justified. He started shooting at people. He was going to try to kidnap me and Elle." Macey paced restlessly back and forth across the room.

Since Macey was just a witness, they weren't interviewing her at the station but in one of the common rooms at the center. The living room where Deacon had held them hostage and been shot was still a crime scene, but other than that, the rest of the house was open to the residents still living here.

Macey had been reluctant to leave her room and her daughter to answer their questions, and Ryan couldn't help but wonder if the woman had something to hide. He just didn't know what it could be. Or it was nothing, and he was just projecting his own issues on to Macey. She had been through something traumatic; it made sense that she just wanted to forget about it and keep her child close.

"When did you and Deacon meet?" Paige asked, trying to focus Macey who was circling the room so frantically it was starting to make him dizzy.

"Middle school," Macey answered shortly.

"You've been together since then?" Ryan asked. That was a long time to have been a couple. No wonder she was struggling to deal with what had become of the man she loved.

"No. His family moved away before we started high school, but he was the first boy I was ever interested in. He was my first kiss, my first crush, my first love." Macey finally stilled and stared off into space, no doubt thinking about better times and what Deacon had been like back then, how happy they had been, and of their dreams of the future. Dreams that had ended up turning into a nightmare.

"When did you meet up again?" Paige asked.

"The summer after we graduated high school."

Doing the math, Ryan said, "You must have gotten pregnant with Elle right away."

Macey turned her back on them, and Ryan knew this was what was giving him the feeling that she was hiding something. There was a secret about her daughter that she didn't want them to discover.

Paige's mind was obviously going down the same track his was. "Macey, yesterday when Deacon was holding a gun to your head, he kept calling Elle *his* daughter. Was there any reason for that?" his partner asked.

Macey didn't say anything, but her shoulders began to shake, she was crying.

"Macey?" Paige prompted gently. "Was Elle adopted by you? Was she the daughter Deacon had with another woman?"

Both he and Paige had adopted children, and they knew that adopting a child didn't make them any less yours, or make you love them any less than if they had come from your body. He and Sofia—who was biologically Sophie's aunt—had adopted Sophie when she was a baby because they were the only family she had. And after an assault by her stalker that almost killed her, Paige had been left unable to have children of her own and had adopted two little girls about five years ago. They both adored their families, and there wasn't anything they wouldn't do for their children. It was clear that Macey felt the same way about Elle.

"Yes," Macey said softly, finally turning to face them. "Deacon was with another girl in high school. She got pregnant, but she didn't want to raise the baby, so she left Elle with Deacon. Elle was only three months old when I met her for the first time, and I just fell in love with her." Tears were streaming silently down Macey's pale cheeks, but her smile was bright as she spoke about her daughter. "When we got married a few months later, I legally adopted Elle. I *am* her mother, the only mother she's ever known."

"Does Elle know?" he asked. This was a sensitive subject for him and his family. Paige's girls knew they were adopted. Hayley had been five when Paige and Elias brought her into their family, so she had always known. Arianna was only five years old now, but she knew as well, just not the details of who her biological parents were. But he and Sofia hadn't told Sophie that she was adopted yet. It was just such a convoluted story, and one that still caused a lot of pain to his wife, but Sophie was ten now, and as horrible as it was going to be for her when she learned the truth, it was something she deserved to know.

"No." Macey's smile vanished, and fear filled her face. "And you can't tell her."

"If it has nothing to do with this, then we won't," Paige assured her. "What kind of father was Deacon?"

"Perfect," Macey answered quickly. "He was the perfect father; he doted on Elle. He adored her, spoiled her, but at the same time, he wasn't afraid to be her father and not her friend. He set out rules and he expected her to follow them."

"Did he discipline her?" Ryan asked. How had this perfect father turned into the abusive man who caused his wife—who clearly still loved him—to flee?

"If you mean physically, then no, but he gave her time out when she was small. He took away privileges and her phone and things as she got older."

"What about with you? What kind of husband was he?" Paige asked.

"He was everything I could have ever asked for in a husband. He worked hard so I could be a stay-at-home mom. He provided us with everything that we needed. Once Elle was in school, I took a part-time job to help with the finances, but he was the main breadwinner. He loved to surprise me with flowers or a special date night that he had planned, and he loved holding hands. It was such a small thing, something so simple, but it always made me feel so loved." She smiled ruefully.

"When did things start to change?" he asked.

"About a year ago, it was like my Deacon was gone and this monster was in his place. He became volatile and emotional; he'd be fine and then he'd suddenly have a violent and explosive outburst. It was terrifying. Then he'd calm down—he'd cry and apologize and beg for forgiveness. At first these outbursts were rare, but then they started getting more and more frequent … it got to the point I was terrified to be around him in case I said or did the wrong thing and set him off."

Ryan hated that victims of abuse felt that way. It wasn't Macey saying or doing the wrong thing that set off her husband's violent temper. It was Deacon who did it. "What he did wasn't your fault," he reminded her.

"I know," she nodded. "But I'm not sure it was Deacon's fault either."

"You thought something was wrong with him?" Paige asked.

"Yes," Macey said. "I couldn't think of any other explanation for his sudden change in behavior."

While it was no doubt easier for Macey to attribute her husband's abusive behavior to something else, Ryan had seen the man and believed she was right. Something was causing Deacon's abusive moods, but whatever it was, was a moot point. He was dead. There was no way to fix it.

"You said Deacon hurt Elle?" Ryan asked.

"That was the last straw. I didn't want to leave. I wanted him to get help, but every time I brought that up, he'd lose it. I didn't want to take his daughter away from him, but when he put his hands on her, I knew I didn't have a choice. I would never let my daughter stay in a place that wasn't safe. So that day, as soon as he left, I just took her, and we ran. I thought we would be safe here. I thought that maybe having lost us, Deacon would finally seek help, and that maybe one day we might be able to reconcile; to get back the family we had before."

Now that dream was over. Her husband was dead, and there was no chance of reconciliation. Macey and Elle's family had become just the two of them, but at least, they were both alive and safe.

Thanks to Sofia.

Ryan just had to figure out how to fix things with his wife before his family fell apart just like the Staines' family had.

* * * * *

10:48 A.M.

This was it.

He was so close.

If everything went according to plan, then in just a few minutes he would be snapping handcuffs on Wade Jeebes and dragging the man off to prison.

Xavier couldn't wait.

This had been a long time coming. The black-market baby ring had been around for at least four decades now. Originally, it had been run by Daisy Xander's family, who, other than Daisy, one of her brothers and her cousin, had all been killed half a century ago, and now the head of the operation was Wade Jeebes.

Seven months ago, Daisy's past had come back to haunt her, and although she and her family were safe now, thousands of runaway teens weren't. The ring worked by abducting teenage girls who ran away from home. They were kept in cages and artificially inseminated. The babies were then sold to wealthy couples who were unable to have children of their own.

When Wade fled, he'd taken one of the girls with him. Sixteen-year-old Colette White. The girl had run from one bad situation just to end up in another, and when he had learned that no one was looking for her, he'd been determined that he would do whatever it took to save her.

"I hope she's still alive."

Xavier looked at Paige, at the fierce determination on her face. Paige had been with him when they had rescued seventeen-year-old Heather Blight. It had been Heather who'd told them about Colette. They had both been equally as determined that if Colette had no family who cared about her, then *they* would care about her. They would find her, and they would rescue her.

"So do I," he agreed.

"I wonder how many other girls are going to be in there."

More than he cared to think about. And however many were there now, there had no doubt been others over the last seven months that Wade had killed for one reason or another. Unlike the Allen family who had run the ring before Wade, he didn't see this as just a business venture or the girls as simply tools of the trade. He wanted to use them to satisfy his sadistic desires.

"There's only one way to find out," he said. He was ready to go in there.

When Wade had disappeared, he and Paige had started watching all IVF and adoption agencies within a hundred-mile radius. They tracked all couples who were wealthy, who had tried without success to become pregnant, and who had not yet legally adopted a child. They then started approaching all families who, while their adoption agencies had not gotten them a child, they suddenly had a baby.

A week ago, they'd managed to get a lead.

That lead eventually led them to this house.

Since they had no idea how Wade was going to react and what

he was going to do when they stormed his house, they had a team of officers with them.

"Let's do this," he said.

With well-oiled precision, everyone pulled out their weapons and spread out. Half of them would go in through the front and half through the back. There was also a basement door, which he and Paige were going to enter through.

Simultaneously, they all breached the house.

When they stepped through the basement door, they found themselves at the top of a short flight of steps. Covering each other, he and Paige were halfway down when a figure appeared at the bottom.

Adrenalin flooded through his system, and he was about to fire when he realized that the person wasn't a threat.

It was a small child—a toddler—not more than a year and a half or so. Wade and his wife Holly had a daughter Genevieve. This must be her. If she was wandering around down here then there had to be an adult with her.

They crept silently the rest of the way down, and when they stepped out into the basement, Xavier was surprised to see a tall blond boy of about thirteen or fourteen sitting cross-legged on the floor outside one of the cages.

"Don't move, son," he said. The boy didn't look like he had a weapon, but that didn't mean he shouldn't be deemed a threat until he couple prove otherwise.

The kid started and jumped to his feet, a look of panic on his face.

"I'm Detective Montague, this is Detective Hood, what's your name, son?" Xavier was pretty sure he knew who the boy was, but he didn't want to jump to conclusions.

The boy just glared at them. If looks could kill, he and Paige would be dead several times over. There was no mistaking the similarities; the boy was the spitting image of his father. The Allen genes were strong. This had to be Blaze Allen, Daisy's nephew.

"Get down on your knees, Blaze," Xavier ordered. Blaze looked surprised that they knew his name, but he was only a kid, and the pressure of having two guns pointed at him was enough to get him to comply.

While Blaze looked too young and innocent—deadly glare aside—to do either of them any real damage, he was taking no chances and snapped a pair of handcuffs on the kid. If what they believed about him was true, then he was already an active part of this operation and thus not to be taken lightly.

"Are you really cops?" a voice asked.

Now that Blaze was safely restrained, he had a chance to take in the rest of the basement. This one was different than the Allen one, in that, instead of there being four cages, there were a dozen. Inside each of them stood a terrified, but hopeful looking girl. The girls ranged from early to late teens. There were blondes and brunettes and redheads, Asians and Hispanics and blacks. It looked like Wade wanted to cover every available market.

All the girls were naked, and even though it was a hot day, it was cool down here. Several of the girls had their blankets wrapped around their shoulders. At least half of them were noticeably pregnant. The rest might be as well, and one girl held a small baby in her arms.

"Colette?" Paige asked, stepping closer to the girl who had spoken.

The girl's blue eyes widened. "You know who I am?"

"Heather told us all about you." He smiled and stepped closer.

A smile broke out on her thin face. "I didn't think anyone was looking for me. I didn't think my parents would have reported me missing, and I didn't think there was anyone else who cared."

"Someone cared," he assured her.

Colette's eyes shone with tears, and the smile she gave them made every sleepless night he'd spent working this case more than worth it.

"Thank you." The words were so heartfelt; they had to be the sincerest thanks he'd ever received. "You found Heather? She's alive? She's okay?" Colette asked anxiously.

"She's alive and doing great. We were able to find her baby boy, and she's living with her mother and raising her son," Xavier told her.

"And we're really getting out of here?" Colette asked.

"As soon as we get the all clear from upstairs that Wade is in custody," Paige assured her.

Just then someone yelled down the stairs, "Suspect in custody."

"It's over?" Colette looked like she hardly dared to believe it.

"It's over."

"Just like that?"

"Just like that." Xavier was surprised Wade hadn't put up more of a fight, but there had been no gunshots. Maybe Wade knew when he was beaten. "If we can't find the keys, we'll get firefighters in here to cut through the bars and get you out."

"Blaze knows where they are," Colette said.

Xavier looked over at the boy who eyed them defiantly. "Where are the keys, Blaze?"

The only answer he got was a glower.

Colette chuckled. "Don't be fooled by his act. He's a good boy; he's just afraid of Wade."

He was surprised to hear that. He had assumed that the kid was in on what used to be his family's business, but maybe he'd just been doing what he had to, to survive. "Where are the keys, Blaze?" he asked again, more gently this time.

The boy glanced at Colette who nodded so Blaze inclined his head at a safe mounted on the wall at the bottom of the other set of stairs. "The code is 9264," he said.

Paige went to the safe and punched in the code. Immediately, the door swung open, revealing a large ring full of keys.

Other officers started to fill the room, and Paige started pulling keys off the ring and passing them out. One by one the girls were released from their cages and led out of the basement to be examined by paramedics and then either delivered back to their parents or into the care of child protective services.

"My mom and dad are both dead," Blaze spoke up quietly. "What's going to happen to me?"

Right now, Xavier couldn't answer that. He didn't know what was going to become of the boy. All he knew was that Blaze Allen was another victim of the black-market baby ring.

* * * * *

11:00 A.M.

Jack hated hospitals.

Hated them.

They were horrible places filled with death and destruction. They were places where hope died—where you walked out leaving a piece of yourself behind. A piece that you could never get back. A piece that left a gaping hole inside you which didn't grow smaller over time but bigger with each day you had to live without the person who made you whole, who made you you.

That was exactly how Jack felt every time he had to walk out the hospital's doors leaving Laura behind.

His wife was the best part of him. She made him a better person, a better cop, a better father, and a better husband. She made his life better, and the very idea that she might leave him was crushing. It weighed on his chest and made simply breathing an effort. Which in a way almost made him feel better because it didn't seem fair that he could breathe when Laura was struggling to stay alive.

He hadn't slept last night, just sat beside Laura's bed in ICU. He'd held her hand and tried to will her into waking up. He'd still be there, but he'd had to go and pick up his kids.

Not being at Laura's bedside killed him. What if she died while he wasn't there? What if she died alone and scared? He couldn't cope with that possibility, so he had left Mark with Laura while he went to get Zach and Rosie from Xavier and Annabelle's house where they'd spent the night.

Jack didn't really want the kids to see their mother like this—unconscious and hooked up to machines—but if Laura didn't make it, then he wanted their children to have a chance to say goodbye.

A tug on his hand redirected his attention to his daughter.

Forcing his lips to curve into something that vaguely resembled a smile, he asked, "Something you want to ask me, honey?"

Rosie nodded and looked solemnly up at him. His daughter was the spitting image of her mother. She had the same long dark hair, the same large violet eyes framed by long black lashes. She made the same facial expressions down to the way her eyes crinkled when she was trying to explain something, and the other person wasn't getting it. And the way her mouth moved when she was concentrating really hard. They had the same laugh, and they cried the same way. They made the same soft little snoring sound when they slept, and the same annoyed huff when they were angry.

If he lost his wife, he would always have this miniature version of her but how was his daughter going to learn to grow into the same compassionate, loving, caring, giving woman her mother was without having her mother as her role model?

"Daddy?" Rosie tugged on his hand again, and he realized he had zoned out and missed whatever she'd said.

"Sorry, baby, what were you saying?" he asked and tried to keep himself focused this time.

"I said," Rosie spoke with exaggerated patience, another trick she had learned from her mom. "Is Mommy sleeping?"

Jack stopped walking toward Laura's room and led the children over to the nearest chairs where he sat and stood them both in front of him. He needed to make sure they were prepared for what they were going to see when they got to their mother's room.

"Mommy isn't sleeping," he told his daughter. "She's unconscious. It looks like sleeping, but it isn't really the same."

"How is it different?" Zach asked. While Rosie had taken after Laura, his son was his own little mini me. Zach was the spitting image of him, with the same blue eyes, the same blond hair, the same dimples, and the same desire to help and protect others that he'd had at seven. His son was definitely a little cop in the making and would no doubt follow in his father's and grandfather's footsteps and join the police force when he was old enough.

"Well, when we're asleep we can be woken up by loud sounds or someone touching us but being unconscious isn't like that. It's kind of like being in a very, very deep sleep where nothing can wake you up until your body is ready. And there's no way to make your body ready except to give it the medicine and the rest that it needs." He was trying to explain something no child should have to worry about in a way his kids could understand.

"So, Mom isn't going to wake up?" Zach asked, his forehead furrowed as he tried to take in the implications of that.

He had always believed in being honest with his kids and treating them like the smart, mature people he knew they were, but this was the hardest thing he had ever had to say to them. "I don't know. She might wake up, and we are all praying that she will, but she might not."

"So, we can't just shout her name really loud to wake her up?" Rosie asked.

"No, we can't."

"Or we can't tickle her or poke her on the cheeks like I do when I wake up early and my tummy is rumbly for breakfast?" she asked, her little face all earnest.

His daughter was trying so hard to understand something that a five-year-old shouldn't even know about. Bringing them here was so much harder than he'd expected, and he had already thought it was going to be the hardest thing he had ever had to do as a parent. "I'm sorry, honey, but none of those things are going to wake Mommy up."

Rosie nodded soberly, and Jack thought that maybe he shouldn't be doing this. His kids were so young—just seven and five. They shouldn't have to see their mother this way. Maybe bringing them here was going to do more harm than good.

Just then Zach reached out and took his hand. "It's okay, Dad, we can do this."

He couldn't help but smile at that. Here he was trying to be the strong one to support his kids through this and there they were being strong for him. "Okay, let's go see Mom."

Holding hands, the three of them walked through the hospital halls. They walked past other families, some beaming, a spring in their steps, a smile they couldn't wipe off their faces. They were the ones who'd been reunited with their loved ones Then there were the ones whose steps were slow and heavy, who had a black cloud hanging above their heads and dead, empty eyes. They were the ones who'd just stepped off a cliff and were now plummeting down into a bottomless pit.

Jack prayed his family would wind up being one of the former, one of the lucky ones.

When they reached the door to Laura's room they stopped, and he stooped and got down on one knee, so he could look Zach and Rosie in the eye. "Are you guys ready? You know Mom might look different, not quite the same as usual."

Both little heads nodded.

"Do you have any last questions you want to ask before we go in and see her?"

This time both little heads shook in the negative.

"And you know that it's okay if you've changed your mind and you don't want to go in and see Mom like this. Uncle Mark can take you down to the cafeteria instead."

The siblings exchanged glances, then Zach answered, speaking for himself and his little sister. "We want to go in and see Mom."

His kids amazed him every single day. They were so much stronger, so much more mature and capable than he gave them credit for.

Jack stood and opened the door. The kids stepped inside and both of them paused, taking in the sight of their mother in a hospital bed and all the machines attached to her.

While Zach hung back a little, Rosie walked to the bed and climbed up onto the chair where Jack had spent the night and took her mother's hand. "Mommy, it's Rosie. I know Daddy said that you were sleeping so deep that you wouldn't wake up if we shouted or tickled you or even if I poked you. But can you wake up if I say please? Because you always say please is the magic word. Please wake up, Mommy."

Tears stung his eyes. His sweet innocent little daughter was ripping out his heart. He should have covered that "please"—magic word though it may be—wasn't going to wake Laura up. Rosie didn't seem concerned that her mother didn't immediately sit up like Sleeping Beauty, which reminded him he probably should have discussed that with the kids too.

"Can I hug Mommy?" she asked.

Jack was going to tell her it probably wasn't the best idea, but Mark helped her climb up onto the bed and said, "You can but they have to be really gentle hugs, okay? Your mom has a sore tummy and we have to be careful not to hurt her."

Rosie nodded, and when she was on the bed she lay down, stretched out at Laura's side. Zach still hadn't moved, and Jack took his son's hand and led him over to the bed.

"You want to give Mom a kiss, bud?" he asked Zach.

His son nodded and very carefully leaned over and kissed his mother's cheek. "I love you, Mommy," he said seriously.

How could Laura leave this?

They had the perfect family, the perfect lives; she had to come back to them.

If being around their children wasn't enough to wake her up, then nothing would.

* * * * *

12:21 P.M.

"What's for lunch, Mom?"

Daisy looked up from the ironing to see her youngest, almost eleven-year-old Tony, lounging against the breakfast bar. She was surprised to see him out of his room. All summer if she didn't have an activity planned, he spent his time in his room playing video games. Her last little baby would be starting middle school next month. It was so hard to believe. It seemed like just yesterday she was cradling him in her arms and staring into his tiny little face, and now he was quickly approaching his teenage years. Where did the time go?

"Mom. Lunch," Tony repeated when she didn't immediately provide an answer.

"Lunch is whatever you make yourself," she told him.

"But, Mo-om," he whined.

She couldn't help but laugh. She usually hated when the kids whined at her, but today she was just happy to be alive and happy that her kids were alive and that they were healthy and in one piece.

They were lucky. Life was precious and could be stolen away at any moment. What had happened with her sister-in-law Laura was proof of that. Her heart was breaking for Jack and the kids, and she was praying fervently that Laura would pull through.

"You know the rules," she told Tony. "When you're off from school, it's your responsibility to make your own lunch."

"Can't you just make it this one time?" Tony wheedled.

"No, Tony. You're nearly eleven; you're more than capable of making yourself a sandwich."

"But I wanted a BLT wrap, and I can never make it roll up properly. It always falls apart when I make it. Couldn't you do it for me?"

"No, Tony." She could do it, but they were trying to teach the kids to be responsible for themselves and their needs and not have Mom or Dad always running around doing everything for them. The same rules had applied to Brian, who was now sixteen, and Eve and Elise who were thirteen. The others had never put up this much fuss, but Tony was the baby of the family and they'd babied him more than they should have. But no more. He was going to learn the same way the others had.

"Please, Mom, please—"

"Tony, stop harassing your mother."

They both looked in the direction the voice had come from and saw Mark standing in the kitchen doorway. "This is a nice surprise." Daisy went to kiss her husband. She hadn't expected him to come home until Laura was out of the woods.

"Jack and the kids are with Laura, and I wanted to give them some time alone as a family, so I thought I'd pop home for a few minutes to see mine." Mark wrapped an arm around her waist and dragged her close, kissing her again and then just holding her. She knew that he would be tying himself up in knots because there wasn't anything he could do to make Laura better.

"You want something to eat?" she asked, snuggling closer. After spending six months away from her family last year, she couldn't get enough of being in her husband's arms. "I'd be happy to make *you* something."

"Actually, I'd love a sandwich."

"Sure." She loved cooking for her family even if they usually ate a meal that had taken her an hour to cook in less than ten minutes. She was going to miss it when all the kids were off at college. Then it would just be her and Mark, although there were some benefits to having no kids in the house. Too bad all four of them were home now. If they'd been alone, she'd have taken advantage of this little visit and gotten a little action before her husband went back to the hospital.

Mark laughed. "The kids are all home."

"How do you always know what I'm thinking?" She grinned up at him.

"Because I was thinking the same thing. Guess I'll have to settle for a quick shower and a sandwich."

"You go have your shower, and I'll make lunch. The ironing can wait, and I'll eat with you."

The doorbell rang just as she headed for the fridge and Mark headed for the stairs. "I'll get it," he said.

Daisy was just pulling things out of the fridge when Mark returned with Xavier in tow. Immediately, she knew that something was wrong. Not that it was unheard of for one of their friends to turn up at their place in the middle of the day, but the look on Xavier's face said this wasn't a social visit.

"What's wrong? Is it Laura?" she asked in a panic. Xavier could have gone to the hospital to check in on Jack and Laura had died while he was there.

Xavier smiled. "No, last I heard she's still hanging on. I just have something that I need to talk to you about."

A knot formed in her stomach. Xavier was a cop, and cops never had anything but bad news to tell you. She knew that from experience that had nothing to do with all the cops in Mark's family.

"What is it?" she asked. Already her hands were getting cold and clammy.

"Relax, its nothing bad," Xavier told her.

She'd believe that once she knew what it was that he had come to tell her.

"Want me to stay?" Mark asked, noticing her growing agitation and taking her hand.

"Yes," she replied immediately, then looked to Xavier to see if he was going to have a problem with that.

"That's fine. Really, Daisy, it's not bad news, just news."

The three of them all took seats at the kitchen table, and Daisy waited anxiously for Xavier to start talking.

"Ever since we found out about Wade, Paige and I have been looking for him, hoping to find Colette White when we did," Xavier began. Daisy knew who Colette White was and she wasn't surprised that Xavier and Paige had been trying to find her.

"You found Wade and Colette?" she asked. If Wade Jeebes was finally in police custody, then it was over. Really over. The nightmare her family had started had finally ended.

"We did."

"And Colette was still alive?"

"She was. Alive and six months pregnant."

Daisy couldn't help but wince at that. She felt partially responsible for the girl's predicament. Colette was the same age as her oldest son, and if her family hadn't settled on abducting teenagers and impregnating them as a get rich quick scheme, then Colette wouldn't be alone and pregnant with a child conceived by medical rape.

"It's not your fault, Daisy," her husband rebuked. "You weren't responsible for your family's actions, and you aren't responsible for Wade Jeebes' actions either."

She nodded, more to pacify Mark than because she agreed with him. A lifetime of blaming yourself for something wasn't easily overcome. She was working on it, but it took time. "And Wade is in prison?"

"He won't be going anywhere. Besides Colette, there were eleven other girls there; they can all testify against him. Heather too."

"And he won't be getting out on bail?" she asked a little nervously. Daisy didn't really think Wade was a threat to her. He didn't seem like he blamed her for anything, but the thought of him still being out there scared her. She wanted him safely locked up where he couldn't hurt anyone else.

"I doubt he'll be getting bail, not with all the charges against him, and he's probably considered a flight risk. You don't have to worry about him, Daisy," Xavier assured her. "Wade's wife Holly is also in prison, and their daughter Genevieve is in the custody of social services."

She was happy to hear that. At least that little girl stood a chance now. If she had been raised by her parents, she would either have wound up helping them abduct girls or as one of the baby incubators. Either way, she would have been a victim.

While everything that Xavier had told them was all good news, the knot in her stomach hadn't gone anywhere. There was more he hadn't said yet, and whatever it was, she wasn't going to like it.

"What haven't you told me yet?" she asked.

"Wade was too old to lure in the girls, so he needed someone else to do it for him." Xavier averted his gaze and she knew this was the part he was dreading telling her.

"So, who was he using as the lure?" While she knew this was the bad news part, she couldn't figure out why. Who would Wade have been using that would affect her?

"Daisy, your brother had a son; he's thirteen."

Thirteen meant that he had reached the age where he would have been brought into the family business.

"His name is Blaze," Xavier added.

Blaze.

Her nephew.

She had a nephew.

A nephew who had helped to abduct and impregnate teenage girls.

It wasn't over.

As long as there was an Allen who sold black market babies, it would never be over.

* * * * *

12:56 P.M.

Amy Frankstone stared at the bottle of pills in her hand.

To take them or not to take them; that was the question.

She had heard that somewhere before, well not the "take them" part but the rest of it. What was the saying again? Oh right, to be or not to be; that is the question.

For the life of her, she couldn't recall who'd said that or where she'd heard it, but it was true.

It had been the question she'd been asking herself all her life.

She hadn't led an easy life. She was the middle of three children and the only girl. One might have thought that that fact would have made her special, but one would have been wrong. She hadn't been anything special in her family; instead, it had been the opposite.

Her brothers were all handsome, smart, and athletic.

She was not.

Instead of inheriting the warm brown eyes and chocolate brown hair of the rest of her family, her hair and eyes were mud colored, ugly to look at. *She* was ugly. She knew that; she'd been told it hundreds of times over the years. She wasn't academic and had struggled just to make passing grades, and she was too clumsy to be good at sports.

Amy had absolutely nothing going for her.

Her mother had told her that every day.

Every. Single. Day.

If you tell someone something often enough, they start to believe it, and Amy believed the cruel words without a doubt. She was worthless, had no prospects for her future, and would never amount to anything.

With no hope for her future, she had given herself to the first man who had shown any interest in her whatsoever.

She had been seventeen, he had been twenty-seven. She'd

thought he was everything—smart, successful, good-looking. It turned out she'd been wrong. The only thing he'd been was charming, and even that was an act. Behind closed doors where no one could see him, his true colors came out.

He wasn't charming; he was just abusive. He beat her. He forced her to perform sexual acts she didn't want to perform, and he cut her off from the rest of the world. He made it clear that, in return for providing for her financially, her job was to cook and clean and serve him and cater to his every whim.

But one day she decided she would rather live on the street with nothing to eat and no warm place to sleep than stay in his house for a second longer.

Unfortunately, she'd been too slow packing to leave. When he'd come home and realized that his hold on her was broken, he beat her so badly she nearly died.

Which turned out to be the best thing that ever happened to her.

In a way.

Those days in the hospital had been the first in her life where she'd felt safe and free. Mark Xander, the doctor who operated on her and saved her life referred her here, and she started getting counseling from Laura Xander, and for the first time ever, she had someone tell her that she was worth something. When she was discharged from the hospital, she came here, and things had been looking up.

Her ex was in prison. She was taking college classes here at the center, and she got her first job which made her feel so much better about herself.

There was only one problem.

She couldn't stop taking painkillers.

The assault that had nearly killed her had left her with a broken back, and she had been in a lot of pain for a long time. But almost a year had passed now, and her pain was minimal; and yet, the thought of giving up the medication filled her with terror.

It didn't make sense.

Amy knew she didn't need the pills. She was safe here and in a place where she could see herself having the same future as everyone else. Job, house, partner, kids, pets, she could have it all.

At least, that's what she'd thought.

Until yesterday.

When that man with the gun had come storming into the place where she lived she had realized she was never going to be truly safe.

If you were going to spend the rest of your life in a perpetual state of danger, then what was the point?

Why not just end things and be done with it?

It would be so much easier.

Amy unscrewed the lid and tipped some of the pills out into her hand.

She could do it.

She had enough pills.

Part of her badly wanted to just swallow them all in one go then go and lie down in her bed and wait for it to be over.

But she couldn't.

She had fought so hard to get to this point. Why give up now?

Amy wished that she could talk to Laura. Laura was so smart, and she always knew what to say, when to be tough, and when to be gentle. But she couldn't talk to Laura right now because the woman was in a hospital bed fighting for her life.

Laura might not be here, but Amy knew what she would say if she were. Don't give up.

She tipped the pills back into the bottle.

Just as she was putting them away, there was a knock on her door. Amy really hoped it wasn't the cops; she had already given them her statement. What else was there to say? Deacon had shot her and he'd been going to kill them all. Sofia had done the right thing when she'd killed him.

Setting the bottle of painkillers on her coffee table, she went to answer the door.

"Hi," she greeted the woman on the other side. She wasn't surprised to see her here. After what happened yesterday, they both needed some support right now.

"Hi." The other woman gave a tight smile.

"Want to come in?" she asked. Their rooms here at the Matilda Rose Women's and Children's Center weren't just bedrooms. This place had been custom built and each of their rooms were really more of a small apartment. There was a kitchenette, space for a kitchen table, a small living area, enough for a lounge suite and an entertainment stand, a separate bedroom, and a bathroom. Some of the larger rooms even had two bedrooms for those who were staying here with children.

"If I'm not interrupting."

"You're not," she assured the other woman and held the door open wider so she could enter, then they both went to sit side by side on one of the sofas.

"How's your arm?"

"It's fine. It wasn't really much more than a scratch." That was true. Although it had bled a bit, the paramedics who checked her out hadn't even recommended that she go to the hospital. They had just bandaged it and told her to see her doctor in a couple of days to make sure it was healing well and there were no signs of infection.

"You were lucky."

That was also true. "*Everyone* in that room was lucky," she corrected, and the other woman nodded.

"That's true," the woman murmured. The toll yesterday's events had taken on her were obvious. And who could blame her?

"How are you doing? Are you coping okay?" Being able to focus on someone else was helping her to feel more grounded. She enjoyed helping others and she and Laura had even talked about the possibility of her getting a degree in counseling or psychology so she could make helping others her job.

"I guess I'm doing as well as could be expected given what almost happened."

The woman said the words, but they clearly weren't true. She didn't look like she was doing very well at all. "What do you need? What can I do to help?"

"Have a drink with me?"

Amy didn't usually drink. She didn't really like the feeling she got afterward, of being drunk and not completely in control. Her ex had never allowed her to drink. She was there to please him, not to do anything that he thought would give her any pleasure. Then since she had been taking painkillers for the last year, she was always wary of mixing the two together, but she hadn't taken anything since this morning and one little glass of something shouldn't be a problem. Besides, if it helped her friend feel even a little better after the horror she had just lived through, then she would do it even if it wasn't really something she would have otherwise chosen to do.

"Sure." Amy smiled. "Although I'm not sure I have anything."

"Not a problem." The other woman pulled a bottle of wine from her bag and held it up. "I came prepared."

"Then let's have a drink and try to forget that yesterday happened."

* * * * *

2:44 P.M.

After spending some time at the hospital with Jack and Laura and their children, Sofia was feeling even worse than she had been this morning.

There was Jack, keeping vigil at his wife's bedside, praying like he had never prayed before that she would somehow pull through and come back to him and their children. And then, here she was dreading having to go home tonight because she'd have to face her husband who, for some inexplicable reason, she couldn't stand to be around right now.

She was the worst wife in the history of the world.

What was wrong with her?

Deacon had been a dangerous man. He'd intended to kill them all and kidnap Macey and Elle. She had prevented that from happening. She had done a good thing. So why didn't it feel like it?

It wasn't like she thought that taking a life—however justified—wasn't going to affect her. She just didn't understand why it was making her push Ryan away. She loved her husband and their lives together with their little family, so why did even the thought of having to be around him make her feel like someone had covered her in spider webs?

She wished she could talk to Laura. Her sister-in-law was her favorite person to talk to because Laura was the perfect mix of logical and empathetic. Laura better not go and die on them. Their family would never be the same without her. Jack would never get over losing her, and Zach and Rosie would have to grow up without their mother.

It was too horrible to think about.

Sofia shook her head as though she could physically dislodge all thoughts of losing Laura.

It didn't work.

Maybe keeping busy would help. After leaving the hospital, she'd dropped Sophie and Ned, as well as Zach and Rosie, off at Annabelle's, and come here to the center. It felt kind of odd to be back here after what had happened. She wondered if she would ever feel settled here again, if she would ever not get that tightening in her stomach when she walked through the doors, if that sense of dread would pass.

Although she had intended to go and check on Amy, Teagan, Tara, Kimberly, Macey, and Elle, her feet had other ideas and she found herself standing at the open living room door. There was still police tape blocking entry, so she just stood in the doorway.

Everything looked so normal.

Someone had cleaned up all the blood so there were no traces left of the life that had ended in that room just twenty-four hours before.

That seemed wrong.

Good or bad, Deacon Staines had been a human being and to just wipe away all traces of his death so quickly didn't seem fair. At one point in time, he'd been a good husband and a good father. Whatever had led to the change in him shouldn't define him and the person he was.

This was silly, and it wasn't helping her.

She had to find a way to let it go.

Resolutely, Sofia headed for Amy Frankstone's room. She was worried about the woman turning to painkillers to dull the shock of what had happened.

When she reached Amy's room, she knocked on the door and then fidgeted with the hem of her T-shirt while she waited for the other woman to answer.

After waiting a full minute without any sign of Amy, she started to worry.

Had something happened to her?

Had she taken too many painkillers?

The last time she'd seen Amy, the woman hadn't seemed suicidal, but that was yesterday. Who knew what mental state she was in now.

She really should have made sure that someone checked in on her before now.

"Amy?" She knocked on the door again, louder this time. "It's Sofia. If you can hear me, can you call out, so I know you're okay. You don't have to let me in. I just want to know that you're all right."

When there was still no answer, she thumped on the door one last time.

"Amy, if you don't answer, I'm going to come in."

There was still no response, so she rifled through her bag for her keys. Although they respected the privacy of everyone who came to live here, their guests had fled from a myriad of horrible situations and a lot of them were suffering from depression or addictions. This wasn't the first time she had stood at one of the doors knocking, getting no answer, and worrying about the safety of the person inside.

"I'm coming in, Amy," she warned one last time before she slid the key into the lock and swung the door open.

She'd been right to worry.

Amy lay on the floor, partially propped up against the side of the sofa. There was an empty bottle of pills on the coffee table and an empty bottle of wine beside it.

A mixture of painkillers and alcohol could have killed her.

Sofia rushed toward her, dropping to her knees and reaching to feel the younger woman's neck.

There was no pulse, and Amy's skin was cold.

She had been dead for a while.

"I need help in here!" she screamed at the top of her lungs. She wasn't sure how many people were around or where the nearest one was. "Someone call an ambulance."

She was pretty sure it was pointless, but she couldn't do nothing, so she grabbed hold of Amy and dragged her away from between the sofa and the coffee table and lay her out, then she started CPR.

Was she doing it right?

She had taken first aid training, and she knew how to do CPR, but she'd never had to do it on a real person before. Now she couldn't remember how many breaths and how many compressions.

Sofia lost all track of time, and what felt like hours, was probably not more than a minute or two.

"What happened?" Kimberly Ute appeared in the doorway.

"I think she took too many pills and mixed them with alcohol," she said as she pumped on Amy's chest.

Kimberly rushed over, and everything blurred into one great big fog. They did CPR, and eventually some paramedics showed up and she was gently guided away from the body.

She had expected them to take over with the CPR, maybe shock Amy with a defibrillator, but they didn't do any of that.

"Why aren't you helping her?" she demanded. Logically, she knew the answer, but she couldn't accept it yet.

"I'm sorry, ma'am," one of the medics said, shooting her a sympathetic glance.

Gone.

Amy was gone.

Dead.

Just twenty-four hours after surviving being held hostage at gunpoint, she was dead.

An uneasy feeling settled over her.

She wasn't sure why.

Maybe it was because she hadn't seen how on the edge Amy had been. She had known the woman had been through a lot, and that she was still battling her addiction, but she hadn't known that she was contemplating taking her own life.

She had really messed up.

She should have known.

It was her job to know everything about the needs of the people who lived here, and she had failed big time with Amy.

"Sofia?"

She blinked and saw Ryan was right in front of her.

Immediately, she stiffened.

"I'm sorry about Amy, are you okay?" His blue eyes were so full of concern but all it did was make her withdraw further. At some point she was going to have to figure out why she kept pulling away from Ryan before she ended up ruining her marriage.

"I'm fine," she said, stalking from the room. She couldn't be around Amy's dead body for another second. The guilt was crushing her.

"Are you sure? I mean, after yesterday and then today finding one of the women—"

"I said I was fine," she snapped. Why did Ryan always have to push to talk about things when it was clear she didn't want to?

"Why were you going into her room?" Paige asked, sensing the tension and stepping in to smooth things over.

"I just wanted to check on her after yesterday," she said, focusing on Paige and pretending her husband wasn't there.

"What did you find when you went into her room?"

"The door was locked … no, wait, I thought it was, but when I put the key in, I didn't have to turn it. Inside I just saw Amy slumped over on the floor, the pill bottle and the bottle of wine were on the table. I assumed she had mixed the two, and when I checked, she wasn't breathing so I started doing CPR," she summarized.

"Did anything seem off, suspicious, unusual?"

"No, nothing I can think of. Why?" she asked. Amy had committed suicide, hadn't she?

"There was a wineglass on the table and one that had been cleaned and was sitting beside the sink," Ryan told her.

Two wineglasses.

There was no reason for Amy to have two glasses out. And now that she thought about it, she didn't even remember seeing Amy drink in the year she'd been living here.

That didn't necessarily mean anything.

Maybe the cleaned wineglass was from the night before, and maybe Amy had been drinking because she couldn't cope with being held hostage at gunpoint.

Or maybe it was actually murder.

* * * * *

3:15 P.M.

Seven months was a long time.

A *really* long time.

Especially when you spent it kept in a basement, in a cage, never allowed out, never seeing the sunshine or feeling the gentle breeze against your skin—and impregnated against your will.

Colette stretched out in her hospital bed and placed her hands on her swollen stomach. She was six months pregnant. In just three months, she was going to be a mother.

A mother.

The thought terrified her.

It still didn't seem real.

In just three months, she would be giving birth to a baby.

A baby.

A real baby.

For the last six months she'd kind of been blocking it out because she knew that once the baby was born, she only had one week with it before it would be taken away, and she wasn't sure how she felt about that.

But now, no one would be taking her baby.

That was a good thing.

Right?

Now she could raise her baby herself.

That was what she wanted.

Wasn't it?

Colette was so confused.

She didn't know what she wanted to do with her baby. She wasn't sure how she felt about him or her. She remembered back just after she had been kidnapped, and she'd asked Heather if she had loved her baby. Heather had admitted that she did, so maybe she would love her baby too.

And if she didn't, she could always put the baby up for adoption.

Maybe she should do that anyway.

How was she going to raise a baby?

She had no money and no job. She wasn't even legally an adult yet, and she had no family to help or support her. She was probably going to wind up in the foster care system for the next year. Even if she became an emancipated minor, she hadn't graduated high school, and she could never earn enough to support her and her child. And who would look after the baby when she worked? She didn't have a support system to help her.

She didn't have anyone.

She was all alone in the world.

She had run from her home after her father's drinking buddies started making trips to her bedroom. Instead of having them prosecuted, her father got the inspired idea that he could make money off her. When she couldn't take it anymore, she'd run, straight from the frying pan and into the fire. From the hell she had lived at home to the hell that had been her life in Wade's basement.

No one had reported her missing.

No one had cared that she was gone, and no one would care that she was back.

That reality of her new life slowly sank in.

She could never go back to her parents' house; she would be no safer there than she had been at Wade's.

She was terrified, almost as afraid as she had been in the cage in the basement knowing that all her future contained was having baby after baby until they decided she was obsolete, and they'd kill her.

Her heart began to race in her chest, and she began to breathe a little too fast. What was going to happen to her and her child?

"Knock, knock," a voice spoke as the door to her hospital room opened.

A familiar voice.

Surprised, Colette turned to see Heather Blight.

"What are you doing here?"

"I came to see you." Heather tentatively came to sit in the chair beside the bed.

Tears brimmed in her eyes. If Heather hadn't told the cops about her, then no one would ever have known she existed. No one would have been looking for her and she probably would have spent the rest of her life—however long that would have been—in that basement.

But now she had a chance at life.

It was up to her what she did with that chance.

Even if she had to fight to get where she wanted to be. Even if she was always going to be afraid. Even if she was going to struggle to trust anyone again. Even if the scars of this ordeal were always going to be visible, at least she had a chance.

Because of Heather.

"Thank you," she said. The words didn't seem like enough. How did you thank someone for saving your life?

Heather grinned. "Of course. I didn't really do anything anyway. It was Xavier and Paige who found you; I just told them about you when they found me."

She could downplay it all she wanted, but if Heather hadn't told the cops about her, then they wouldn't have been looking for her. In her mind, Heather was just as responsible for her being rescued as the cops were.

They hadn't spent long together—only a few days seven months ago but spending any amount of time with someone under such intense circumstances bonded you for life.

"How have things been since you went home?" Colette asked. She needed hope right now, and if Heather had been able to reacclimatize into the real world, then maybe she could too.

"They've been good," Heather replied. "But hard. My mom wants to make up for not believing me and for me running away because of it and everything that happened. She's been really supportive, but even though she tries, she doesn't really understand."

"It's hard to explain to someone just what it was like, but at least, she's trying. It's great that you have someone there for you." Colette couldn't help but sound a little wistful. She wished she had someone who was going to help her through this.

"I'm so lucky to have her. I don't know what I would have done if she wasn't there. She's been so great. She drives me to all of my appointments with my therapist, and she helps me out with the baby so I can go back to school. Well, not back to *school* school; I'm not ready to be around large groups of people yet, but she found me a tutor so I can continue my education and graduate. I'm pretty far behind where I should be, but my tutor is great, and I'm really loving just doing the same things as other girls my age. Being excited about schoolwork is something I never thought I'd be." Heather giggled.

Heather was moving on with her life. Getting her education, raising her son, getting help. Colette couldn't help but be a little jealous.

"So, my mom and I were talking, and . . ." Heather trailed off when they both heard the sound of crying even before the door opened.

"Sorry to interrupt," a pretty middle-aged woman who was an exact older version of Heather hurried through the door, a squiggling, crying baby in her arms. "Tate wants his momma."

Colette stared in raptured silence at the beautiful baby. He had grown so much since she had last seen him. As soon as Heather took him in her arms, he stopped crying and nuzzled closer to her, a huge smile on his sweet little face.

She could have this.

She could be holding her baby in her arms and have him or her looking at her like Tate was looking at Heather, like she was the most special and important person in the world.

Maybe she would keep her baby after all.

As long as she loved it, of course. If she couldn't be around it when her baby was born, she'd put it up for adoption. She wouldn't subject her child to having to grow up in a home where it wasn't loved.

"Hi, sweetheart, I'm Christie, Heather's mom." Mrs. Blight kissed her on the cheek.

"Hi." She smiled back, suddenly shy. It had been a long time since she'd been around people other than her captors and fellow victims.

"Did you ask her?" Christie asked her daughter.

"I was going to when you came in," Heather replied, settling her son on her lap.

Ask me what, Colette wondered. After everything that she'd experienced in her life, she didn't hold out high hopes that whatever they were going to ask her was something good.

"Would you like to come and live with us when you get out of here?" Heather asked.

What?

Colette was sure she must have heard wrong.

Why would these people invite her to live with them?

She was a stranger to them. She'd spent a few days locked in a cage in a basement seven months ago with Heather, and that was it.

"What? Why?" she asked nervously, part of her brain believing this must be some sort of trick.

"Because you need a family, a safe place to recover and rebuild your life," Christie told her.

"But I'm ..." She trailed off and dropped her eyes to her pregnant belly.

"We're aware of that." Christie laughed.

"Really?" This seemed too good to be true.

"Really," Christie said.

"Really," Heather echoed. "Our babies will be able to grow up together, kind of like siblings."

"You deserve this, Colette." Christie took her hands and

squeezed them tightly. "You deserve to be happy; you deserve to live with people who care about you, and you deserve a chance to finish school and go to college and do whatever you want to do with your life."

This seemed to be too good to be true, but it seemed like it really was true.

It was really happening

She was going to have a family.

She was going to have a chance.

She was going to have a life.

* * * * *

4:03 P.M.

Paige hoped that talking with Heather and Christie Blight about Colette would work out.

Ever since they'd found Heather close to death on the basement floor of the Allen house, she'd kept in touch with her. She'd seen the teenager grow a lot over the last seven months. Heather still had a long way to go to get to a point where she could live a normal life, but every step she took in that direction was a win in her opinion.

She didn't make it a point of getting involved with all the victims in all the cases that she worked. She didn't have the time or the emotional strength to get invested in all of their lives, but every now and then, there was someone who just touched your heart in some way, and that had been Heather. She had asked Laura to take on Heather as a patient and that had been the teenager's first step toward getting her life back. From there, she resumed her studies, so she could graduate high school. She started taking trips out of the house after a couple of months and was bit by bit regaining her confidence.

Heather was a strong, young woman and a wonderful mother,

and Paige knew that she was going to end up with the life she deserved. She hoped that with some love and support, Colette White could make the same progress.

When they learned about Colette last January, they had looked into the girl's history and found that her father was a drunk who couldn't hold down a job, and her mother was addicted to meth. Neither of them was in a place where they could help and support their daughter, and given what they had allowed to happen to their daughter, she would never have allowed Colette to return there anyway.

Which left foster care as the only option.

Then she'd had the idea of seeing whether Heather and her mother would be willing to let Colette come and live with them. Paige hadn't been sure how receptive they would be to the idea, but she'd thought it would be good for all of them. Christie Blight was trying to make up for the mistakes she'd made with her daughter, and Heather needed someone who understood what she had been through, and they had both jumped on the idea of having Colette stay with them.

She was so happy knowing that everything had worked out so well for all five of them, including Heather's baby and Colette's unborn baby. Now they just had to sort out this new development on the hostage situation.

"Coffee," her partner announced as he set a cup down on her desk and then dropped down into his chair.

"Thanks." She took a long drink of the hot liquid, enjoying the way it burned her throat as it was going down. She had always loved hot drinks—the hotter, the better.

"So, what do we think?" Ryan asked. Her partner looked distracted and she assumed it was because he and Sofia were having problems. She wasn't sure of the cause although she assumed it had something to do with yesterday's events. They were all stressed out with what had happened and Laura being in the hospital. She'd try to check in with Sofia later and see if there was anything she could do to help.

"Logic says it was suicide," she replied. "We know that Amy Frankstone had been battling an addiction to painkillers ever since her ex almost beat her to death. With the broken back and the long, slow recovery she was continuing to get a prescription from her doctor, and as far as I'm aware she took one daily."

"That explains the pills, but what about the alcohol?" Ryan asked. "Amy had been living there for almost a year now, and no one has ever seen her drink anything—not even on New Year's."

"But even if she doesn't drink, if she intended to commit suicide, she could have used the alcohol just to mix with the pills," she contradicted.

"She could have. I guess it boils down to whether or not the hostage situation yesterday was enough of a trigger to push her to take her life."

"No one said she'd been having a hard time lately; in fact, other than the addiction, she seemed to be doing well, getting better. She had even come to one or two of my self-defense classes." She hated knowing that Amy Frankstone might have gotten to a point where the only option she felt she had was to end things. How had none of them seen it? Between being a cop and raising two daughters, she didn't get to spend as much time at the center as she would have liked to. She taught weekly classes there, and she enjoyed seeing the women gain confidence and strength as they made progress in their journey toward getting their lives back.

Ryan noticed the drop in her mood and reached over and patted her hand. "How are you doing? I know you spent time around Amy; whatever happened to her, this was certainly a shock."

"Yeah, it was. I just, I don't know, Ryan. I'm just not sure that I buy that Amy would kill herself. She was looking forward to what the future held for the first time since I met her. Yes, being held hostage would have been a shock and something that she would have struggled with, but was it enough to make her commit suicide? I don't know. I don't think it was. I don't think she'd do it. Think about it, possibly, but not actually go through with it. She'd found something that she was interested in and good at. She and Laura had discussed her maybe becoming a counselor helping other women who had been through the same thing she had. Her life was moving in a good direction. I don't think she'd do it." Paige didn't feel like Amy would have ended her life, but was it because her cop instincts were telling her it was murder or just because she didn't want to believe it?

"Which bring us to the possibility that this was murder," Ryan said.

"There's no proof that it was."

"Well, not proof exactly, just the second wineglass."

"Which could mean anything."

"It could, but we already know that Amy didn't drink, so why would she have poured herself some wine, drank it, washed the glass and left it on the counter, then later used a different glass to pour herself more wine and mix it with the pills to kill herself?"

Paige didn't have an answer to that. "Maybe she'd tried it earlier but backed out, then the second time, she was successful."

"Were there any other bottles of wine in her room?"

"I don't think so."

"Then where did this one come from? I checked, and no one saw her leave the property between the paramedics checking her out after the hostage situation and when Sofia found her body. That means that she had to have had the wine there already. But she doesn't drink, so why would she? And if she did have wine there, then it would suggest that she had been contemplating this for a while, only no one had any indications that she was suicidal."

"Which suggests murder."

"But who would kill Amy?" Ryan asked.

"Her ex is in prison; he was charged with attempted murder for the assault on Amy."

"If she was murdered, could it be related to the hostage situation?"

That was what had been weighing on her mind. "I don't see what else it could be, but I also can't see why Deacon Staines trying to get his wife and daughter back would lead anyone to murder Amy."

"It doesn't make sense." Ryan shook his head. "But what are our options? One, she committed suicide. Two, she was murdered by some random person—either another resident or someone who somehow broke in undetected. Or, three, her murder is connected to the hostage situation."

"For her to be murdered less than twenty-four hours after the hostage situation implies that the two were related. But who would kill Amy because of it, and why?"

"We need to know more about the Staineses," Ryan said. "Maybe that will help us find out if there was anything about them or the hostage situation that might have led someone to kill Amy."

"I never spent a whole lot of time with either Macey or Elle. Macey was pretty protective of her daughter and she was fairly introverted. Neither of them attended any of my self-defense classes."

"Sofia seemed to know them better than anyone else," Ryan said, but he looked conflicted about the prospect of having to talk to his own wife.

"Then let's go see her." She didn't want to add to Ryan and Sofia's problems, but maybe the quicker they got this situation resolved, the quicker they could work things out.

* * * * *

4:51 P.M.

"Why do you need to ask me about the Staines family?" Sofia

asked her husband and his partner as they all sat down in the living room.

After discovering Amy's dead body and giving her statement, she'd left work, unable to spend another minute there. She had always loved her job, loved giving people who needed it a safe place to live, a place where they could sort their lives out and have the future they wanted, but now she couldn't stand to be inside that building.

What had been a place of hope had quickly become a dark, gloomy place of death.

She just wanted to forget about it, even for just a few minutes. She was so tired. She hadn't slept in thirty-six hours, and lying down and going to sleep sounded wonderful, but she had too much to do, and even if she *did* go to sleep, she was more than likely going to have nightmares.

Sofia had picked up Sophie and Ned on her way home, and Zach and Rosie. They were going to babysit her nephew and niece tonight to give Annabelle and Xavier a break. She had offered to take the babies as well, so they could have a night to themselves, which gave her the added bonus of keeping her busy enough that not only would she not have to think of anything else, but she also had a legitimate reason to keep her distance from Ryan. Maybe she'd see if Paige wanted to bring Hayley and Arianna over. She might even call Mark and say his kids could spend the night too. They'd make it a big sleepover with lots of food and lots of fun—something they all needed right about now.

She had been hoping that Ryan was going to work late tonight and had been surprised when he showed up with Paige. She was confused about why they wanted to talk to her about the Staineses. Deacon was dead. What was there to talk about?

"We're looking into the possibility that Amy's suicide is related to Deacon Staines and the hostage situation," Paige explained.

"Because of the wineglass," she said, remembering what they'd told her at the center earlier today.

"It's not definitive proof of anything, so we're not saying that Amy was murdered, but we have to look into it given the inconsistencies in what we know about Amy and how she died," Ryan added. He looked like he wanted to come and sit beside her, wrap his arm around her shoulders, comfort her, but he was keeping his distance, and for that, she was exceedingly grateful.

"What do you want to know about the Staineses? Haven't you already spoken to Macey?" She wasn't sure what they wanted from her.

"What do you think about Macey? What's she like?" Paige asked. "I don't know her very well. She never attended any of my classes, but you spend so much more time there, so you know her better than I do."

"I don't know her that well," she contradicted. "The best person to ask would have been Laura." The same look of concern that she knew was on her own face appeared on the faces of her husband and her friend.

She honestly didn't know how they were all going to cope without Laura. Sofia didn't think her sister-in-law was aware of it, but she was the glue that held their family together. Yes, they would still be a family without her, and yes, they would still all love and care about one another and spend a lot of time together, but it was Laura who made them what they were. She was so easy to talk to, and she was everyone's go-to person when they needed advice or they needed to vent or they were worrying about something. There was no one who could ever take Laura's place or give them what she gave.

"Laura was counseling both Macey and Elle. She'd know if they were hiding anything that might have gotten Amy killed," she said, shoving all thoughts of Laura dying and leaving them out of her head. Laura would survive. She was the toughest person Sofia knew; if anyone could make it through this then it was her.

"Why don't you just tell us what you do know," Ryan suggested, reaching out to touch her hand and she quickly pulled it back out of reach, then deliberately looked at Paige so she didn't have to see the hurt in his eyes. She knew she wasn't being fair to him. She owed him an explanation, at least, but what would that explanation be? She didn't even understand her own behavior.

"Well," she began slowly, trying to recall all the gossip that had circulated the house about Macey Staines. "There was a rumor going around that Macey wasn't really a victim of domestic abuse. I'm not sure who started it or why they thought that, but I know of at least four other women who believed that Macey wasn't a victim and that she had hurt herself to make her story more believable when she left her husband."

"What did you think?" Ryan asked.

"Well, I saw her when she first arrived, and from the look of the bruises, it didn't look to me like she had caused them herself."

"So, you don't think that the rumors were true?" Paige asked.

"You saw her when she arrived; you were there that day. What did you think?" she asked her friend. "You've seen a lot more victims than I have. Do you think she could have done it to herself?"

Paige thought about that, then said, "To me the bruises she had looked like they had been caused by someone else, but I can't say for sure. I didn't get a really good look at her, and even if I did, I'm not a doctor."

"Did she see a doctor?" Ryan asked.

"No, she wouldn't. Those first few weeks she didn't even come out of her room. She would barely speak with anyone, and when she did, it was mostly monosyllabic. Again, Laura would know more about her. Macey took an instant liking to Laura, just like everyone does. I'm sure she opened up more about herself and her life, but she never spoke much to me. Oh," her eyes widened as she thought of something. "Yesterday was the first time that Macey had left the property since she arrived. I think she went out to the store. It was also the first time she had left Elle. I was surprised when she gave permission for her daughter to go to the water park with the other kids."

"Did you think that behavior was odd?" Ryan asked.

"Not really. We have a lot of women who arrived at the center so traumatized that they can't bear to let their children out of their sight for fear that something will happen to them. Especially if their abusive partner isn't in prison and still out there. And a lot of the women who stay at the center are afraid to leave their rooms at first. They're embarrassed or they don't want anyone to see them, or they have just been beaten down—physically and emotionally—that they kind of forget how to interact with people. Even once they come out of their shell enough to leave their rooms, leaving the center is a whole other story. It becomes their safe place. We never rush any of the women or their children who live there. It takes them however long it takes to reintegrate into society."

"The timing is odd though," Paige said thoughtfully. "You're right, Macey hadn't left the property before yesterday, and she never let Elle out of her sight."

"Elle didn't go to school?" Ryan asked.

"She took classes with the tutor," she replied. "Again, that is not uncommon, particularly in those first few months. We were hoping that she would be ready to let Elle go to school when the new school year started."

"It's a pretty big coincidence that the very day she decides to go out is the very day her husband finds her, holds a room full of people hostage to try to get her back, then the very next day one of those hostages is killed," Paige said.

Sofia couldn't deny that. "You think that Macey might have killed Amy? Why would she do that?"

"I don't know yet," Paige replied.

"Or it was Elle," Ryan suggested.

Elle? She was only fifteen. "You really think Elle would kill Amy?"

"Maybe. Macey didn't like to let her daughter out of her sight, but was it because she was afraid *for* Elle or afraid *of* Elle?"

That was a possibility, she supposed. "Even if there was more to what was happening in the Staines family than we knew, I still don't get what killing Amy would achieve."

"Maybe Deacon said something they thought might incriminate them," Ryan suggested.

"We were all there and nothing stood out to any of us. He sounded like a crazy man desperate to get his family back," she reminded him.

"Maybe we didn't know what we should be listening for. And if someone thinks Deacon said something he shouldn't have, then that means more people could die. There were eight other people in that room besides Deacon, and one of them is now dead. That means the rest of us could be in danger too."

Her husband's words sent a shiver through her.

If he was right, then she, Ryan, and Paige, as well as Tara, Teagan, and Kimberly, and maybe Macey, too, could all be in the sights of a killer.

* * * * *

9:07 P.M.

She was going to have to be careful.

Very careful.

The first kill had been easy because no one was looking for her. No one was expecting someone to start killing off the hostages. No one knew there was more to the story of the Staines family.

But there *was* more to the Staines family.

Which was exactly why she needed to take out *all* the people who'd been in the room when Deacon went storming in with a gun.

They had heard things that they shouldn't.

Things that might give her away.

She couldn't have that.

They might not realize that they had heard anything they weren't supposed to know because they didn't know what they should have been listening for, but whether they knew it or not, what they heard, could destroy her, and she wasn't going to let that happen.

Which left her with no other choice.

She had to do this.

She had to silence them before they realized what they'd heard and put the pieces together.

It wasn't that she particularly wanted to. She wasn't a killer. Well, she guessed that technically she was, since she had taken a life, but she'd only done it out of self-preservation, so she didn't really think that counted.

It had been surprisingly easy though.

She'd been terrified the entire time that something would go wrong. The possibilities had been endless. Someone could have come in at the wrong time and she would have had to decide whether to pull out, or if things had gone too far she would have had to kill them too. Or Amy could have put up a fight, and she would have had to knock her out or hold her down or something. Or she could have refused to drink the wine which again meant she would have had to force it down her throat, no doubt leaving bruises, which would tell the cops immediately that it has been a murder and not a suicide.

Luckily, it had all gone smoothly, and Amy Frankstone was now dead. Amy had been receptive to having a glass of wine even though it was common knowledge the woman didn't drink. While Amy was getting the glasses, she'd quickly emptied out all the pills in the bottle and crushed them, tipping them into the bottle of wine. Then she'd poured them both a glass but never touched hers; instead, she rambled on about how she "felt" about the whole hostage situation thing. As soon as Amy slumped over, she had quickly washed her glass and fled. In hindsight, she probably should have put it away, but she'd been so nervous to get out of there before anyone saw her.

She was hoping that the cops believed it was a suicide, which would buy her a little more time. It wouldn't last though. As soon as she made her second kill, the cops would know something was up. Best case scenario, they'd think it was a coincidence that two women who had both been held hostage by the same man died within forty-eight hours, but they would still investigate it closely. Worst case scenario, they would know that both deaths were murders and they would come looking for her.

Now it was time to move on to the second kill. She would rather have left some time in between each murder, lulling everyone into a false sense of security, but time was not on her side. She had no choice but to do this as quickly as she could.

These first ones were the easiest. Killing the cops was going to be a whole lot harder. She still had no idea how she was going to manage it, but she wasn't going to worry about that. She would cross that bridge when she came to it.

At the door to Tara May's room, she paused and drew in a long, deep, steadying breath.

She had to settle her nerves before she went in there.

This one would be harder than the first because whether people believed it was a suicide or murder, the residents of the center were bound to be on edge.

"You can do this," she whispered aloud.

She could.

She was sure of it.

She just had to remain focused.

Amy had made things easier for her by having an addiction to painkillers. It had been easy to decide how to kill her and make it look natural. Things wouldn't be quite so easy this time. But there was one little thing she knew about nineteen-year-old Tara that gave her a way she could kill her and still make it look like suicide or an accident.

Okay, no more putting it off. It was time. Things would look suspicious if she stayed outside Tara's room for long. If anyone saw her, they'd tell the cops and then they'd be on to her.

Curling her hand into a fist, she rapped on the door.

But no one came.

Was Tara not in there?

It was nearly half past nine. Where could she be? She'd checked the common rooms on the way here, and they had all been empty. After everything that had happened, it seemed like people were uncomfortable and hiding out in their rooms.

Should she knock again?

Maybe Tara had gone to bed already.

She really didn't want to stay out here any longer. Every second she was here, she was tempting fate, and the chances of someone seeing her grew.

She was just about to turn and leave when the door swung open.

"Oh, hi." Tara beamed. "Sorry, I was just about to hop into the bath."

Perfect.

That was exactly what she had been hoping.

She knew that Tara loved baths and that she often took one at the end of the day to relax, and after what had happened yesterday and today, they all needed something to help them relax.

"Should I go?" she asked, feigning regret for disturbing Tara.

"No, of course not, come on in. I can take a bath later." Tara let her in and closed and locked the door behind her. Apparently, paranoia was starting to become the norm around here. Before Deacon stormed the place with a gun, she didn't think anyone ever locked their doors.

"Thanks." She faked a smile and took a seat at the table with Tara. "Sorry for interrupting your evening."

"Not a problem." Tara smiled back. Beamed, really. She smiled a lot for someone who'd grown up in a home where she was beaten daily and sexually assaulted from the time she started school, then fled from her family only to wind up with a man who locked her in a room and assaulted her daily until she managed to break out a window and jump from the third story. She had broken both her legs in the fall, but she'd been free. It didn't seem like someone should still be so optimistic after all of that.

"I was just kind of feeling a little lost after everything that happened with Deacon and then Amy. I just kind of needed some company," she said, trying to look sincere.

"Yeah, I can understand that," Tara clucked sympathetically. "It's been such a rough couple of days. Everything with Deacon was bad enough, but then to be followed so quickly by Amy's death, it's been such a shock for all of us."

"I can't believe Amy would commit suicide," she said.

"I know, it seemed out of character." Tara looked thoughtful. "There's talk going around that maybe she was murdered," she whispered conspiratorially.

"Really?" She hoped she looked shocked at that and not terrified. If a rumor was going around that it was murder already, then it was a sure thing that the cops were already pursuing that as a possibility. She had hoped for a little more time, at least until this murder or even the next before they started seriously looking at the deaths as murders.

"That's what I heard, and I guess it sort of makes sense. I mean, I talked to Amy after the whole hostage thing, and she was okay. She was upset and shaken like everyone was, but she wasn't suicidal. At all."

"Did you tell the cops that?" she asked, fishing for information.

"I sure did. If someone's walking around where we live killing one of us, then they better do something about it," Tara said fiercely.

"Definitely," she agreed, nodding her head vehemently to try to hide the fact that she was thinking this was quickly unraveling into a nightmare. She was really going to have to pick up the pace if she was going to finish this before they came for her.

She had to finish what she started.

She had to.

The stakes were too high for her to fail.

It was imperative that she silence everyone who could destroy her; she wasn't going to lose.

Under no circumstances was she going to walk out of this mess as the loser.

She would do whatever it took to get what she wanted.

AUGUST 16TH

7:28 A.M.

It hadn't sunk in yet.

Her husband was dead.

Deacon was dead.

Dead.

Gone.

Forever.

It didn't seem real.

Macey Staines was beginning to wonder if it would ever feel real.

She still couldn't believe he'd done what he had. Tracking her down here, nearly killing Laura Xander, shooting the security guard, holding a gun at her head. It was all so un-Deacon-like.

The Deacon she had first met back in middle school had been a sweetheart. Yeah, he had driven her crazy and they had bickered almost constantly, but that had been because, even at eleven, he had owned her heart.

When she'd come home from school the first day of sixth grade and told her parents that she had met the man she was going to marry, they had all but laughed in her face—in the nicest way possible since her parents were great people. They'd thought she was just a kid. What would she know about falling in love.

But she had been in love, even back then. Even as young as she had been, she'd recognized her soul mate.

Deacon had been her first kiss, he had been the first—the only—guy she'd ever had sex with. He was not only the first man that she had loved, but the *only* man she had loved. He had given her an amazing daughter and a wonderful life.

He was the love of her life, but ...

Sometimes love wasn't enough.

He had changed everything.

Macey wasn't exactly sure that she could pinpoint the exact second when things had started going downhill. It was like one day everything was fine, and the next, everything had spun so far out of control that she didn't think that it was possible to rein it back in.

What had happened was all Deacon's fault. *He* was the one who'd destroyed what they had. *He* was the one who'd ruined the perfect life that they had.

Part of her hated him for it.

It was so disconcerting to see the man that she loved do all the things that he'd done to her and to their daughter.

Leaving was the right thing to do.

She was sure that it was.

And at the same time, she felt like running had been the biggest mistake of her life.

Some days *she* felt like the crazy one.

Like what had happened and what she had done were too insane for words.

But what was done was done.

She'd made her choices, and now she had to live with the consequences.

Well, she and Elle both had to live with the decisions she'd made.

It terrified her that the cops knew she wasn't Elle's biological mother. What if they tried to take her away? She had legally adopted Elle, so in the eyes of the law, she was the teenager's mother. But what if they found out what she had done and used that as a reason to take her daughter?

Macey was so terrified of losing Elle.

Worrying about it consumed her.

It was almost always on her mind, every second of every day. She even dreamed about it at night. It was the worst thing that could happen to her. She honestly didn't know what she would do if anyone threatened to take her child. She *did* know that she wouldn't go quietly. She wouldn't just stand quietly by and let them take her daughter; she would do whatever it took to make sure it didn't happen.

Just like she had always done.

She might not have any biological children, but she was the fiercest mama bear around.

No one messed with her little girl.

When Elle had been seven, her two front teeth had fallen out—just like a lot of other kids her age, but unlike a lot of other kids her age, her teeth had taken almost a year to grow back in. The kids in her class had teased her relentlessly about it, and she had stormed the school, demanding they do something about it. Then, she called the parents of every single child who had teased her daughter and demanded that they make their children apologize.

In the eighth grade, one particular boy had made it his mission in life to harass Elle. He was relentless. He followed her from class to class taunting her. He stuck notes on her locker door; he started rumors about her. Whenever he walked past her in the halls he would snap her bra straps. He was making her life a living hell, and she wouldn't stand for it. She had again approached the school first, and when their response was unsatisfactory, she had gone to the boy's parents. When they hadn't seemed to care, she'd gone to the police to have the boy charged with sexual harassment.

There wasn't anything she wouldn't do for her daughter.

Anything.

She would fight; she would lie; she would steal. She would even go so far as to kill if that was what she had to do for Elle. Her daughter was her number one, and with Deacon dead now, her daughter was the only one she cared about. Elle was her life and protecting her was her focus.

Everything she'd done from the moment she had held that tiny little baby in her arms was for her daughter, and everything she would do from now until the day of her death would be with Elle in mind.

Which is exactly what she was doing right now.

When she got to the door of Tara May's room, she knocked briskly. She counted to thirty and then swung the door open and stepped inside, closing the door behind her.

Macey headed toward the bathroom.

She stopped in the doorway.

Tara lay in the bath. Water was splashed all over the floor, and the hair dryer was plugged into the socket and in the bath was Tara.

Dead.

She was dead.

Macey turned and left the bathroom. Once she was out in the hall, she screamed at the top of her lungs.

"Help!" she screamed. "I need help. Please. Come quickly. It's Tara, it's Tara. She's dead."

It didn't take long for her screams to start rousing people. Doors opened, and women and their children started spilling out into the hall. The place was large, and the rooms spaced out, but the commotion started to spread. More and more people came, all of them milling about not quite sure what to do.

"What's going on?" Kimberly suddenly appeared beside her.

"There was an accident. Tara's in the bath. She must have had the hair dryer plugged in and it fell in with her. She's dead," Macey summarized.

"I have to go check on her." Kimberly started for the door to Tara's room, but Macey grabbed hold of her wrist and stopped her.

"It's too late. She's already dead. The water was already cold;

she probably took a bath last night and accidentally knocked the hair dryer in."

"We should call paramedics." Kimberly nodded slowly, accepting that there was nothing she could do to help. Kimberly was a nurse, and it was her natural instinct to help people, but this time, Tara was beyond help. "The cops too. They'll need to come, check the room out, make sure that it really was an accident."

"What else could it be?" she asked.

Kimberly's brown eyes widened. "Deacon broke in here and held us hostage, then the next day Amy is dead, and now Tara. The cops are going to think that's suspicious. They'll probably send their crime scene people to go through that room with a fine-tooth comb in case it wasn't just an accident and Amy didn't commit suicide. Someone could be trying to kill us all. We were in there, too, Macey. We could be in danger."

"Yeah, you're right. I guess I wasn't thinking." Macey reached over and patted Kimberly's shoulder. "I'll go and call the cops. I guess you should go in and make sure she really is dead."

Once Kimberly had disappeared into Tara's room, she sank back against the wall, letting it take her weight.

This was so stressful.

She had never been this on edge in her whole life.

She had to keep reminding herself that she had started this, and she had to see it through to the finish.

Regardless of what had happened between them, she still loved Deacon, but now she had no choice but to keep going down the path she'd chosen.

"I'm sorry, Deacon," she whispered aloud. "I'm sorry that it came to this. I'm sorry for the part I played in your death. I did it all for Elle. I hope that wherever you are, that you forgive me."

With a heavy heart, she pulled her cell phone from her pocket and dialed 911.

* * * * *

EIGHT

8:13 A.M.

Another day, another death at his wife's center.

Eight people held hostage. Two of them now dead—one in a supposed suicide, the other in a supposed accident.

This wasn't a giant coincidence like someone was trying to make out.

Someone was killing off those who'd been in the room while Deacon Staines had been brandishing a gun and demanding his wife and daughter leave with him.

There were six of them left now including himself, his partner, and his wife, and Ryan wouldn't allow anyone to hurt his wife. Even if things between them were pretty rocky at the moment.

Sofia had cooked up the scheme of having all the kids stay at their place last night, so she had a reason to keep her distance from him. Ryan wasn't stupid. It hadn't taken a genius to figure out what she was up to, but when he'd confronted her on it, she had denied everything. She claimed that she was just trying to help everyone out by taking the kids and giving them all a break. She'd gone full-out. They'd made homemade pizzas, chocolate cupcakes, watched movies, played board games, then everyone had slept together down in the living room.

So far, he hadn't had a chance to get her alone long enough to pin her down and get her to talk to him. Ryan knew how important it was to keep the lines of communication open. He hadn't done that in his first relationship, and he hadn't realized that his fiancée was suicidal until it was too late. He had lost the first love of his life; he had no intention of losing the second. He'd find a way to help Sofia deal with taking a life before it got to the point where it destroyed the love they shared and their family along with it.

"There was no break-in," Paige said as they stood in the living room area of Tara May's small apartment.

"She knew her killer, probably opened the door and let them walk right in here," he agreed.

"Just like with Amy Frankstone. There were no signs of a break-in there either—one of the reasons it looked like a suicide at first glance. Amy's death wasn't a suicide, and Tara didn't accidentally let the hair dryer fall into the bath while she was in there. Why would she have had the hair dryer out anyway? It was night. She was going to bed. She wouldn't have dried her hair with the dryer then gone to sleep; her hair was going to be a mess when she woke up in the morning regardless, and besides she had it in a bun on top of her head like she didn't even intend for it to get wet. Someone is killing off the hostages one by one. We're on that list, Ryan. We were in there too. We heard or saw whatever it is this killer thinks is going to incriminate them. I mean, that has to be it, right? It has to be out of self-preservation that someone is killing us off. I can't think of any other reason … it's the only thing that makes sense."

His partner was wired this morning. He understood why. Paige was right. If someone was killing off the hostages, then they were on that list. She had two daughters who were only ten and five, and the prospect of being killed and leaving behind young children was a terrifying one.

It was the same fear he felt.

And if the killer got to him and Sofia before they caught her, then his children would be orphans.

There was no way he was going to let that happen.

They *would* find who was doing this.

If they followed Paige's logic that the killer was someone who thought Deacon Staines had said or done something that would incriminate them and was taking out everyone before they themselves got taken out, then their suspects were limited. The only people left who had been in the room when Deacon was brandishing his gun were himself, his partner, his wife—all of whom he knew weren't the killer—Teagan, Kimberly, and Macey

Staines.

As Deacon's wife, Macey was the most likely to have something to lose and was currently their number one suspect.

"CSU are going to go through this place. If Macey was in here, they'll find some trace of it," he said to Paige.

"Unless she already took care of that and gave herself a reason to have been in here," Paige countered.

Unfortunately, Paige was right.

Macey had been the one who discovered the body. If she had been the one who killed Tara, then she had provided herself a logical reason for her fingerprints or hairs to be found in the apartment.

Which was pretty diabolically genius.

If Macey really was the killer and she had just waited a little bit in between kills, or at least waited a while before killing Tara, then she might have gotten away with it. Amy committing suicide so quickly after the hostage situation might have raised a few brows, even without the extra wineglass, but that would have been it. Everyone would have just assumed it shook her up so badly that she couldn't take it anymore. But by killing Tara May the very next day, it was too suspicious. They were never going to ignore it and let that death pass as an accident.

"Why don't we ask her about it, see what she has to say. If we don't find any forensics we could use, then we're going to need to trap her or get her to slip up and reveal something we can use," Ryan said.

"If it *is* Macey who murdered Amy and Tara because she was worried we learned something that could be used against her, possibly something that would have her end up losing Elle, then why not just run? I mean, she wasn't a suspect or anything. All anyone saw her as was a battered wife who'd tried to do the right thing and left with her daughter, only to have her abusive husband track her down and try to kidnap her. If she'd gone, it wouldn't really have looked suspicious. We'd have just thought that she couldn't stay here after her husband had died here. That's how I would have seen it, and I've spent a little bit of time around Macey. It doesn't make sense that if she felt threatened, she would stay here and kill people."

"Or she just doesn't feel safe running yet," he suggested. "She is genuinely afraid of losing Elle. Maybe she thinks if she doesn't take care of these perceived threats and tie up all the loose ends, then she and Elle will never be safe." As much as this was their working theory, he'd been in the room with Deacon Staines, and he'd gone over what had happened with the others who'd been there. He didn't hear a word that implicated Macey in anything other than being Deacon's wife and making him angry by taking their daughter and running.

"Maybe. Hopefully we get something out of her that we can use. I just wish that we knew more about her."

Paige didn't need to add that it would be so helpful if Laura had woken up by now to tell them what she knew about Macey and Elle. Wanting his sister-in-law to wake up to help them with this case wasn't the biggest reason he wanted her to wake up, but he had to admit it was on the list.

"Macey?" Ryan said as they approached her. She was standing and leaning back against the wall. Elle was standing beside her, quietly watching everything that was going on.

As soon as they said her name, Macey straightened. "I was just going to talk to Tara. After what Deacon did, and then after Amy's suicide, I guess I just needed some reassurance that she was okay. I didn't want what my husband did to hurt anyone else. When I knocked, and she didn't answer, I was worried, I went in and found her in the bathroom. I knew she was dead. There was no steam, so the water had obviously gone cold. She'd been in there a while. I came out, called for help, and then dialed 911," she summarized briskly.

Ryan already knew where Macey had been this morning. What he wanted to know was where she'd been last night. Tara had last been seen alive around eight when she left the library and headed off to her room saying she was going to have a long, hot, relaxing bath and then make it an early night.

"Where were you last night?" he asked.

Macey's brown eyes grew wide, and her gaze darted to Paige who she probably felt more comfortable with. "You think *I* killed Tara?"

"Where were you last night, after eight?" he asked again.

"Elle and I went straight to our room after dinner. After everything that had gone on with her dad, we just needed some quiet time together, just the two of us. We watched a little TV and then we both went to bed."

"And you didn't leave after that?" Paige asked.

"I didn't leave until this morning when I went to check on Tara."

"Can you confirm that your mom was in your apartment all night?" He directed this question to Elle.

"She's a heavy sleeper." Macey replied before her daughter had a chance to speak. "A herd of elephants wouldn't wake Elle once she's asleep. But I'm telling you the truth."

"Elle?" Paige asked the teenager.

"I *am* a heavy sleeper, but my mom wouldn't kill anyone," Elle said quietly, not meeting anyone's eye, not even her mother's.

For now, they were going to have to leave it at that. It wasn't necessary to ask for a set of fingerprints to use to see if she'd been in Tara's apartment because they already knew she had been. If this was a murder, then the woman had thought of everything. Unless they found fingerprints on the hair dryer cord, any prints were useless.

But as suspicious as he was of Macey, something was off with Elle.

Was Macey covering for Elle?

Was Elle covering for Macey?

Or were the two of them in on this together?

* * * * *

2:59 P.M.

Finally, she'd been able to sneak away.

She was sick of her mother's overbearing, overprotective, smothering attentiveness.

Elle was fifteen now. She really didn't need her mother to hover by her side like she was three years old.

Fifteen.

She was *fifteen* years old.

She wanted space. She *needed* space, especially after the mess her mother had made of their lives.

Her dad was dead.

Dead.

Elle knew that her dad wasn't perfect. She wasn't stupid; she knew what he'd done and that he had changed dramatically from the man he'd been her whole life.

Growing up, she'd always thought that she had the perfect family. Her mom had always been home when the bus dropped her off after school, there were usually homemade cookies for an after-school snack, and every night she had a home cooked meal. On school breaks her mom always made sure to take her out to fun places: museums, the zoo, the aquarium. Although her dad worked a lot so that her mom could stay home and she could have all the toys and clothes she wanted, he always made it to every one of her baseball games and dance recitals, and he often helped her with her homework.

A lot of her friends didn't have that. Their parents were divorced or they fought a lot or they were too busy with work and too tired at the end of the day to spend much time with them.

Elle had felt so lucky.

And then everything had changed.

She blamed her mother.

Fair or not, she did.

When she was being honest, she admitted that she wasn't completely blameless in the destruction of her family. But she was the kid and they were the parents. They were supposed to take care of her. Not the other way around.

But ever since they'd left their home and her dad, things had been the wrong way around. She'd had to be the strong one and look after her mother who had changed so much, she hardly recognized her anymore.

Maybe it was the weight of carrying such a big secret that had finally worn her mother down. Elle didn't know, but she wanted to go back to being a normal kid.

Leaving her home had been hard. It hadn't just been leaving the only house she'd ever lived in and everything in it—clothes, mementos from her childhood, her favorite stuffed animal, her laptop, her iPad, her cell phone—her mom hadn't let her bring anything but the clothes on her back. She had left her school and all her friends, including Andrea whom she'd been best friends with since first grade, and Brandon, the cute guy in her math class, whom she'd been dating for almost a month.

Ever since they'd been living at the center for abused women and children, she had been all alone. She hadn't been allowed to go to school, she wasn't allowed to leave the property, and most of the time, she wasn't even allowed to leave her mother's sight.

She hated it.

She had no one to talk to.

Well, no one but Laura Xander.

The woman had quickly become more than just her therapist. She was her confidant and the only one Elle had to talk to.

She really needed to talk to Laura now, but her dad had stabbed Laura, and now she was in the hospital fighting for her life.

Elle couldn't imagine her dad stabbing anyone, and yet in a

way she could. The father she had known before she and her mom left had been violent and unpredictable. A raging maniac one minute and then a crying, quivering mess the next, begging for their forgiveness.

Picturing her dad brandishing a gun and holding it at her mom's head all because he wanted them back, both scared her and made her feel kind of special and loved. No matter how her dad had changed, one thing had never changed, *could* never change—he loved her.

Even now, Elle believed he still loved her. He was in heaven now watching over her; he was her guardian angel. Some people might have thought she was crazy for thinking her dad was in heaven after all the bad things he'd done, but she knew that deep down inside he was still the loving, caring father he had always been. The changes in him weren't his fault.

What was going to happen to her and her mom now?

Since her dad was dead, there wasn't really any reason for them to have to stay at the center. They'd been living there so they would be safe—although that apparently had been just an illusion since they clearly hadn't been safe there. But now that Dad was gone, they were no longer in danger. So where would they go?

Her mom had never really had to work to support them, so how was she going to get a job?

Where would they live?

Would they still have a nice house to live in?

Would she still go to the same school?

Could they go back to their old house?

Could they afford it?

Could she at least get all her stuff from there?

Would she be able to see Andrea?

Would they still be best friends? It had been six months since they last saw each other, and in the world of high school, that was a long time.

And what about Brandon? Did he still think about her? Had he moved on? Did he have a new girlfriend? If she came back, would he want to get back together with her?

What would happen when everyone found out about her father?

What would the other kids say about her?

Her dad was violent; he had killed someone. Would that mean the kids thought she could do those things too?

Could she?

Her dad's blood ran through her veins, so *was* she going to go crazy and start killing people too?

She just wanted to be like all the other kids her age, but she wasn't sure if she was. She didn't know if she was a normal kid anymore. Could you still be after everything that she'd been through?

How would she face the kids at school again? Where would that leave her if they couldn't accept her?

Being a teenager was tough.

Especially when you'd been isolated from your support system.

She really needed to talk to someone.

"Elle? What are you doing here?"

She jumped at the voice. Immediately assuming something was wrong, that someone was going to get her, after what had happened, she couldn't help but expect the worst.

"Elle? Are you okay?"

A large hand landed on her shoulder and she looked up into the face of the person looming above her and let out a sigh of relief. After months of barely speaking to anyone, she couldn't seem to summon her voice, so she just gave a small nod in response to his question.

"Does your mother know you're here?"

"No," she whispered in a small voice. Her mother was going to be furious when she realized she snuck away from the center to come here. "Please, don't tell her, Detective Xander."

He smiled down at her. "Jack," he reminded her. He had asked her dozens of times over the last six months to call him Jack, but he was the first cop she'd ever met, and he made her a little nervous, so she always stuck with addressing him formally. "Did you come here to see Laura?" he asked.

"Yes. I know she's hurt, and it was because of my dad, so if you want me to—"

"Of course not," Jack interrupted. "You aren't responsible for your father's actions. Laura cares about you. You can go and sit with her for a while if you want, and I'll go call and check in with my parents who are watching Zach and Rosie."

Elle couldn't help but flinch when she thought of those two sweet kids. They spent a lot of time at the center after school, and during the day over the summer break, so she had seen them around a lot. They were both great kids, and she didn't want them to lose their mother. She knew what it was like to lose a parent and it hurt.

A lot.

It was like a piece of her was gone now.

She wondered if that pain would ever go away.

Whenever she thought too much about her dad, she couldn't help but think about all the things she would never get to do with him. He wouldn't be there at her high school or college graduation; he wouldn't walk her down the aisle at her wedding; he wouldn't hold her baby in his arms.

She only had one parent left now—a mother who was getting increasingly difficult to be around.

She prayed that Laura survived so that Zach and Rosie wouldn't have to experience what she was currently dealing with.

"Take as long as you like with Laura." Jack shot her a sympathetic glance.

Why was he being so nice to her when it was her dad's fault that his wife might die?

Elle wondered if Laura had told him the things they'd talked about in their sessions. She knew that your therapist wasn't supposed to break confidentiality, but did that include not talking to their spouse?

The possibility made her uneasy.

She didn't quite like the idea of anyone knowing the things she had talked about.

It left things kind of up in the air.

It left her exposed.

And that was unacceptable.

She had told Laura things she didn't want anyone else to ever find out.

When Jack headed off down the hospital hall, she slipped into Laura's room, not quite sure what she was here to do.

* * * * *

3:41 P.M.

Jack disconnected the call and then stood and stared at the phone in his hands.

The background image was a family selfie that they'd taken when they'd gone on a family vacation to the snow last winter. He loved the cold and anything to do with snow sports, and he had wanted the kids to learn to ski and snowboard from an early age. Laura didn't mind the cold and she knew how to ski, but she wasn't as into it as he was. She'd gone along with the vacation and the kids taking ski and snowboard lessons for him.

Zach and Rosie, on the other hand, had mixed reactions to the idea of sliding down a hill on a piece of plastic. Zach had been horrified and refused to even give it a go, spending the entire trip sticking close to the hotel, building snowmen, perfecting the art of making snowballs, and creating a fort made of giant ice cubes with Laura.

Unlike her big brother, Rosie had relished the idea of skiing and turned into a little daredevil giving both him and her coach several scares in the week they were there, when she took off after the big kids and sailed down slopes even he would have been hesitant to try.

That trip could have been the last they ever took as a family.

If he had known that, he would have savored every second of it so much more than he had. He would have taken thousands of photographs and videos. He would have committed every single second of it to memory. He would have treasured up each moment, so he could hold them in his heart when he needed to remember the happy times they'd shared.

If he had known what was going to happen to Laura, he would have done so many things differently. He would never have argued with her. Looking back on it now, nothing was worth wasting time being angry with the person you loved. He would have spent a couple of minutes longer in bed each morning holding his wife. He would have come home a little earlier from work each day to spend more time with his family. He would have said *I love you* more. He'd have held hands more, made love more, and he would have expressed his love for Laura more in his words and in his actions.

But now it was too late.

Laura hadn't stirred once in the forty-eight hours since she'd been stabbed, and he was starting to think maybe she never would.

In his mind, he was already starting to process and think about how he was going to juggle a demanding job with being a single parent and not over relying on his friends and family who he knew would always be willing to help in whatever ways they could, but he didn't want to take advantage.

A single parent.

Even the sound of the words terrified him.

Jack didn't want to admit that this could be his new reality.

He wanted his wife back.

Mark and the other doctors didn't seem to know much of

anything. Every time he asked for an update, he got something vague along the lines of: Laura had lost a lot of blood; her injuries had been severe; it would take her body time to recover; they didn't really know what was going to happen, and they would just have to wait and see.

Well, he was done waiting.

He shoved his phone into his pocket and headed back to Laura's room. He was hoping to catch Elle Staines before she left. He'd been surprised to see her standing outside Laura's hospital room when he'd come out to call and check on the kids, but he supposed it made sense. Elle had been one of Laura's patients, and from what he understood—although his wife never talked about anything any of the people she counseled told her—the teenager didn't really have anyone else to talk to, so she had come to rely on Laura.

From the look on the girl's face as she looked through the window, she was blaming herself.

Jack knew all about that.

He was blaming himself for Laura's attack. Although the logical part of his brain knew that it wasn't his fault, that there wasn't anything he could have done to stop it from happening. The emotional side of his brain hadn't caught on yet. Probably never would.

He might be having no luck convincing himself to let go of the guilt, but maybe he could help Elle let go of hers. When he opened the door to Laura's room, he was surprised to see it empty other than his wife. Elle was gone already?

"Mark, did you see Elle Staines? Did she leave already?" he asked, stepping back outside to where his brother was standing. Jack was sure his brother had taken time off from work because Mark hadn't done anything but stay here with Laura and him.

"She just left, about thirty seconds before you got back," Mark replied. "Why?"

"I was hoping to talk to her. How did she seem?" Hopefully

spending some time talking to Laura, even if she couldn't talk back, had helped to calm the girl, give her some sort of reassurance.

"A little twitchy and jumpy. I asked her if she needed a ride back to the center, and she just shook her head and pretty much ran off down the hall."

That seemed odd.

Why would she be nervous?

It wasn't like Laura could have said anything to upset her.

"Is something wrong?" Mark asked.

"No, I don't think so, I just—" He broke off when an alarm went off in his wife's room. "Laura?" He dashed into the room, his brother on his heels.

Machines were beeping frantically.

Laura lay unmoving in the bed.

Completely unmoving.

She wasn't breathing.

Mark ran to the bed and immediately began working on Laura.

Doctors and nurses flooded the room.

They all seemed to know what they were doing; they all seemed to have a purpose.

All except him.

He was Laura's husband, and there was nothing he could do to help her right now.

That left him feeling so impotent that he wanted to rip off his own skin piece by piece, just so he could feel something else.

If this was it, if Laura was dying, then he needed to be there for her. He had to hold her, he needed her to know that she wasn't alone, that he was with her to the very end, and beyond that.

Jack tried to rush toward her, desperate to have his wife in his arms one last time.

Before he could get to her, he was grabbed from behind and yanked back.

"Stay back, Jack; let us work," one of the doctors told him.

"I can't." How could anyone ask him to do that? "She needs me."

"Right now, she needs you to stand back and let us do our jobs."

"I just need to touch her," he pleaded. He wasn't beyond begging right about now.

"I'm sorry," the doctor said and then tried to drag him from the room.

He resisted.

Who wouldn't?

They were trying to take him away from the woman he loved when she needed him the most.

Laura needed him.

She needed to know how much he and the kids needed her.

She needed to feel it, to feel him.

She needed to know just how much he needed her to fight.

He struggled to get away from the arms pulling him back. They felt like tentacles wrapped around, squeezing the life out of him. Laura was his life; without her, he didn't see how he could survive.

Jack fought harder, and more arms took hold of him, forcibly removing him from the room.

He didn't stop fighting.

He couldn't.

All he could think of was Laura.

Part of his brain hoped he wasn't hurting anyone lashing out as he was, but that thought got lost amongst the chaos.

Laura.

Get to Laura.

It was like a mantra in his head, repeating itself over and over again.

"Jack, stop. Jack, listen to me."

Slowly, the voice penetrated the fog he was trapped in.

Mark.

There was only one reason his brother would have left Laura.

His knees buckled, and he would have dropped if people weren't still holding him.

Laura was dead.

Gone.

Forever.

He thought he might be screaming … He was definitely crying … He could feel the wetness on his cheeks.

His wife was dead.

The woman he loved gone.

He was freefalling like he'd jumped from a plane without a parachute, only there was no end in sight for him. He was just going to fall and fall forever, stuck in a perpetual state of agony, waiting for relief that was never going to come.

How was he going to tell his kids?

How was he going to help them deal with this loss when he had no idea how he was going to deal with it?

"Jack, listen to me. Laura is still alive."

He froze.

The world froze along with him.

"Are you hearing me? Laura isn't dead. Her heart stopped, and she stopped breathing, but we were able to resuscitate her. Jack, she's not gone."

Relief had his knees buckling once again, and this time he was lowered to sit, and he leaned back against the wall, the relief so intense it stole his breath for a moment.

Laura wasn't gone … She hadn't left them … She was still alive … He still had her.

Suddenly, something occurred to him.

What if this wasn't an accident?

What if someone had done something to Laura?

"Elle." He launched himself to his feet, so angry he saw red. "Where is Elle Staines?"

* * * * *

4:26 P.M.

"Jack?" Ryan burst through the door into Laura's hospital room.

He'd received a phone call from Mark ordering him to get to the hospital as soon as possible. He and Paige had dropped what they were doing and come straight here. His younger brother hadn't given many details, just said that Jack needed them.

The only reason Ryan could think of that Jack would need him was that the worst had happened, and Laura had died.

They had run their lights and sirens and made record time from the precinct to the hospital, but now that they were here in Laura's room, he saw that she was hooked up to a ventilator and machines were still beeping their insistences that she was alive.

"She's still alive," Jack confirmed. "Just. She stopped breathing … Her heart stopped beating … I thought she was gone." The stark terror in his brother's face and tone shook him. He hoped he never found himself in this same position.

"But she's okay," he said, half question, half needing clarification because from the sound of things they had lost Laura only to get her yanked back at the last moment.

"For now, at least. Where's Elle?" Jack asked.

"She's sitting in a room waiting for us to interview her. They found her just about to get onto the bus to presumably go back to the center. Apparently, she didn't offer any resistance when she was asked to come back in, didn't even ask why. You really think she did something to Laura?" Ryan couldn't imagine the quiet teenager doing anything even close to attempted murder.

"I don't know, but she was alone in here, then about a minute after she leaves, Laura suddenly goes into cardiac arrest. Mark said she looked nervous when he saw her leaving. I don't know for sure that she did anything, but someone has been killing off hostages—we're guessing to keep them quiet—well, Laura was there as well. Deacon stabbed her, but maybe he said something to her first, something someone thinks could incriminate them. Maybe they decided it was better to take her out before she could wake up and take them out."

It made as much sense as anything else the last few days. "If Elle did anything to Laura, we'll find out. We won't let her get away with it," he promised his brother.

Leaving the room was both difficult and a relief. He felt bad leaving his brother alone to sit as his wife's side, clutching her hand and praying that she would live. He felt like he should be there to offer whatever support he could. And yet, at the same time, being there with Jack with Laura in a coma was hard. He kept picturing his and Jack's positions reversed with him sitting there begging his wife to live.

The fact that he and his wife were having problems didn't help.

Things between him and Sofia weren't getting better. They were getting worse, and what made things even harder, he had no idea how to go about fixing them.

If Sofia refused to talk to him, then what could he do? He couldn't make her open up, and as much as he wished she would talk to him, so long as she talked to *someone,* he was good. He just wanted her to find a way to come to terms with what had happened and that she had done the right thing. Ryan wished he had tried to take a shot. In the course of his job he had shot to kill before, and while he hated when things came down to that, he did what he had to. Just like Sofia had done.

"Everything okay with Laura?" Paige asked the second he opened the door to the small office where his partner was waiting for him with Elle Staines.

"She's still alive," he assured her, noting that Elle was discreetly listening while pretending that she was more focused on her hands, which were folded neatly and resting in her lap.

Ryan didn't know the teenager well enough to decide if he thought she'd actually attempted to murder Laura. But he didn't think Sofia would have allowed the girl to live at the center where so many vulnerable women and children lived, and where their children spent time after school and during school vacations, if she believed that the girl was dangerous.

"Elle, is there anything you want to tell us?" he asked as he and Paige both pulled up chairs and set them close enough to Elle to make her feel on edge and boxed in.

"No," the teenager replied quietly and a little sullenly. His kids might not be teens yet, although Sophie was heading quickly toward being a preteen, but he had teenage nephews and nieces. He spent time around the teens at the center and plenty of teens in his job. Whatever was going on with Elle Staines went beyond just being a brooding teenager.

"Why did you come here?" he asked.

Elle just shrugged.

"Does your mother know you're here?" Ryan asked. Maybe they'd been wrong, and it wasn't Macey who was killing off the hostages. Maybe it was Elle. The girl certainly wouldn't be seen as a threat by anyone, so it would make sense that both Amy and Tara would have let her in, probably to comfort her after the death of her father. Their killer didn't need to be physically strong to kill someone with drugs and alcohol or to drop a hair dryer into a bathtub. So, the fact that Elle was as thin as a rake and probably weighed maybe one hundred pounds didn't discount her.

Elle shrugged again, but then gave a single shake of her head.

Ryan was starting to get frustrated. Laura was his sister-in-law. They'd been friends since they were babies, and his wife and his partner, as well as himself were on this killer's list, if indeed she was working her way through the hostages. He wasn't in the mood to play games.

"What's going on, Elle?" Paige asked, with a lot more patience than he could muster.

The girl looked up nervously. "What happened to Laura?"

"She stopped breathing," Paige replied.

"But she's still alive?" Elle asked, sounding like she needed reassurance.

"Why did you come here?" Ryan repeated his earlier question.

"I just needed someone to talk to," Elle answered.

"You couldn't have talked to your mother?" Ryan asked.

Elle rolled her eyes in response.

Right. Teenagers didn't talk about things with their parents. "What about one of your friends?"

"I don't have any friends."

For a teenager, that would be tougher than tough. They needed friends; it was how they defined themselves, and it was how they functioned. "What about some of the other kids from the center? You aren't close with any of them?"

Elle shook her head.

"What about Tara?" Paige asked.

Elle wouldn't meet their gaze, but she shook her head again. "The only person I had to talk to was Laura."

"What did you two talk about?" he asked.

"Everything. That's why I came."

Her acknowledgment could either show that she had nothing to hide as she had admitted that she had told Laura things that perhaps she didn't want anyone else to know. Or, it further incriminated her.

"Mark said that you seemed nervous when he saw you leaving Laura's room," Ryan confronted her. "Why were you nervous?"

"I was worried what my mom was going to say if she found out that I snuck away from the center without telling her. I just wanted to get back there as quickly as I could. I'd already done what I came here for."

Ryan couldn't get a read on the girl. She seemed sincere and yet at the same time he sensed that she was hiding something.

"Did you hurt Laura, Elle? Did you do something to her to?

Did you try to kill her?" he asked.

"I would never do anything to hurt someone," Elle said but without a lot of conviction.

"You were the only one in the room, Elle," Paige pushed. "Did you maybe do something by accident? Did you touch Laura? Did you touch any of the machines?"

"All I did was sit beside her bed and talk," Elle said.

"Did you see Tara May or Amy Frankstone after your father's death?" They may as well confront her about the other deaths and see if they could get her to crack.

"No."

"Was your mother really sleeping last night when Tara was killed?"

"I don't know."

"What about when Amy was killed, were you two together then?"

"I can't remember. I guess."

"Would your mother have any reason to be worried that someone might find out something about her that she's desperate to keep secret?" If they could find a motive, then maybe they could prove that all of these deaths weren't suicides or accidents, but murders.

"I—"

"Don't say another word, Elle." The door was suddenly flung open and Macey Staines stormed in.

"Elle was in the room just seconds before Laura stopped breathing, Macey," Paige informed her.

"And you think my daughter tried to kill her?" Macey demanded. "Come on, Elle, we're leaving. Now."

"We're not finished talking to her," Ryan said.

"Oh, yes, you are. If you want to talk to either of us again, you can go through my lawyer." With that, Macey stalked over, grabbed her daughter's arm, and dragged her from the room.

Laura was alive for now, but if Elle wanted her dead, then she wasn't safe. None of them were. There was still a killer out there hunting them, and if the killer stuck to schedule, then another one of them would be dead by the morning.

* * * * *

10:10 P.M.

"I'm going to bed," Ryan announced.

"Okay, goodnight," Sofia said stiffly. She has spent the evening working, finalizing details for the charity ball and attending to other things she'd been procrastinating on. She had someone who did all the finances for the center, and people who took care of the administration side of things, but in the end, it was her center and she made sure that she went over everything.

"Are you coming?" her husband asked.

"No, I'm still working." She knew she couldn't keep making excuses to avoid Ryan. Last night having all the kids had meant they were busy enough that there wasn't any time where he could get her alone.

Tonight, it was just the four of them and avoiding him had been much harder. They had eaten dinner as a family then watched one of the kids' favorite movies. Together she and Ryan had put Sophie and Ned to bed, tucked them in, read to them, then she had immediately announced she had work to do. She had expected him to try to push her to talk the second they were alone, but he hadn't. He just turned on the TV and watched sports.

"Where are you sleeping tonight? Our bed or the couch?" he asked her. He was always one to be direct and not bother with beating around the bush.

She could lie and hope that Ryan was already asleep before he realized that she wasn't going to join him, but in the end, he was going to find out anyway. "The couch."

Ryan sighed and ran his hands through his blond hair. Then he directly met her eye. "I understand that taking a human life, no matter how justified—and what you did *was* justified—takes a toll on you. I get it. I do. I've been there. But shutting me out and withdrawing isn't helping you. I know you'd usually talk to Laura at a time like this, but since you can't, you have to find someone else to open up to. You can't keep going on like this."

Sofia felt herself bristle.

Why was Ryan always so understanding?

Couldn't he just leave her alone and let her wallow in the stifling depression that was settling over her?

"You can talk to me, Sofia." He took a tentative step toward her. "I'm right here. I know what you're going through. I'll listen to anything you have to say. I'll give you my opinion, or if you just need to vent without me saying anything, then you can do that too. Whatever you need, but you have to do something."

Maybe she should.

Maybe he was right.

Maybe isolating herself wasn't the right thing to do.

It would be so easy; all she had to do was start talking. Ryan was a good listener. And really, she didn't need him to say anything. She just needed to talk and keep talking until she figured out why shooting Deacon Staines was affecting her this way.

She should do it.

She knew that.

Instead, what came out of her mouth was, "I just need some space right now."

Ryan sighed. "Fine, I won't push you into talking. But that doesn't change anything. You still need to figure out a way to deal with this. I get that we all deal with things differently, so I'll try not to impose my ways on you. I'll try to let you process what happened in your own time and in your own way."

"That wasn't what I meant."

"Then what did you mean?"

Nervous now, she had to clasp her hands together to stop them from fidgeting. "I was thinking that I might take the kids and we'd go and stay at a hotel for a while." Sofia found herself holding her breath as she awaited her husband's response to the idea that had been floating around her head, at first not quite fully formed, for the last forty-eight hours.

Ryan just stared at her.

For so long, she couldn't resist the urge to fiddle with her bracelet and her rings.

At last, Ryan cleared his throat. "How is taking Sophie out of the only home she has ever lived in to stay at a hotel at a time when she's traumatized and needs stability going to help her?"

"Maybe a change of scenery will help her," she retorted.

"It won't. She needs familiarity right now. She needs her routines; she needs her room and her things; she needs her family and her friends. She needs her normal life."

Ryan was probably right but *she* didn't want her normal life right now. She needed a timeout. "Sophie needs her mother," she said.

"I'm not saying she doesn't. Look, Sofia …" His voice had gone hard as had his expression. "You're an adult, and I can't make you stay here. If you want to leave, there is nothing I could do to stop you. But I will not, under any circumstances, let you take my kids and leave. *This* is their home, and I am their father. Go and stay in a hotel if that's what you feel like you need to do, but those kids are not going anywhere."

With that, he turned and left.

Leaving her staring after him.

She hadn't expected him to be thrilled with the idea of her and the kids going to a hotel for a while, but she hadn't really expected him to outright refuse to let her take Sophie and Ned.

Sofia would never keep her kids from their father; they adored him, and Ryan was everything she could wish for in the father of her children. She just needed some time to think, and she needed her kids, but it seemed like she couldn't have both. She was going to have to make a choice.

Space or her children.

What kind of choice was that?

Obviously, she would choose her kids over anything, but what kind of mother was she going to be able to be to them if she couldn't get herself together?

She needed to sort out what was going on with her; everything she loved depended on it. She still loved her husband despite this sudden intense need to not be around him, and she loved her children and their family. She didn't want to lose the life she had.

Grabbing a pillow and a blanket, she stretched out on the couch. She left the lights on; she didn't want to fall asleep in the dark. When she was a little girl she used to sleepwalk. She hadn't in decades, but sometimes when she was stressed, her sleep was filled with night terrors.

Sleep.

She'd almost forgotten what that was like.

She hadn't really slept since she'd killed Deacon Staines. Every time she closed her eyes, everything that had happened played out like it was stuck on repeat.

Maybe if she got some rest, she'd be able to think more clearly and actually figure things out.

Clearing her mind of everything, she was just drifting off when she heard a scream.

Sofia bolted upright.

Sophie.

She didn't even process what she was doing. Sofia just launched herself off the couch and ran up the stairs, two at a time.

Ryan was already throwing Sophie's bedroom door open and switching on the light by the time she reached the second floor.

"Mommy, Mommy," Sophie was sobbing over and over again.

"Its okay, Sophie." Ryan was kneeling by the bed when she got to her daughter's bedroom door.

"No!" Sophie shrieked. "Where's Mommy? Where's Mommy?"

"I'm right here, baby, right here." She rushed to the bed and wrapped her arms around her daughter.

"You were dead," Sophie sobbed into her shoulder.

"You were dreaming, sweetheart," she soothed.

"He shot you … there was blood … you were dead." Sophie continued to cry hysterically.

Lifting her daughter into her arms, she sat on the bed and rocked Sophie like she hadn't done since she was a baby. "You were dreaming, honey. It was just a dream. I'm here. I'm okay."

"I was so scared. I saw him shoot you." Sophie pressed herself closer, nuzzling her wet face into Sofia's neck.

"I know it was scary, sweetie, but you can see that I'm okay. Sometimes dreams feel so real, but they aren't. Why don't you lie back down and try to go back to sleep. You need your rest."

"Don't leave me." Sophie clutched at her.

"Shh, sweetheart, I'll stay in here with you tonight."

"On the bed with me?"

"On the bed with you, holding you tight in my arms all night long," she promised. "I'm not going anywhere … I'd never leave you." As she said the words, she realized they were true. She couldn't leave her daughter when she was suffering like this. Which meant she either had to find a way to let go of this unfair hostility she felt toward Ryan, or she would have to leave, meaning there would be a nasty custody battle.

She wasn't letting her kids go and neither was Ryan.

AUGUST 17TH

3:23 A.M.

She hoped she'd made the right decision.

Teagan Vonce wasn't sure that she had; she wasn't sure she had ever made a right decision in her life.

She was going to be sixty-three next month, and when she looked back she found she had nothing to be proud of—no achievements, and she'd never done anything of merit for herself or for anyone else.

Leaving a bad situation after four decades was terrifying, but she'd done it.

One day she had been standing at the sink in front of the kitchen window, scrubbing the dishes just the way her husband liked them. She'd seen her neighbor, a woman about her age, playing with her grandchild—a little boy of about three—in the street. The two were laughing and chatting and they looked like they were having so much fun. They looked like they loved each other so much.

And it hit her.

There wasn't a single person on the planet who loved her.

She had been shocked.

At first, she had tried to deny it, but it was true. It was her reality. She was alone in the world except for a husband who had isolated her from everyone who used to love her, who manipulated her, and who abused her emotionally, psychologically, and physically.

That moment had been the wake up call she needed.

She had given up the family who had adored her, encouraged

her, believed in her for a man who only wanted to control and destroy her. She knew she should have left him the second he laid his hands on her, but pride had gotten in the way. Her family and her friends had warned her about him, but she had stubbornly refused to believe them, thinking she was in love. When she realized she'd been wrong and they had been right, she hadn't wanted to let them know it. So she'd allowed him to isolate her until all she did was spend her days fighting a losing battle to keep herself and the house perfect so he wouldn't get angry with her.

It had taken her almost a month after her revelation to do something about it.

Knowing that she had to make a change didn't necessarily mean she had the courage to make said change.

She had waged an internal conflict.

Should she leave, or shouldn't she?

Forty years of being belittled and told she was worthless, of being manipulated, and beaten down until she felt like she was nothing was a hard thing to overcome.

After so many decades spent in an abusive marriage and being in her sixties she had wondered whether it was worth doing anything. Surely, she may as well just last it out, probably only another ten years or so if she was lucky, then she'd be dead anyway.

Teagan had so very nearly chosen that route.

The easy route.

The route that would have confirmed every horrible thing her husband had ever said to her.

But she hadn't given into the fear.

She had waited until he went to work one day then grabbed her things and ran.

At the time she hadn't known where she was going; she just knew that she had to get away—far, far away.

Living on the streets those first few weeks had been tough but no harder than living in her house with her husband had been.

Then she'd met a cop.

Detective Paige Hood.

The woman had told her about the center for abused women and children that she helped to run with some friends and brought her to the first safe place she'd been in years.

She had taken control of her life for the first time.

And that's what she was doing now.

The safety the center had offered was nothing more than an illusion.

Danger and violence had touched it too.

One woman's husband had tracked his wife down there and held a gun to her head, demanding that she return. Although she had somehow survived that, two of the other people who had been in that room were now dead.

Would she be next?

She couldn't take that chance, so she had run.

Teagan didn't have much money, but she had taken what she did have and paid for a motel room. The small amount of money she had wouldn't last long, and she knew she couldn't stay here more than a day or two. Right now she had no plan; she was just doing what she had to do to survive. Maybe once the cops found who had killed Tara May and Amy Frankstone she would go back to the center, or maybe that place was now ruined for her beyond repair.

Right now, though, she could at least get a good night's sleep without worrying about someone coming to kill her.

She snuggled down into the motel bed. She'd spent forty years going to bed nursing injuries and afraid that the man she shared her bed with would wake in a rage. It was so nice to know that now she could go to bed and sleep safely and soundly.

She drifted off.

Sometime later, years of practice listening out for threats had her snapping awake.

A split second too slow.

The figure above the bed pressed a pillow to her face.

Instinct had her clawing at the hand that was smothering her; she kicked her feet and struggled with everything her abused sixty-year-old body had.

If she had done anything of note with her life, it probably would have flashed before her eyes. Instead, she saw nothing but empty blackness.

Darkness had been her life for the last forty years. It seemed only fitting that she should be consumed by it in the end.

* * * * *

3:52 A.M.

She wondered how long it took to smother someone.

It was taking longer than she'd thought.

All the murders she'd committed had taken longer than she'd thought they would. Who knew death was such a slow process.

She pressed harder down against the pillow. She knew Teagan Vonce's air supply was already cut off but maybe that would speed the process up a little.

Eventually, the woman's struggles began to slow. Her thrashing became weaker, and although she kept trying to claw at the pillow, she was only connecting maybe one out of every three or four times now.

"Come on," she muttered aloud. This was getting ridiculous. The woman was old and in her sixties. She should be dead by now.

Another minute ticked by and still Teagan continued to struggle.

"Why won't you die?" she growled, annoyed. It would be so much easier to just shoot the woman. She didn't own a gun, but she could have stabbed her, surely that would be faster than this. But that would look too suspicious. She had to keep playing things safe if she was going to have hope of making this work.

Although it was looking less and less likely that she could actually do this.

The cops already knew that Tara and Amy had been murdered; they just weren't sure yet who'd done it.

"Are you dead yet?" she asked, not sure why she was asking. If Teagan was dead she couldn't reply. The woman had stopped fighting, so maybe she was dead.

Tentatively, she removed the pillow.

Was Teagan dead?

She wasn't quite sure.

It wasn't like she was any expert in dead bodies even if this was her third kill.

This was the most up close and personal kill she'd made. With Amy, she had just put the crushed pills in the alcohol and sat back and waited for her to die. With Tara, she'd talked her into getting in the bath while they chatted—which, she was proud to say, she had accomplished after quite a bit of persuasion. Then when the woman was distracted, had just taken the hair dryer, that had helpfully been sitting plugged in on the counter, and tossed it into the bath.

But this time she was actually touching her victim.

Feeling the life drain out of her.

Wait.

Teagan wasn't dead.

Her chest still rose and fell with each shallow breath that she took.

Why wouldn't this stupid woman die?

She already had enough to deal with, trying to keep her secrets, trying to take out everyone who could potentially destroy her, trying to figure out how to take them out.

Teagan had made things a little trickier by moving to a motel, but she'd handled it like the talented killer she was becoming.

Returning the pillow to Teagan's face, she pressed as hard as she could. Smothering her like this was probably going to confirm for the cops that these deaths had all been murder, but there was nothing she could do about that. She just had to kill her; she couldn't worry about how it would look to the cops. And if luck was on her side—and so far, it had been—hopefully they wouldn't even find the body for a while, at least until she was done.

Finally.

Teagan was dead.

She could feel it.

Somehow, she could feel the woman's life slip away.

It felt odd, indescribable, but she could feel it.

That was three down now.

She was getting closer.

* * * * *

9:11 A.M.

Ryan was finding it particularly difficult to concentrate today.

All he could think about was his conversation with Sofia last night.

She wanted to leave.

He had seen it in her eyes.

This had gone beyond just her struggling to deal with taking a life and had now impacted their relationship to the point where things might be over.

Really over.

He had never thought he would ever think those words. He had believed that his marriage was rock solid. He had believed that the love he and Sofia shared was strong enough to weather anything life threw at it.

Apparently, he'd been wrong.

It didn't look like their marriage was going to weather this, which gutted him.

His family was the most important thing in the world to him. It was the *only* thing in the world to him.

Right now Ryan didn't know what the future held for his family, but he did know that under no circumstances would he allow Sofia to take his kids and leave. They were both Sophie and Ned's parents. Neither had more right to the children than the other, but right now their daughter needed her home; she needed to feel safe in her surroundings. Last night's nightmares were proof of that. If Sofia insisted on leaving then he foresaw a custody battle in the near future—neither of them was going to give up the kids without a fight.

He couldn't believe he was really thinking about the possibility of having to sort out a custody arrangement. Of not being able to have his kids there every day, to not see them in the morning and kiss them goodnight every night when he put them to bed. And what happened if Sofia remarried one day? He didn't want any other man playing dad to his children; they had a father and he wasn't going anywhere. And how was he going to manage the practicalities of being a single father? His job had unpredictable hours which weren't conducive to school drop-offs and pick-ups, and extracurricular activities, and home cooked meals, and all the other things that went with kids.

Okay, he had to stop himself before he drove himself insane.

Right now all of this was worrying about something that hadn't even happened yet.

Hopefully Sofia would get herself some help and they could repair the damage done. And he couldn't deny that damage *had* been done. While he understood that she was struggling and that taking a life was messing with her head, that she had decided her method of dealing with it was to bail on him, their marriage, and their family—that hurt, and it rocked his trust in her.

Struggling was one thing; it was part of life. But that was exactly when they were supposed to turn to each other, seek strength from each other. Instead, Sofia wanted to walk away from everything they'd built and shared.

If she really loved him, then leaving him would be the last thing on her mind.

Although he didn't want to be thinking this way, he was having doubts about her and whether or not she really did love him.

"Ryan."

"What?" He blinked and looked at his partner.

"I've been calling your name for the last two minutes. What were you thinking about?" Paige asked.

"Nothing." He knew it was a bad lie and he knew she wouldn't believe it, but he hoped she would just leave it alone. He really didn't want to discuss the state of his marriage right now.

"Things not getting any better with Sofia?"

"No, not really—worse, actually."

"You want me to talk to her?" Paige offered.

He appreciated that, he really did, but Paige was friends with both of them, and it didn't seem fair to get her involved because she would end up having to choose sides. "Thanks, but I don't think there's anything you could do. I think that until she acknowledges that she needs help, there's no way to help her."

"I'm sorry things have gotten so bad."

"Thanks." Obsessing over the state of his family wasn't productive. If they didn't find who was killing the hostages, then he'd be worrying about more than just a divorce and custody case. He and Sofia could both be dead and neither of them raising their kids. "I wish that Teagan Vonce had stayed at the center."

"Me too," Paige said, looking sad. She had spent time with Teagan at the center, and although the older woman had only been there a couple of weeks, Ryan knew that Paige had already started to bond with her. "Why would she leave? We could have protected her if she'd stayed. I would have made sure that I or another cop was on her apartment so the killer couldn't get to her. But she left and now ..." Paige trailed off.

She didn't need to finish her sentence; he already knew how it ended.

Teagan Vonce was dead.

Her body had been discovered around six o'clock this morning. She had been suffocated. Unlike the last two crime scenes, this time the killer had to break in. The door had been forced open, possibly with a crowbar. Which made sense, if their killer was Macey or Elle Staines. They hadn't known Teagan as long, and she wouldn't have been as receptive to opening the door to them. And with two of the hostages already dead, then Teagan would have been warier, more on edge, looking for dangers where the other two hadn't had any reason to.

"We need to figure out which one of them it is," he said.

"Are we sure it's one of them?"

"Who else could it be? What would anyone else have to gain by killing off the people who had been in the room with Deacon?"

"I don't know. I can't think of anyone else who would want to kill us off, but I don't like that we don't have a motive," Paige said. "Yes, I can't think of anyone else who the killer could be but that doesn't mean I know what Macey or Elle would have to gain by killing us."

"Self-preservation."

"But why? What do they have to lose? Deacon didn't say anything in that room that made either of them look guilty of anything." Paige shook her head in frustration. "Okay, let's just go with it's one of them. Which one do we like?"

"Macey seems like the more obvious choice. She's an adult. She would be the one who's more likely to be able to pull this off. Plus, it seems like she would be the one who would have something to lose. What would Elle have done that her father would have let slip that would be worth killing over? At least with Macey, we know that she isn't Elle's mother. Maybe Deacon knew something that would cause her to lose her daughter. That would be something worth killing for."

"I would have agreed that Macey was the more likely suspect until Laura. I know we don't know for sure that she did anything to Laura, but Elle was in the room alone, then she leaves in a hurry looking nervous and seconds later Laura goes into cardiac arrest. It's too coincidental to ignore. Laura had been counseling both Macey and Elle, and she was alone with Deacon before he stabbed her. We don't know what, if anything, he said to her. If anyone knows anything incriminating, it's her."

Paige was right.

Either of them could be the killer.

Until they had something concrete, there was no way to know, and they were running out of time. They could go back and forth indefinitely without making progress. They needed something. Anything. Even something small. They just needed something to point them in the right direction.

Then like a godsend, Francesca Marks came rushing over to their desks. Frankie was a fifty-four-year-old medical examiner he always enjoyed working with. She was dedicated to her job, as well as to her family. She'd gone through years of infertility treatments to finally get pregnant and carry her daughter to term, and that little girl, now eleven years old, was the light of her life.

The look on Frankie's face clearly said she had something for them.

"Hey, guys," she beamed, pulling up an empty chair and dropping down into it.

"What do you have?" Paige asked, hope in her brown eyes.

"Deacon Staines was being poisoned with mercury." Frankie's dark eyes twinkled. "Symptoms include mood swings, nervousness, irritability, emotional changes, insomnia, headaches, abnormal sensations, tremors, weakness, and decreased cognitive functions."

Poisoned?

That certainly added a different light to things.

Some of the women at the center hadn't believed that Macey was really a victim of domestic violence. Maybe they were right. Maybe Macey was really the abusive one. If she had been poisoning her husband that could be what she was afraid they would figure out.

Deacon had said over and over again that he had never hurt his wife, and he had seemed unbalanced and like he was on something. What Frankie had just told them about mercury poisoning could explain Deacon's behavior that day and in the months leading up to it.

This could be what they needed to end this before anyone else died.

* * * * *

10:02 A.M.

"Hey."

"Hey," she returned. Daisy shivered as her husband sat down beside her. She'd been on edge ever since she learned she had a nephew.

"You doing okay?" Mark asked, slipping an arm around her shoulders and tugging gently, encouraging her to lean against him.

She honestly didn't know the answer to that question.

She was and she wasn't.

On the one hand, she was so very glad that the business her family had started was closed forever now. Babies would continue to be sold on the black market and girls and women would continue to be abducted and used in the sex trade market—but at least one group of people doing it had been stopped, and that made a difference, however small.

On the other, she was now faced with an impossible dilemma. Should she take in her brother's son or not?

Daisy didn't know what to do.

Every time she thought she had made up her mind, she rethought her decision. She had gone back and forth so many times in the last forty-eight hours that her head was spinning.

"It's okay if you don't want to have Blaze come and live with us," Mark said.

"But if I don't, what will happen to him?" She didn't want more harm to come to the boy if he went into foster care and didn't get placed with a nice family.

"He's a strong kid. I'm sure whatever happens he'll be okay," her husband consoled her.

"What kind of person am I if I turn him away?"

"You're the same amazing, kind, caring, thoughtful, brave woman you've always been."

Mark was only saying that because he was her husband and he loved her.

How could she abandon a thirteen-year-old kid who had already lost both his parents and the only home he'd ever known?

If she did, wouldn't that make her just like the people she'd tried so hard not to be like?

Wouldn't it make her just as uncaring and heartless as the rest of her family?

Didn't it make her selfish?

"No."

"No what?" she asked, confused, tilting her head so she could look up at Mark.

"No it doesn't make you selfish or heartless or whatever other names you're calling yourself. It makes you a human being who's trying to do what's best for her family and balance that with figuring out what she can do for her nephew."

Daisy smiled and rested her head on Mark's shoulder. She had really lucked out with him. He was without a doubt the best husband a girl could hope for. He had forgiven her for lying to him, for hurting him and their children when she had left, for putting herself in danger, and for making wrong decisions based on fear that had let a killer hunt free.

Most days she didn't feel like she deserved Mark's unconditional love, but she was so grateful to have it.

"What are you scared of?" her husband asked, his hand trailing softly up and down her bare arm, making the skin go all goose pimply.

"That he's like them," she whispered. It was a horrible thing to think about a thirteen-year-old kid, but she couldn't help it.

"Like the rest of your family?"

"He helped. He worked with Wade to trick innocent young girls into going with him so they could kidnap them."

"So did Liam," Mark reminded her.

That was true.

Her cousin Liam had been forced to help play the role of young homeless teen to lure in vulnerable runaways, making them feel safe when they shouldn't, lulling them into a false sense of security so her family could swoop in and abduct them. Liam hadn't wanted to do it and tried to put a stop to what their family was doing, which almost got him killed. And although she hadn't known until recently, he had even helped her get away.

Even though he had done what he needed to survive and worked in the family business, Liam was a good guy. After living with the guilt of the choices he'd made and what he'd done, Liam was finally moving on and finding the happiness he deserved. He was dating the woman he had loved for most of his life but been afraid to pursue a relationship with, and he'd recently confided to her that he was planning on proposing.

If Liam had done unspeakable things but was still a good person inside, then it was possible that Blaze was too.

Who was she to deny him a chance to redeem himself and have a normal life?

But what if Blaze *wasn't* a good person inside?

Unlike Liam, Blaze had never known anything but the dark world of kidnapped runaways and black-market babies. He hadn't gone to school; he didn't have any friends; he hadn't spent time around teachers or other normal adults. How could he even know what the real world was like? He had been brainwashed to believe that his world was normal. What would he be like? How would he adjust to living in her home, with her family? Could she trust him around her children? How would he cope at school?

There were so many what ifs and she wasn't sure she was brave enough to give things a go. Which made her feel awful. Blaze was her own flesh and blood. Surely she owed it to him to at least give him a chance. She could get him some psychological help and invest time in him, and hopefully, he would learn to adjust. But was it fair to her four kids to take time away from them to put into their cousin, especially after everything she'd put them through last year?

Daisy groaned and snuggled closer to her husband. "I don't know what to do, Mark."

"You don't have to decide right now. Blaze can stay where he is in the group home and we can get to know him and then just see where things go."

"What time is it?" she asked. They were meeting Blaze here at the hospital at half past ten and she was nervous. She didn't know what to expect. She hadn't been close with Blaze's father, and now to have to decide whether she could take on the responsibilities of raising a child who'd had anything but a normal life was one of the most stressful decisions of her life.

"We have about ten minutes before we have to go and meet Blaze and the social worker." She hadn't wanted to meet Blaze at her home. She wasn't ready to have him that close to her family just yet, so they had decided the hospital was neutral ground for the first meeting.

"You look tired." Daisy traced her fingertips along her husband's stubbled jaw. She knew there was no use asking him to come home and get some rest. He wouldn't until he knew that Laura was going to be okay. "How's Laura doing?"

Mark's chest expanded as he drew in a deep breath. "She's not doing well."

"How not well?"

"I don't think she's going to pull through," he admitted.

"You think she's going to die?"

"Her chances of waking up now after all this time are slim. If we take her off life support, I expect that she'd die pretty quickly. She lost too much blood and her body is too weak."

She had known that Laura's condition was precarious, but she hadn't realized that things were quite so bad.

Daisy couldn't help but remember last January when Mark had been shot trying to save her life and she'd sat here in the hospital at his bedside praying that he would be okay.

She had been lucky.

She had gotten her husband back.

But it didn't look like Laura's family was going to be as lucky.

She wrapped her arms around her husband's neck and kissed him deeply. She loved him so much that sometimes it physically hurt. The thought of losing him was too much. As a kid she and her best friend had had one of those heart charms that had been split into two pieces so they could each wear one on a chain around their necks. That was what her love for Mark was like. It was like her heart now had two pieces—one beat inside her chest and the other walked around in Mark.

"Poor Jack," she said when she ended the kiss. She didn't want to imagine what he was going to feel when he found out that he was probably going to lose the woman he'd loved since childhood.

"We'll all be there for him and the kids; we'll help them through this."

They would but it wouldn't ease Jack, Zach, and Rosie's pain.

"I wish there was something I could do." Mark sounded despondent. Daisy knew he wouldn't take Laura's death well. Not only would he lose a sister-in-law and a friend he'd had since he was born, but he would feel partially responsible. He was a doctor, and in his mind it was his job to fix everyone, especially family, and that he couldn't save his brother's wife would eat away at him.

She wouldn't let this destroy him. She would do whatever she had to, to make him see that this wasn't his fault, that he had done everything within his power to save Laura.

But Laura wasn't dead yet.

And as long as she was alive there was always hope.

Sometimes hope was all you had, and you had to cling to it. You had to let it shed light on the darkness inside you so that that darkness didn't consume you.

As long as there was hope then you could get up and face each day.

And if that hope was extinguished, then you had to turn to what was left.

Love.

Even if Mark couldn't save Laura, he would still have their children and he would still have her. Their family's love would get him through.

And if Jack lost Laura, then he would still have his children. Together the three of them would make a new family that would never forget the missing piece or fill the hole losing Laura would leave, but at least they would still have each other.

Hope and love were every bit as much a part of living as oxygen and water and food. Without them you were dead inside even if your body remained alive.

"Dr. and Mrs. Xander?" A young woman approached them.

Together they stood. "Yes. Are you the social worker?" Daisy asked.

"I am." The woman shot them a warm smile. "Blaze is waiting to meet you."

Love and hope. If they could help Jack and his children through the worst loss imaginable, then maybe they could help her family too.

Hand in hand, she and Mark went to meet her nephew.

* * * * *

11:21 A.M.

All of the pieces of the puzzle were falling into place.

She was so close to getting what she wanted.

None of this had been easy, but she had started this journey and she had to see it through to the end.

The mercury poisoning had been a brilliant idea.

She wasn't even really sure where the idea had come from. She had just needed something to take out Deacon and that had suddenly popped into her head one day.

Sourcing it had been a little tricky, and then getting him to ingest it had also taken a little finagling, but she had been driven to achieve her goals and she had done whatever she had to in order to make it happen.

She had taken a lot of risks to get to this point; every step of the way had been fraught with danger. If she had been caught, she would have lost exactly what it was that she was fighting to get.

To see how her life was playing out, poisoning people, killing people, plotting more murders. Ten years ago, five years ago, even a year ago she wouldn't have seen this happening. She would never have thought that she was the kind of person who would do things like this, but desperate times called for desperate measures.

Getting Deacon so messed up he didn't know what he was doing and couldn't control himself had been vindicating. He deserved to suffer after what he'd done to her. She was glad that she had taken him down. She was, however, sorry that innocent people had gotten messed up in this; that wasn't what she had intended. People had died because of the ball she had started rolling. She might not like it, but it was what it was, and it certainly wasn't going to stop her. More people *would* die, but she wasn't backing out. Nothing could stop her.

When this was over, she would finally have what she had always wanted.

One bad decision shouldn't mean that you lost everything, that what was most important was ripped away from you.

It wasn't fair.

She was determined to right that wrong, even if it meant killing more people.

She had to figure out how to take out her next target. With Teagan Vonce dead, that was the last of the easy targets. Security had been increased at the center which made doing anything there much more difficult. Then there were the cops. Killing them was going to be hard, so hard that she was contemplating not bothering. Surely if anyone who had been in the room with Deacon had realized what they'd heard, they would have come forward by now.

Maybe she was safe.

Maybe it could be over.

But what if it wasn't?

Doubt.

That was what was killing her.

She couldn't let go of the doubt.

She had trusted her instincts once before and been wrong. So wrong that she had been badly burned by those she had trusted.

She couldn't make that mistake again.

She had an idea of what to do to get rid of the cops. She would just have to pray that it worked, and that when this was over, it would all have been worth it.

* * * * *

12:33 P.M.

"Come on, Laura. Don't make me do this," Mark begged his sister-in-law.

How did you sit your brother and the rest of your family down and tell them that you didn't think that their loved one was going to survive?

He was a trauma surgeon, so he'd definitely done his fair share of family notifications, but this was the first time he'd had to do it with his own family.

As much as he wanted to put this off and procrastinate for as long as possible, he couldn't avoid doing this forever.

It was time to man up.

He was a doctor. If he couldn't fix Laura, then the least he could do was make sure that he was the one to break the news.

How exactly he was going to do that, he wasn't sure yet.

Everything that he normally would say to the family of someone whom he'd operated on but been unable to save seemed wrong. This wasn't just any family. It was *his* family, and he wanted to be able to break the news gently, take some of the pain away.

Which, of course, he knew was pointless.

There was no easy way to say this.

Nothing he could do was going to take away the pain.

The pain was only going to get worse.

There were so many decisions that Jack needed to make. Did they keep Laura on life support? Did they keep hoping that if they waited long enough, she might wake up on her own? If they kept her on the ventilator, then for how long? Indefinitely? If her brain scans showed no signs of activity, then at some point, they had to discuss things like organ donation.

These were not the kind of questions anyone expected to be dealing with at the age of forty-one. Jack and Laura should have had half their lives still ahead of them. There was so much they still had to do. They should be watching their kids grow up, graduate, go to college, get jobs, fall in love, have kids. They should be able to enjoy their retirement together, and then when they were old and gray have to face making these kinds of choices.

It was time.

He couldn't stall any longer.

Everyone was waiting for him.

When he had spoken with Laura's doctors earlier this morning, they had come to the decision that it was time.

Time to have *the talk*.

The talk that changed lives.

The talk where you sat a family down and broke the news that their loved one was probably beyond saving.

While his colleagues had offered to do it, he had declined. This had to come from him. It wouldn't make it easier, and yet, in a way it would. This wasn't just a doctor giving bad news. This would be a family member who loved and cared about the patient and was grieving right along with you.

And he was.

Laura had always been a part of his life. Just like Ryan, and almost every other guy at their school, he'd had a crush on her when they were teenagers, but even back then, it had been obvious that Jack and Laura were meant to be. He had been satisfied with just being friends, and he'd been thrilled when Jack had reconnected with Laura and she'd come back into their lives. Now they were all so close that her death would leave a hole in his day-to-day life. So often they picked up each other's kids after school or babysat on weekends so that one of them could have a date night.

"Prove me wrong, Laura. There's still time."

With a last look at his sister-in-law, he left her room and headed for the waiting room where he'd told everyone to wait for him when he'd called them all after he and Daisy had met her nephew.

While he wanted to keep giving Laura one more day and one more day and one more day, he couldn't. He couldn't let his family keep living with false hope.

"Hey." He attempted a smile as he opened the door and fourteen anxious and nervous faces looked up at him. Jack, his parents, Ryan and Sofia, Daisy, Laura's parents, and Laura's sister and her husband, Paige and her husband Elias, Xavier and Annabelle. His family. He would do anything for any single one of them, and yet, the one thing they needed him to do he couldn't.

"What's wrong with Laura?" Jack asked. Everyone else was sitting except for his oldest brother who was pacing the room at a near frantic speed.

"Come and sit," he said, joining the others. He hated the resigned looks on their faces. He hated that those resigned looks were well founded.

"No," Jack all but shouted. "What's wrong? She was still breathing when you asked me to leave her room so you could examine her. Did something happen?"

"Nothing happened," he replied.

"Then why are we here? Why did you call everyone? If Laura's still the same, then why are you wasting our time and keeping me from getting back to her?"

"That is why we're here." Mark worked to keep his tone as 'doctor-y' as he could while still letting some of what he was feeling come through. "We're here because nothing has changed. Laura has been here for seventy-two hours now, and there have been no changes in her condition. She's not heavily medicated; there's nothing preventing her from waking up."

Jack said nothing, just continued pacing the length of the room.

"What's her brain scan like?" Laura's father asked.

"It's okay; it's still showing signs of activity. She's not brain dead, but she's not waking up."

"But she still could wake up," Jack said.

"She could," he agreed. "But, Jack, it doesn't look like she's going to." Mark drew in a deep breath. "In my medical opinion, I don't believe that she's going to wake up."

"I don't believe that," Jack immediately protested.

Everyone else looked shattered but not necessarily surprised. Most of the couples turned to each other and offered whatever consolations they could. All except for Ryan and Sofia. Both sat stiffly, looking just as upset as everyone else but all but ignoring one another. Mark had no idea what was going on with the two, but when he had a chance, he would try to find out. Now wasn't the time to be pulling apart. Now was the time when they needed each other the most. They were a family and family supported family no matter what.

"You don't have to, you really don't," Mark said, returning his attention to Jack. The urge to tell his brother what he wanted to hear was strong. It was something he'd had to learn how to do when he first became a doctor. You couldn't sugarcoat things; you had to be honest. You didn't want to hurt people, but lying to them and misleading them *would* hurt them in the long run. Honesty wasn't just the *best* policy, it was the *only* policy. "I'm not telling you that things are completely hopeless, but I *am* telling you that in my medical expertise and experience, I don't think she's going to wake up. I hope she does … I pray she does … but I want to give you all realistic expectations."

Jack said nothing.

He would almost rather his brother raged and argued and fought against what he'd just said. He didn't want to be right. He wanted Laura to beat the odds and come back to her family. Although medically speaking, he knew that Jack's belief in his wife couldn't actually bring her back, he felt like Laura would know if they gave up on her and the last string keeping her alive would snap. If anything was going to save Laura it was love, and Jack's love might just be enough to bring her back. He wanted his brother to be prepared for the worst—the likely—but still hope for the best.

"Can I go back to Laura's room now?" Jack asked tightly.

"Of course."

His brother nodded once and left.

With Jack gone, everyone else started to whisper amongst themselves, no doubt discussing the bad news and their lingering hope that he was wrong.

Mark felt drained. That was the most emotionally exhausting thing he'd had to do in a long time.

"You okay?" Daisy's hands landed on his shoulders and she began to knead.

Some of the tension faded under her touch. "I hated having to say that to him."

"I know you did, but it was the right thing to do. If it were me, I'd want to be prepared."

Her voice wobbled when she said that, and he knew she was thinking about last winter when it had been him in a hospital bed and Daisy wondering whether she was going to lose him.

"Come here." He took her hand and tugged her around to sit in his lap. "I love you," he said, kissing her harder than he probably should in a room full of their family.

"I love you too," she whispered against his lips when they ended the kiss.

"How are *you* doing?" he asked, tucking her hair behind her ear and letting his fingertips linger on her neck. Mark knew how stressed she had been about meeting the nephew she didn't even know existed until a few days ago and the pressure she was feeling having to decide on whether or not to bring him into their family.

"I'm okay. I liked Blaze, and I want to believe in him. I want to believe that not everyone in our family was evil, that there's hope for him. Even if I'm wrong about him—and since we're planning on getting to know him over the next few weeks and then come and have him live with us, I really hope I am—there's something to be said even for false hope. Yes, we need to keep it tempered with some realistic expectations, but when we give up completely, where does that leave us?"

His wife was right.

Sometimes even false hope served a purpose.

Despite all his medical training and experience and the fact that he knew the odds were not in Laura's favor, he found himself clinging to hope he wouldn't have if this had been any normal patient.

However small the chances, he hoped that their false hope turned out to be real hope and that Laura proved them wrong and woke up.

* * * * *

1:51 P.M.

Elle eyed her mother warily.

Her mother eyed her back just as warily.

They were in a standoff of sorts.

Ever since they had driven back from the hospital yesterday, they hadn't really spoken. They had exchanged a couple of necessities but that was it. All they had done was sit in their apartment. They hadn't gone anywhere—they'd eaten; they'd taken showers; they'd slept; and they'd sat and stared at each other.

There was a cop on their door, so she wasn't worried about the killer breaking in and killing her.

What she was worried about was that the killer was *already* in here.

Was her mother a murderer?

The woman who had always been there for her, who would sit up with her all night when she was sick, the woman who baked homemade cookies for her, who had helped her with her homework. Her mother had always been there to support her one hundred percent.

When the kids at school had teased her about how long it had taken her two front teeth to grow in, her mom had gone to the school then called all the parents of the kids who teased her to make their kids apologize to her.

And when Gervase Hayden had started relentlessly harassing her last year because when he tried to pressure her to have sex she refused, her mom had been there for her then, too. Gervase had started making up lies about her and spreading them through the school and making her life miserable, but her mom had been there. She had gone to the school and Gervase's parents and even the police to make sure that the person who was hurting her was punished.

Her mom had always been there.

How could the woman who had always been so loving and caring be a killer?

But if it wasn't her mom who killed Tara and Amy and Teagan, then who else could it be?

Who else had something to gain by murdering the people who had been there when her dad had come for them?

No one.

There was no one.

Sitting here trying to rack her brain to come up with an answer to that question wasn't going to magically produce an answer.

Her mom was the only suspect.

What happened at the hospital yesterday confirmed it.

She hadn't done anything to Laura Xander. It was purely coincidence that just after she'd left the room that Laura had gone into cardiac arrest. She loved Laura. She would never do anything to hurt her. She had just sat there and poured her heart out to the older woman's unconscious form. She had only looked nervous when she left because she had stayed longer than she had anticipated, and she knew her mother would have noticed her absence.

Elle had been waiting for the bus when several doctors had come running up to her and all but dragged her back indoors.

She'd been afraid, thinking that the killer had struck again. Left alone in a room with nothing but her imagination for company, she had started to wonder if it was her mother who had been the next victim. When she had learned it was about Laura, she'd been shocked.

Until her mother showed up.

Then all of the pieces had started to fall into place.

Her mom didn't want her talking to the cops because she was worried that she was going to say something incriminating.

Her mom was the killer.

There was no other explanation.

She was probably pleased that Sofia had shot her dad. Her dad was sick. There was no other explanation for his abrupt and completely uncharacteristic changes in behavior. Now she was plotting to kill off everyone she thought had the power to bring her down.

Then what?

What was her mom's end goal?

What was she going to do once everyone else was dead?

Was her mom going to kill her too?

Was she going to kidnap her and run off with her someplace?

Was she going to keep her locked up?

Was she going to keep her forever?

What was she going to do to her?

Was she going to hurt her?

Was keeping her prisoner it or was she going to do much worse?

There were too many questions, too many what ifs, Elle felt like her head was going to explode.

She had to get out of here.

She had to get as far away from her mother as she could.

What if her mom had done something to her dad?

What if her mom had *made* her dad sick somehow, so he did things he would never otherwise have done?

Would her mom do something like that to her too?

Maybe that had been her plan all along. Make her think that dad was violent, then run, then lure him here so he got himself killed, then kill off anyone who might realize that she had done something to her husband, and then the two of them would disappear. She would be completely at her mother's mercy with no chance of help or escape.

She had to get help.

She had to tell someone what was going on before anyone else got hurt. Sofia and Ryan and Paige had been in the room when her dad came here with a gun. That meant her mom meant to kill all of them too. Sofia and Ryan had two kids, and Paige had the two sweetest little girls on the planet. She couldn't let her mother destroy those children's families like what she had done to their own family.

Elle was terrified to make a move in case her mom decided she was more trouble than she was worth and decided to kill her now, but she couldn't just sit here a moment longer and do nothing.

Cautiously, she stood, aware of the fact that her mother's eyes tracked her every move. She pretended like she was just going to the kitchenette to grab a glass of water, but at the last minute she made a dash for the door.

She was too slow.

Her mother jumped up and blocked her path.

"Where are you going?" her mother demanded.

"Uh …" Elle panicked, unable to come up with a lie quick enough. "For a walk," she finished lamely.

"You're up to something." Her mother narrowed her eyes.

Why did her mom always have to know what she was going to do before she did it? "I'm not."

"What did you do, Elle?"

"Nothing." She shrugged and wouldn't meet her mother's eye.

Did her mom suspect that she had told someone something she shouldn't?

"Did you kill Amy, Tara, and Teagan? Did you do something to Laura?"

Was her mom bluffing to see how much she knew? Her mother was the killer, so she knew that Elle hadn't done anything to anyone.

Should she confront her mom about what she knew?

Would that make things worse?

She couldn't lie her way out of this. Her mom knew when she was lying. She'd never been able to get anything past her.

They were in their apartment at the center; there were people about and a guard outside their door. If she screamed for help then someone would hear her, someone would come, someone would save her.

"It was you." She confronted her mother, finally meeting her gaze squarely.

"What was me?" Her mother looked confused.

"You killed them," she growled, angry now. How dare her mother think it was okay to do what she'd done. It wasn't fair to pretend to be a wonderful, amazing, caring mother to your daughter for her whole life only to then let your true colors be revealed.

"Killed who?"

"You know who."

Her mom's eyes grew wide. "You think *I* did this? That I killed Amy, Tara, and Teagan?"

"And daddy too." Now that she'd spoken up, she felt free, liberated. She wasn't backing down.

"Your father? I didn't kill your dad. He got shot because he stormed in here to kidnap us."

"You did something to him. He was always sweet and kind and loving. You did something to make him angry and violent."

"I have never done anything to anyone," her mother said.

"You did," she screeched. Hot, angry tears burned the backs of her eyes. Her mom had single-handedly ruined her life and so many other peoples'. And she thought she had gotten away with it. Elle would never let that happen.

"What's going on in here?" The door suddenly swung open and Ryan and Paige stood there.

"It's Mom. Mom is the killer," she screamed, relief almost knocking her over. She was safe.

"I tried to protect you, Elle, but I can't let you keep hurting people. It's my daughter, but she's not well; she needs help. What Deacon did to me, to her, it messed her up. Please go easy on her."

Elle stared at her mother in shock.

She was lying.

How could she do that?

Her mother was ruthless.

Before she could open her mouth to protest her innocence, Ryan spoke. "You're both coming down to the station with us."

This was unbelievable.

Her mother did something to her dad to make him lose his mind, got him killed, murdered three innocent people, and now she was going to pin the blame on her.

That wasn't going to happen.

She had always been a daddy's girl, and she was not going to let anyone get away with hurting him even if that person was her mother. She was going to tell the cops everything she knew and then watch her mom get carted off to prison.

* * * * *

2:22 P.M.

Macey was in shock.

Her daughter thought she was a killer.

177

Her own daughter.

Her child.

Her baby.

Thought she was a murderer.

After bringing her and Elle down to the station, the authorities had separated them, and she had been left in an interview room.

She felt like a criminal.

In the car ride here, her daughter wouldn't even look at her, let alone speak to her. All Macey wanted was to get to Elle, to talk to her, to find out what was going through her head.

She had to make things right with her daughter. Elle was the center of her world and the reason behind everything that she did. She couldn't stand the thought of her baby girl being angry with her, or worse, still hating her.

Macey knew that she was probably being watched. They obviously thought that she was the killer, and she knew that she should probably project an air of outward calm even if it wasn't what she was feeling inside, but she couldn't.

She was nervous.

Anxious.

Scared.

Terrified.

And the only thing she could do that even made a dent in her anxiety was to move about the room. Every few minutes she would make herself go and sit in the hard metal chair by the table, fold her hands and rest them neatly on the table and wait.

But it never lasted.

Her nerves got the better of her, and after only a minute or so, she would be back up pacing the room restlessly like a caged animal.

She knew they were making her wait on purpose. They wanted to see how she reacted and try to get a read on her before they came in here and interrogated her.

Macey knew what impression she was giving them.

Her behavior was telling them that she was guilty.

She couldn't take the waiting any longer.

The pressure was getting to her.

She wanted to just open the door and walk out of here, grab her daughter, and go home—wherever home was.

Could she do that?

She hadn't been arrested, so did that mean she was free to just walk out of here if she wanted to?

Would someone stop her if she tried to leave?

If she did leave, could she take her daughter?

Had Ryan and Paige brought in child protective services?

Elle clearly thought that she was dangerous so maybe she didn't even want to go anywhere with her.

How was she going to convince her daughter to leave with her? How was she going to convince her to go home with her? How was she going to convince her that ...

The door swung open and her attention immediately snapped toward it. Ryan and Paige came sauntering in as though they didn't have a care in the world and that leaving her here to stew in her own anxieties meant nothing to them.

She had known them for six months now. While she didn't know Ryan very well since he didn't work at or spend a lot of time at the center, she knew Paige a little. She knew that the woman had nearly been killed by a vicious stalker, and that she had two adopted little girls. The woman had been through a lot but had come back even stronger than ever. Although they hadn't talked a lot, Macey had looked up to her, admired her, and hoped that one day she would find the same reserves of strength that Paige had.

"Take a seat, Macey," Ryan instructed as he and Paige sat down at the table.

Although she didn't want to, Macey joined them. There was no point fighting this; it was happening whether she liked it or not.

"Deacon had been poisoned," Paige announced without preamble when she sat.

Her mouth fell open.

She just stared at them.

Poisoned.

They were telling her that her husband had been poisoned.

"Did you poison Deacon, Macey?" Ryan came right out and asked her.

For a moment, she couldn't answer; she was too shocked.

"Someone had been slipping him mercury, changing his moods and making him unpredictable," Ryan added.

"That's why he hit me," she said, more to herself than to either of the cops.

"Was that the plan?" Paige asked. "Did you want to make him so unstable that he would beat you, so you had an excuse to take your daughter and run?"

"Your *adopted* daughter," Ryan added.

His emphasis annoyed her.

Like because she hadn't given birth to Elle, she wasn't really her mother. She was *every* bit as much Elle's mother as if she had carried her inside her body for nine months.

Macey was surprised Paige let her partner say things like that. Paige knew the pain of not being able to get pregnant and have biological children. She knew firsthand just how much you could love a child that didn't grow inside you. She was a member of the adopted mother's club, and she knew that being a parent had nothing to do with your ability to procreate.

"I legally adopted Elle. In the eyes of the law, I *am* her mother whether I gave birth to her or not," she snapped, throwing a glare Paige's way. She got that this was their job and that they thought she was a killer, but that didn't mean they had to attack her in such a nasty way.

"No one is disputing that you're Elle's mother," Paige said, and from the look in her eyes she *did* feel bad about pursuing this line of questioning. "You raised her, you love her, we know that. But maybe you felt like you had to go to the extreme to protect your relationship with your daughter."

Macey rolled her eyes; that didn't even make sense. "You're implying that I had reason to poison my husband because he was going to leave me and try to get custody of our daughter using the fact that I wasn't biologically her mother against me. But you're forgetting that Deacon came looking for me. If he was going to leave me then why would he go to such extremes to try to get me back? Deacon wasn't going to leave me. I had no reason to worry about losing Elle."

"Maybe Deacon wasn't the one who wanted to end things. Maybe *you* were," Ryan countered. "Maybe you wanted out, but Deacon threatened that if you left, you couldn't take his child with you. Maybe he told you that since he's the biological parent and if it came down to who was going to get custody it would be him. Maybe you did the only thing you could think of that would ensure you got to keep your daughter."

"Again, I *legally adopted* Elle. Deacon couldn't just take her away from me. I am her mother just as much as he was her father. But I wasn't planning on leaving. The only reason I took Elle and ran was because he put his hands on her. And Deacon wasn't the only one who had been acting oddly those last few months," Macey admitted.

"What do you mean?" Paige asked.

"Elle had been acting oddly as well. The day Deacon hit her, she was provoking him … on purpose. I told her to calm down and leave her dad alone, but she wouldn't. She kept going at him until he snapped and hit her. I'm not saying what he did was okay—it definitely was not—but it wasn't like my daughter to behave like that."

She expected them to grill her on that, but instead, it seemed like they had another topic to bring up, something else they thought was incriminating. "Why did you go out that day?" Ryan asked.

"Which day?"

"The day Deacon died. Sofia said you hadn't left the center since you got there and then the very day that Deacon breaks into the center brandishing a gun is the exact same day you go out for the first time."

"A coincidence."

Both the cops cocked eyebrows at her.

"Kimberly had been pestering me about trying to go back to living a normal life," she elaborated. "She said it wasn't helpful to me or to Elle. That at some point I had to stop hiding. She said that we would never be able to move on if I couldn't let go of the past and start living a normal life—and part of living a normal life was going out sometimes. So I finally decided she was right. I went to my favorite bakery to get muffins. I guess Deacon must have been staking out my favorite places. He must have seen me and followed me back to the center."

"Macey, you adopted Elle when she was just an infant. That means you were around just after she was born. Do you know who Elle's biological mother is?" Paige asked.

That was a question she didn't want to answer.

"Maybe that was why you poisoned Deacon. Maybe Elle's biological mother came back. Maybe you were afraid that she wanted her daughter back. Maybe you thought that if you could make it look like your husband was beating you then you would be able to get custody of Elle. And if you had sole custody, then there was no chance of the biological mother ever coming back into Elle's life," Paige suggested.

"Do you know who she is?" Ryan asked when she said nothing.

As much as she didn't want to answer, Macey didn't see that she had any other choice. "It's Kimberly," she admitted.

"Kimberly Ute?" Paige looked shocked. "The nurse at the center? The one who you met at the hospital when you went there after Deacon had beaten you? The one who helped you get away?"

"The very one."

She'd told them she had no reason to poison her husband, and she'd told them that it was nothing more than a coincidence that the first day she left the center was the day Deacon found her. She'd told them who Elle's biological mother was. Macey just prayed they believed her.

Because if they didn't, then she was going to lose her daughter.

* * * * *

2:40 P.M.

He refused to believe that his wife was going to die.

Jack knew what Mark had said, and he understood where his brother was coming from. Mark was a doctor, and he believed that medical science knew the answers to everything. But he knew his wife and she was still in there.

And yet, that niggling little doubt at the back of his mind was tormenting him relentlessly.

What if he was wrong?

What if he really was going to lose Laura?

Up until Mark's talk, he'd been living in what would probably be described as a delusional state. He had been waiting for Laura to wake up. The idea that she wouldn't had never really occurred to him. Any time the thought tried to creep its way inside his brain, he quickly banished it.

He didn't even want to think about the possibility that he may soon be a widower.

But this wasn't just about him.

Jack did not want to mislead his kids. They had to be prepared for the worst; otherwise, if the worst did happen, it would be so much harder for them to deal with.

The kids were on the way here, and he was going to sit them down and explain to them that their mother might die.

How he was going to do that, he had no idea.

He was hoping the words were just going to come to him.

How did you explain to a five- and seven-year-old that they might lose their mother?

Zach and Rosie were too young to really even understand what death was, what it would mean to them and their family if Laura died.

"You could just wake up and then I wouldn't have to try to explain it to them," he said aloud, taking Laura's hand and squeezing tightly.

He hated seeing her like this.

All still and limp and lifeless.

Laura was so strong, and although she was often quiet in large groups of people, she always left an impression. What she had been through had changed her from the bright, bubbly, effervescent girl she had been when they were growing up, into the serious, intuitive, empathetic woman she had become. Jack didn't even think Laura realized how much people valued and relied upon her opinions and advice.

"Daddy." The door swung open and Rosie burst through, her long dark hair in pigtails, her favorite rag doll in her arms. She looked so young and innocent. She ran to him and jumped up, throwing herself into his arms.

"Hey, princess." He picked her up and kissed her cheek, then held her as he leaned down to kiss his son. "How you doing, buddy?"

Zach shrugged and turned serious blue eyes to his mother. "Mom hasn't woken up."

"No, she hasn't," he agreed. Zach was taking what had happened to Laura much worse than Rosie was. The eighteen months between them made a big difference in their maturity level and what they were able to comprehend and understand.

"I'll be right outside if you need me," his mother said, shooting him a distraught look before closing the door.

His parents had been his rock his entire life.

They had given him the kind of home and childhood that most people dreamed about. They had been happily married for forty-five years; they had raised him and his brothers; they had helped raise their eight grandchildren. They were always there to offer their love and support and advice, even if it wasn't always appreciated in the heat of the moment. They had always done whatever they could to fix any problem that one of their sons had.

But this was something his parents couldn't fix no matter how much they wanted to. And although Jack knew that his mother would gladly help him break the news to his children that their mother might not survive, this was something that he had to do on his own.

Alone with his kids, he sat down with Rosie on his lap, then lifted Zach up too.

"Daddy, Grandma said that she'd help me pick flowers to bring in for Mommy," Rosie told him.

"I'm sure Mommy would love that, honey." He smiled at his little girl. She had no idea what was going on, but her big brother had an inkling; Jack could tell by the look in Zach's eyes. He drew in a long, deep breath. It was time to bite the bullet and get this over with. "You guys know that Mom is very sick, right?"

"Right," Rosie agreed, her little face somber.

Zach just nodded.

"She's sick enough that she might die," he said. He wanted so badly to sugarcoat things, to protect his children from the reality of what might happen just like his brain had been trying to do for him. But it was time for all of them to face reality.

"Mom's going to die?" Zach looked stricken.

"Maybe. Uncle Mark thinks that she might. Do you understand what being dead means?"

"It means you're not around anymore," Zach said.

"That's right. It's like the kitten we got last year, Fuzzy, you remember him?" When both children nodded, he continued.

"You remember how Fuzzy got really sick and we had to take him to the vet? The vet told us that there wasn't any medicine that could make Fuzzy better, and that he was going to die. We were all really sad, and we wished there was something we could do, but there wasn't and Fuzzy died. That's kind of what's happening with Mom now. She's really sick, and there's no medicine that can make her better, and even though we're all praying that she'll get better, she might die."

"When Fuzzy died we buried him in a box in the backyard," Rosie said.

"We did, but we wouldn't bury Mom in the backyard."

"What will we do with Mom if she dies?" Zach asked.

This wasn't something he and Laura had talked much about. They were only forty-one, discussing burials and coffins and cremations and donating bodies to science had never really been something that seemed important or relevant to their lives. There had always seemed like there was plenty of time to talk about that stuff and figure out what they wanted to happen to their bodies after they died.

Only now that time might be up for Laura.

"If Mom dies, then we'll have a funeral … kind of like what we did for Fuzzy when he died where we all said something that we loved about him and said goodbye before we buried him. Then Mom would be buried in a cemetery."

"What's a cem-cemtry?" Rosie asked.

"It's a place where you bury people who have died." He almost said that you could go and visit them there and talk to them but thought that was likely to confuse the kids who were already struggling to grasp the concept of death.

"When someone dies, can they come back?" Rosie asked.

"No, sweetheart, they can't. Once someone is dead, they can't ever come back."

"Not ever?" Rosie's violet eyes—so like her mother's—were wide as she tried to comprehend that. Forever was a concept difficult for adults to grasp, let alone small children.

"Not ever. Just like Fuzzy the kitten didn't come back after he died, Mom wouldn't either."

"But we got a new kitten after Fuzzy died. Does that mean we're going to get a new mommy?" Rosie's brow furrowed as she tried to apply the same logic to this situation.

Jack knew that if Laura died, he would never remarry.

After they'd split up in high school, he'd dated occasionally in the fifteen years they had been apart but he'd never felt the same soul-soaking, heart-filling love for any other woman that he felt for Laura.

She was it for him.

She was the other half of his heart.

The other piece of his soul.

He wasn't a corny guy, but she was his soul mate—the one great love of his life—and he knew he would never find another.

"No, sweetheart, you're not going to get a new mommy. Even if I ever got married again and you got a stepmother, *no one* is ever going to take the place of your mom."

Zach nodded seriously but Rosie looked concerned. "If Mommy dies, who's going to take me to ballet? And who's going to read me bedtime stories? And who's going to make me breakfast and pack my lunch for school and tuck me in?"

Tears brimmed in her eyes and Jack felt them building in his own. "Baby, I don't want you to worry about any of those things. Even if Mommy dies, I'm still here."

"But you work a lot … sometimes you're not there when I go to bed." Rosie's bottom lip wobbled.

"Then Grandma or Grandad will tuck you in and read you your story. Both of you have so many people who love you and will take care of you. I don't want you to *ever* feel like you aren't loved, okay?"

"Daddy, I don't want Mommy to die." Rosie wrapped her thin arms around his neck and burst into tears.

"I don't either, baby."

Rosie was crying; Zach was crying; he was crying; and Jack prayed that Laura could feel their pain. He hoped it was what she needed to fight her way back to them.

* * * * *

3:00 P.M.

"Thanks for coming down, Ms. Ute." Ryan greeted the woman as she stepped off the elevator.

"No problem." She smiled at them. Kimberly was a pretty brunette who looked much younger than her thirty-three years. She didn't appear phased to have been called down to a police station and probably assumed it was something to do with Deacon and the murders of the hostages. Which it did, but they were also after background information on Macey and Elle Staines from someone who knew them beyond the center.

"Take a seat," Ryan said as they entered the interview room. This wasn't a suspect interview. They had no reason to believe that Kimberly was involved; they also didn't know for sure she wasn't. She was Elle's biological mother. Maybe she had decided she wanted her daughter back and what better way to do it than to take out both of the obstacles in her way.

"Is this about the murders?" Kimberly asked as soon as she sat down.

"It is," Paige confirmed.

"I can't believe it. It's all so crazy. What Deacon did, and then someone killing the people who were in the room. I'm on the killer's list; I was there too. He's going to come after me." Kimberly looked genuinely concerned about the possibility that a killer might be coming after her. It was also interesting that she had ascribed a male gender to the killer.

"Who do you think it is?"

"I don't know." Kimberly looked distressed. "It doesn't make sense. Deacon is dead. Why would anyone want to kill those of us who were there? But it's what's happening. I mean, Amy, then Tara, then Teagan. He's working his way through everyone systematically. You two are on the list, too. You were there, he'll be coming after you as well."

That was true.

And terrifying.

Not only were he, his partner, and his wife on the killer's radar, but there was no way to know that the killer would stop at that.

Who else would she decide was a risk?

His daughter had been there. She had almost walked into the living room and become one of the hostages herself. If the killer realized that she had been in the building, she could go after Sophie.

If he got even an inkling that his daughter might be in danger, he wouldn't hesitate to send her to a safe house until this was resolved.

Which would inadvertently give Sofia exactly what she wanted.

She wanted to leave.

He could see it every time he looked at her.

The only thing keeping her in their home was the fact that he had refused to let her leave with the kids.

That threat wasn't going to keep her in the house for long, nor was it healthy for their relationship with each other and their children. If Sofia didn't want to be with him anymore, then forcing her to stay was probably going to do more harm than good. He was going to have to sit her down and hash this out. If she was intent on leaving, he couldn't stop her, so they needed to figure out how to do it and cause the minimum amount of disruption to their kids' lives.

"You keep referring to the killer as a he. Any reason why?" Paige asked.

"Oh." Kimberly looked surprised like she hadn't even realized she was doing that. "No, I guess it's just that most serial killers are men, right?"

"They are, but—" Paige agreed.

"But you think this killer is a woman," Kimberly finished. If it were possible, her large brown eyes grew even bigger. "Amy, Tara, and Teagan are dead, so not them. Not you two, or Sofia. So, me? No, Macey. You think *Macey* is killing the people her husband held hostage. Why? Why would she do that? That makes no sense. Well, I guess it makes as much sense as anything else because none of this makes any sense."

Kimberly talked a lot, which was hopefully going to be good news for them. They had talked with both Macey and Elle, and neither of them were convincing him that they were a killer. There were reasons for and against either of them being the killer, but so far, nothing definitive. And Macey's claims that Elle's behavior had also changed around the same time as her father's added another angle. Had someone been poisoning Elle as well as Deacon?

"Macey told us about Elle," Ryan told her.

"Oh," Kimberly said, like that explained everything. "You know that I'm Elle's biological mother."

"We do," Ryan confirmed. "Why don't you start by telling us about Deacon."

"Deacon and I met in high school. We were both fifteen-year-old sophomores. My father was in the army and we moved around a lot. I was quiet and shy, too many times making friends and losing friends made me keep to myself. But then I ran into Deacon one day and we just hit it off. He was so confident, and easygoing, and funny that he immediately put me at ease. We were together up until our senior year. I found out I was pregnant, and I panicked … started to spin out of control. I pulled away from Deacon and my family, and I started hanging out with the wrong crowd doing drugs and drinking. It's a miracle that Elle wasn't born with any problems because of me."

"Why did you give Elle up?" he asked.

"I didn't want a baby. I had wanted to get an abortion, but Deacon begged me not to. He was upset when I went off the rails. He wanted to save me … he begged me to go to rehab, kick my addictions, and raise our baby together, but I didn't want to." Kimberly's gaze dropped to the floor and when she spoke, her voice was barely audible. "I was alone when I went into labor and I'm ashamed to say that I actually considered killing the baby as soon as it was born. I might even have done it if Deacon hadn't turned up just as she was being born. He was so enamored with her that I didn't even fight him taking her. I was eighteen years old and not in a good place in my life … I couldn't be a mother. When Deacon got back together with Macey and he asked me to sign away my parental rights so that Macey could adopt Elle, I was happy to do it."

"You didn't know Macey though," Paige said.

"No, I didn't. But Deacon told me about her, and she sounded like just the mother I would pick for my daughter. I'm so glad that I gave Elle up. If I'd kept her she wouldn't have had a good life. I'm so grateful that Deacon and Macey provided her with the stable, loving home that I could never have given her."

"Do you think Macey is capable of killing?" he asked.

"No."

"No?" Paige repeated.

"I cannot imagine her killing anyone. I mean, why would she?"

"What if she wanted to leave Deacon or he wanted to leave her, and she was worried about losing Elle?" he asked.

Kimberly shook her head. "She and Deacon loved each other and they both loved my daughter. Even if they stopped loving each other, there was no way Deacon would ever have tried to take Elle from Macey. He loved his daughter, and he would never have done anything to hurt her, and taking her away from the only mother she has ever known, would have hurt her."

"You seem to have a lot of love and respect for Deacon, but

you saw firsthand what he had become," Ryan reminded her. "You're the one who brought Macey and Elle to the center because you knew Deacon was abusing them. You were there in the room when Deacon came in with a gun, He would have shot every person in there if it got him his family back."

"The Deacon I knew would never lay a hand on anyone; there must have been something wrong with him. Maybe a brain tumor or something, but he was a good guy."

"And yet you helped his wife and daughter leave him," Paige said.

"I wanted to do something to help him, but whether I gave her up or not, Elle is still my flesh and blood and she had to be my first priority. When I saw them in the hospital where I worked, I knew what had happened. I'd seen those injuries before. I had to protect my daughter and I had to repay Macey for being the mother to my child that I couldn't be. I knew I had to get them someplace safe and I'd heard about the center, so I told them about it. When Macey was ready to leave, I helped them get safely away."

Everything that Kimberly had told them made sense. Although she maintained that she didn't believe Macey would kill anyone or that she would have had any reason to be concerned about losing her daughter, by her own words, Kimberly didn't even really know Macey.

And there was one thing that Kimberly didn't know.

She was right, Deacon's behavioral changes weren't his fault.

He had been poisoned.

Only three people lived in the Staines house.

Deacon, Macey, and Elle.

While he supposed it was possible that Deacon had poisoned himself, it didn't seem likely.

That only left Macey or Elle.

Neither stood out as an automatic suspect, but between the thirty-three-year-old Macey and her fifteen-year-old daughter, the one who was the most likely to come up with the mercury plan, source it, and then administer it was Macey.

Even with Kimberly's glowing report of the kind of person she believed the woman who had raised her daughter to be, Macey was still their number one suspect.

* * * * *

3:54 P.M.

She was lost.

She didn't know how she'd gotten to this place or where it was. All she knew was that she wanted to go back.

Laura wasn't even sure where *back* was.

Or why she wanted to get there.

All she knew was that she didn't belong here.

This place was timeless and endless.

Rolling waves of white.

That was all there was in this place.

And all you did was float amongst the clouds, dazed and confused, and not altogether sure of what was happening.

It was peaceful.

It was quiet.

There was no pain.

No sadness.

No anger.

There was nothing.

Just emptiness.

Just floating.

Just the cool, soft, fluffy clouds.

But something had changed.

Something was pulling at her.

Pulling her away from here.

She wanted to find her way back, but she didn't know how.

She didn't really know anything.

She wasn't even sure who she was.

All she knew was that she had to leave here.

She had to go back.

She had to.

Had to.

A string appeared out of nowhere.

Laura took hold of it.

It felt real.

Substantial.

Not like everything else in this place.

As she held the string in her hand, her surroundings began to change, to slowly morph into something else.

The white began to darken, and not just into one color but several, and in all different shades. Laura saw browns and blues, grays and blacks, greens, pinks, and purples.

The colors were almost too bright for her eyes that had become accustomed to nothing but white.

There were sounds too.

Beeps and kind of a whooshing sound and something that sounded like chair legs scraping across a linoleum floor.

Everything was fuzzy, and although she could hear, the sounds all seemed very far away.

She still wasn't quite sure where she was or even who she was, but one thing she was certain of was that she was no longer in the clouds.

As the world around her began to become clearer as everything came back into focus, she became aware of something in her throat. It didn't hurt exactly, but it felt odd, like it was invading her body.

Her throat might not hurt but the rest of her body did.

And not just hurt.

It burned with such intense agony that she almost wished she were still in the white clouds.

All of a sudden something loomed over her.

A face.

A man's face.

He had blue eyes, blond hair, and dimples.

"Laura?"

The man's face changed, and he looked … happy? Relieved? Hopeful?

She wasn't quite sure.

She might be back, but her mind was taking a little while to remember how to function properly.

"Laura?" the man said again.

His face had changed.

Now it looked concerned?

Yes, he looked worried.

About her.

Why was he worried about her?

Because she had been gone—maybe not physically—but her soul had left her body for a while, only just returning now.

She was in pain.

She'd been hurt.

Stabbed.

Back at the center.

She'd been outside on her daily walk when Deacon Staines had shown up.

She had tried to convince him not to do anything stupid but he'd been determined to get to Macey and Elle.

He'd stabbed her.

She had tried to get to help, but she'd been hurt too badly.

Jack and Ryan had shown up, but she hadn't been able to hold on.

She had faded away and ended up in the white clouds where she had been trapped for who knew how long.

The memories were coming too fast, making her feel disoriented and nauseous.

She clenched her eyes closed in an attempt to regain control.

"Laura?"

A hand rested lightly on her shoulder.

The touch pulled her back to reality.

Jack was here.

He had been the one to bring her back.

Her eyes snapped open, and she tried to talk but couldn't because of the tube down her throat.

"It's okay," Jack soothed as his hand stroked her hair. "It's okay. *You're* okay."

His eyes met hers and she saw how much he had suffered, how much he'd been hurting while she'd been gone. Laura wondered how long it had been. She hated that she had caused her husband and her children pain.

"I can't believe you're awake ... I was starting to think that I would never ..." He trailed off, but she knew what he'd been going to say. He had been going to say that he was starting to think that she would never wake up, that she was going to die.

She wanted to tell him how much she loved him; she wanted to fling herself out on the bed and into his arms; she wanted to apologize and laugh and cry and rejoice in the fact that she was alive.

But she couldn't do any of those things.

The only thing she could do was find Jack's hand and curl her fingers around it.

"I love you so much." Jack leaned over and pressed a gentle kiss to her forehead. "I have to go get Mark. Let him know you're awake."

Laura didn't want him to leave her.

She'd only just come back, and she didn't want to be alone.

Correctly reading her fear, her husband squeezed her hand and kissed her forehead again. "He's right outside. He's been here with you the whole time. I'll only be gone a second."

She tracked him with her eyes as he moved away from the bed

and over to the door. When it closed behind him, she felt herself start to panic. He had been here beside her the whole time; she knew it even though she had no memory of his presence.

What felt like minutes—but was probably only fifteen seconds—the door swung open again and Jack returned with his youngest brother.

"Laura," Mark beamed at her. "You scared us … we weren't sure you were going to make it."

She hated that her family had gone through that.

She hated that her precious children had gone through that. She wanted to see them. As soon as Mark took this tube out of her throat, she was going to ask Jack to bring them to her.

She had to ask about Macey and Elle, too. She had to know if Deacon had gotten them.

Laura tried very hard to be patient while Jack held her hand and Mark stood beside her bed and explained the extubation process to her.

She didn't care.

She just wanted the tube out.

"I'm going to gradually lower the amount of support you're getting from the ventilator, and we'll see how you do breathing on your own. If you do well over the next few hours, we can take the tube out," Mark said.

Hours?

She couldn't sit here and wait hours.

"Hours, Mark?" Jack looked just as unhappy as she felt.

"I need to make sure she's getting adequate oxygenation and that her arterial blood gas is adequate. We need to get her sitting up and see if she can cough."

Laura coughed. Anything to speed this process up.

"There you go, she can cough. Now sit her up and take the tube out," Jack said.

Mark rolled his eyes at both of them. "I'll elevate her bed and we'll wait thirty minutes and see how she does."

For the next thirty minutes, she and Jack just stared into each other's eyes. Mark hovered beside them, checking her vitals every few minutes but she blocked him out. She only had eyes for her husband right now.

When the thirty minutes was up, Mark checked her vitals again. Both she and Jack looked at him hopefully.

"All right, let's try this," he agreed.

He fiddled with the tube, exercising the proper suctioning procedures, and then he was *finally* taking it out. It was an unpleasant sensation and she coughed as it was being removed. But then it was gone.

"Don't try to talk much. You'll probably be hoarse and your throat sore after being intubated. I'm going to put an oxygen mask on you just to make sure you're getting enough oxygen." Mark slipped the mask on. "Okay, I'll give you two some time together. I'll be right outside if you need anything."

Then he was gone, and it was just her and her husband.

"Jack," she tried to speak, but her throat felt raw and she could only croak. Her stomach still burned with pain but she had never felt so good, so alive, in all her life.

"Mark said not to talk," Jack said. He was holding her hand clutched tightly in his, and his other hand compulsively stroked her hair and traced her face as though he couldn't believe he was talking to her.

Laura shook her head. She didn't care if it hurt. There were things she needed to say. "Love you."

"I love you, too, angel."

"Kiss me."

"You need the oxygen mask," he reminded her.

"Don't care."

Jack laughed. The sound was music to her ears. "One quick kiss," he said, then pulled off the mask and touched his lips to hers.

He tasted warm and soft and safe. He tasted of love and hope.

That single kiss did so much to strengthen her.

"Zach and Rosie … want to see them," she said when he straightened up and put the mask back on her.

"As soon as you get some rest, I'll bring them here. They're going to be so happy to see you."

Not happier than she was going to be to see them. "Deacon?"

A shadow crossed Jack's face, and instead of answering her, he said, "You should rest. We can talk more later."

He was hiding something from her. She may have just woken up from a coma, but she wasn't stupid. She knew she needed to rest but not before she got the answers she needed. Pulling the oxygen mask off with her free hand, she asked, "Jack? What happened?"

Her husband sighed but he knew her well enough to know that if he wanted her to rest then he was going to need to answer her questions first. "Deacon got inside after he stabbed you and held some people hostage. He wouldn't be talked down and Sofia had to shoot him. He's dead, but someone has been killing off the hostages. Ryan and Paige think it's either Macey or Elle. Ryan, Sofia, and Paige are on the killer's list; they were all in the room with Deacon. You know both of them better than anyone else. Do you think either Macey or Elle could be a killer?"

Laura wanted to help.

She really did.

Particularly if the people she loved were in danger.

But she was so tired.

Whatever strength her body had accumulated while she'd been unconscious was running out and she so badly wanted to close her eyes and go to sleep, safe in the knowledge that her husband would be beside her bed the entire time. No matter how hard she tried, she could no longer hold her eyes open.

"Sleep now, angel, we can talk about this later." Jack smiled at her and gently tugged the oxygen mask from her hand, fitting it back over her mouth and nose.

Sleep was lapping at the edges of her mind.

Tugging her under.

"Elle knew," she said before sleep could claim her. "She knew Macey wasn't her biological mother."

All her energy used up now, she slipped off to sleep.

* * * * *

5:28 P.M.

Despite everything that had happened the last few days and the fact that she was wildly confused about the state of her marriage, Sofia couldn't stop smiling.

Laura was awake.

It was a miracle.

When Mark had called the whole family to the hospital and explained to them that the chances of Laura surviving were slim, she'd been sure that her sister-in-law wasn't going to make it. She had started to mentally prepare herself for it, and even considered talking to Ryan about sitting the children down and explaining to them that their aunt might die.

Now they wouldn't have to, and the relief she felt was enormous. Not just because she didn't want to have to tell Sophie and Ned that they might lose the aunt they adored, but because she just couldn't cope with talking to Ryan right now.

Her sister-in-law's narrow escape from death should have given her some perspective. She had a husband who loved and adored her, a family that was everything she had wished for growing up. She had everything she'd ever wanted, and she was living her dreams. To give up all of that because she'd had to do something she knew was the right thing to do seemed stupid. How do you walk away from a decade of love, kids, happiness, good times? To throw all of that away, was that craziness?

And yet, every time she thought of going to Ryan and

explaining to him the mess of fears and emotions swirling around inside her, she backed out.

Sofia really wanted to go and visit Laura, see how she was doing and talk to her, but Mark had said that Laura was still very weak and shouldn't be overwhelmed by a lot of people right now. Jack and Zach and Rosie were with her and that was what it should be. Their family needed time to start healing. Maybe tomorrow she would pop by the hospital and see Laura just for a few minutes. She wanted to see for herself, make sure that she really was alive and slowly recovering.

It was coming up six o'clock. She really should go home, get dinner going, spend some time with the kids.

She should.

But her feet didn't move.

Sofia was standing in the huge backyard of the center looking out at the beautiful gardens.

She had grown up here.

Only it had been very different back then. After the mansion that had been in her family for generations burned down, and with no other family left, she inherited not just this property but millions in businesses and stocks and shares. She had known she wanted to do something good with it all. Something that might undo some of the bad her family had done.

Her childhood hadn't been a happy one.

In fact, it had been the complete opposite.

Shortly after she met Ryan, when he was working a case that involved someone killing off the members of her family one by one, she had learned her family was so much worse and so much more complicated than she had ever realized. She wasn't sure she had yet fully come to terms with it all.

Through all of that, Ryan had been her rock.

He had given her strength when she didn't have any left of her own; he'd made her laugh when she had been drenched in tears for days; he'd made her feel loved and cared about when she had gone through life wondering what that felt like.

So why couldn't he help her now?

Why did just the thought of him touching her or talking to her or even being in the same room as her, fill her with dread?

Things couldn't go on the way they were.

It wasn't fair to Ryan, and it wasn't fair to their kids.

They were going to have to sit down and work something out. Sofia knew that he'd said no before when she'd said she wanted to take the kids and go to a hotel for a while, but the killer was still out there, and she was still a target. Maybe she could use that to convince him to let her go. Maybe once she had some space and wasn't being pressured to pretend everything was fine for the sake of the children, she would be able to sort herself out.

And if she couldn't … well, she didn't want to think about that just yet.

Time.

She just needed some time.

Sofia was about to go back inside, grab her stuff, and head home when she spotted something.

A person.

Slinking around the side of the house and hurrying toward the cover of the trees.

It was Elle.

She had a bag slung over her shoulder.

She was running away.

Sofia had heard about the commotion at the center earlier today. Macey and Elle had been accusing one another of being the killer. She also knew that both were suspects and that Ryan and Paige had spoken with both of them.

Although neither had been arrested and both had been released to come back to the center, they had moved Elle into a different room.

If she was running, was that an admission of guilt?

Or was she just running because she was scared of her mother?

She probably shouldn't go running after the girl. She should probably call Ryan or Paige to come and track her down, interview her again, try to figure out if she was guilty.

But she couldn't.

Sensible or not, Sofia took off after the teenager.

"Elle," she called out.

The girl froze and turned in her direction. Even from a distance, Sofia could see that she was weighing her options. Should she make a run for it or should she accept that she'd been found and stay?

Thankfully, Elle made the smart choice and stayed put.

"Where are you going?" she asked when she reached her.

Elle just shrugged.

"Are you running away, Elle?" Over the ten years she had been running the center, this wasn't the first time that one of the kids had decided that life as a runaway was preferable over their current situation. Usually, she had Laura here for backup and Laura always knew what to say to help these kids. But today, she was on her own. It was up to her to convince Elle that running wasn't the answer. Sofia prayed she was up to the job.

This time, Elle gave a small nod in answer to her question.

Sofia was struggling to get a read on the teenager. Elle was so quiet, and Macey had kept her isolated the entire six months they'd been here, so she didn't know Elle very well.

"I don't think you should leave, Elle. We can't keep you safe if you aren't here. Teagan left the center and the killer got to her; but here, you'll be safe. You'll have a cop on your door until this is over."

Elle's gaze dropped to her feet.

"Are you afraid of your mother?"

While she didn't give a verbal answer, Elle looked up and the expression on her face was clear.

That Elle was afraid of her own mother spoke volumes about Macey and what she was capable of. However, if it was Elle and not Macey who was the killer, then maybe this was all just a ploy, a game to convince everyone that Macey was guilty.

"Don't leave, Elle. Let's go back inside together."

The teenager hesitated, once again seemingly weighing her options. Regardless of what Elle thought, she didn't really have any. If she tried to run, then Sofia would call in backup to track her down and bring her back. What she had said was true. Regardless of who the killer was, Elle wasn't safe out on her own.

Elle must have figured that out because she nodded and started trudging back toward the house. Sofia fell into step beside her.

"Is Laura going to be okay?" Elle asked when they were about half way back.

She must not have been told yet. She knew that Elle had been suspected of doing something to Laura to cause her to go into cardiac arrest, and she couldn't tell if the girl was asking because she was concerned about Laura or if she was concerned about something Laura might say if she woke up. "Laura is awake. She woke up a couple of hours ago. She's going to be okay."

There was no outward change in Elle's demeanor so Sofia couldn't figure out which option was the right one. This girl was tough; cracking her was like cracking into a bank safe.

She may not be as good as Laura at reading people, but she could feel the fear rolling off the girl. She wished she had worked harder at building trust so she could get something out of Elle now.

"Elle, if you're afraid, you can talk to me. I may not be Laura, but I can listen, and I can give you my opinion, and I will help you if I can. If you've done something that you shouldn't have, then it's not too late to try to make it right. If you know something about who killed Amy and Tara and Teagan, then you should say something. I don't want anyone else to get hurt. Please, Elle, tell me what you know."

* * * * *

9:04 P.M.

It was late.

Mostly dark outside.

Where was her mom?

Why wasn't she home already?

Her mom was always home before now.

If she was going to be late, she always called, but they'd been home for almost two hours now and nothing.

Not a word.

And Sophie was starting to worry.

Everyone had been lying to her. They hadn't told her that the hostages were being killed off.

Her mom was one of those people.

And now her mom wasn't here and hadn't told them where she was and what she was doing.

She had been at Grandma and Granddad's house when Dad had come to pick her and her brother up. She had been surprised to see him. He picked them up sometimes but usually Mom collected them and brought them home.

But Mom didn't seem to want to be at home since *that* day.

Sophie didn't know why, but she did know it wasn't good news.

She was worried.

She had to find out what was going on.

That meant listening quietly at doors to overhear the grown-ups' conversations. That was how she had found out about the killer. Maybe if she was careful and quiet she could also find out what was going on with her mom.

If her mom was okay.

What if the killer had got to her?

What if she was lying somewhere hurt?

Or even worse, dead?

Dad was upstairs putting Ned to bed, but his phone was down here, over on the table where he'd left it after he'd cooked them dinner and played several games of Go Fish with them.

She wasn't supposed to touch his phone. She had her own iPad to play games on and talk to her friends, but her parents' phones were off limits. But this was an emergency.

What if Mom had called and Dad's phone was on silent and they had missed her call?

She could have called to say she was held up at the center. Sometimes she was, normally when a new family arrived and needed help settling in. Or she could have called because she was in trouble and needed help. The killer could be chasing her right this very second, hunting her down, hurting her, killing her.

She had to check the phone.

Sophie was just about to pick it up when her dad's voice behind her made her jump, "Everything okay, Soph?"

Quickly, she spun around. "Mm-hmm."

"Why don't you go up to bed?"

"No." She couldn't go to bed now. It was summer, and she often stayed up later than this, but tonight she wasn't going to bed until she knew that Mom was okay.

"Sweetheart, what's wrong?" he asked, coming to her and leaning over so he could look her in the eye. "Something has been bothering you all night. You can tell me what's going on."

She knew that.

She knew that she could talk to her father about anything, but she didn't want to worry him. Dad worried about Mom a lot. He tried not to let it show but she knew. It was because he loved her so much, and when you loved someone, you worried about them even when there was no need to.

If he worried about Mom even when he didn't have to, he would be worrying tons now when she might actually be in danger, and Sophie didn't want to add to that.

"Were you going to look at my phone?" Dad asked, glancing at the table behind her.

Sophie tried not to let her face give her away, but she was a terrible liar and her parents and teachers could always tell by the way her eyes twitched and her cheeks went pink that she wasn't telling the truth. Her mom always told her that she was an open book.

"What did you want with my phone?" Dad asked, once again reading in her face the answers he sought. "You know you're not supposed to touch it so it must be something important if you were going to break the rules."

She wanted to be strong.

She wanted to pretend that everything was okay so Dad didn't worry.

She tried really hard to stay calm, but tears were welling up in her eyes and threatening to burst out.

She tried to hold them back.

She really did.

But she couldn't.

Despite her best intentions, they came in a rush. "I wanted to see if Mom called. She's not home and it's late and she hasn't called, and what if the killer got to her?"

"Come here." Dad pulled her into a hug, and she wrapped her arms around his neck and clung to him as she cried. "How did you find out about the killer?"

"I was eavesdropping … I'm sorry." She cried harder.

"Shh." Dad picked her up and sat down at the kitchen table with her on his lap. She was ten years old and really too big to be sitting on her daddy's lap, but yet she made no attempt to move. "Mom is fine, she'll be home soon."

"How do you know?"

"Because Aunt Paige texted me a couple of hours ago to say that they were at the center. I'm sorry, Sophie, I didn't know you were worrying about Mom. If I had, I would have told you that she was okay. I don't want you to worry about her or about this killer. Aunt Paige and I will make sure that no one hurts your mom."

Sophie had never felt so relieved about anything in her life.

Mom was with Aunt Paige. Aunt Paige was a cop, and she wouldn't let anything happen to Mom.

Just a couple of days ago, the most important thing in the world to her had been convincing Mom to buy her the blue dress for the charity ball. Now she couldn't care less about the dress. All she wanted was to make sure that her mom stayed safe. She might have been okay this time, but what about next time?

"Have you been worrying about this since what happened at the center with Deacon Staines?" her Dad asked.

"Yes," she whispered against his neck. She was feeling better, but she wasn't ready to leave her daddy's arms just yet.

"Why didn't you say anything?"

"Because I'm a big girl now, and I didn't want to worry you because I know you worry about Mom, and Mom has been acting weird, and I thought I could handle it by myself," she explained.

"Oh, baby, you're never too big to let the people who care about you help you when you need help. We're a family, we're always going to be there for one another, no matter what."

She felt like there was more to what her dad was saying than what he was actually saying. As she got older, she was beginning to understand that people often didn't say things outright; instead, they kind of tried to hide them in their words.

Before she could ask him what he was trying to keep from her, Mom came walking through the kitchen door.

"Mommy." Sophie ran to her mother and threw herself into her arms.

"Sophie, honey, what's wrong?" Mom asked, wrapping her up in a warm hug that made her feel safe.

"I was worried about you."

"Worried about me, why?"

"She was eavesdropping and heard about the killer," Dad replied.

"Oh, baby, I'm fine. I'm sorry, if I'd known you were worrying, I would have called you. Why don't you go put your PJs on and hop into bed and I'll come and read stories with you for a while."

She pulled back so she could look up at her mother. "Can I sleep with you tonight?" She didn't want to be alone tonight. She was worried that she would have nightmares and she was worried that the killer would come here looking for Mom.

"Of course you can, sweetheart." Mom smiled and gave her another hug. "I'll come and sleep with you in your room."

Having Mom sleep in her room might help her not to have nightmares, but what if the killer came looking for her? She was ten. She couldn't protect her mother, but Dad could. "Can I sleep in your and dad's bed, with both of you?"

Something swirled through her mother's silvery gray eyes. Something Sophie couldn't quite decipher. It was just like with Dad earlier; he'd been hiding what he really meant in his words and Mom was hiding something in her eyes.

As much as Sophie wanted to know what her parents were keeping from her, right now she just wanted to go to sleep cocooned between her parents feeling safe and secure.

"Are you sure, baby? I can bring in the sleeping bags from the garage and we can have a sleepover in your room."

"No." Her mind was made up. "I want to sleep in your bed, with you and Dad. Please."

Mom smiled but it seemed forced. "Of course, sweetie. Go get into your PJs and jump into our bed, and your dad and I will be up in a minute."

"Thank you." As Sophie ran up the stairs, she decided she was going to have to do a little more eavesdropping. Her parents were keeping something from her, and she wanted to know what it was.

AUGUST 18TH

1:36 A.M.

Something was ringing.

The sound entered her dreams, and for a moment, she was confused. She couldn't understand how ringing fit into the jungle.

One minute, Paige was happily swinging through the trees; the next, she was awake.

The phone, she thought groggily.

It was the phone that had been ringing and entered her dreams.

Instantly, she was awake.

Paige was a cop, and this wasn't the first time her phone had awakened her in the middle of the night. Her first thought was her partner and his wife. There was someone working their way through killing all of those who'd witnessed Deacon Staines' death, and both Ryan and Sofia were on that list.

As was she.

She and Elias had decided that until this killer was caught, it would be safer if their daughters, ten-year-old Hayley and five-year-old Arianna, stayed with her parents. So far, the killer hadn't attempted to take out anyone who hadn't been there that day, but she didn't take any chances when it came to the safety of her children.

Her husband was a firefighter, and he was on shift tonight. His protective instincts had him wanting to stay with her, but she was the cop. She was the one who was trained to protect herself and those around her, so she'd insisted that he go to work as normal. Since she was alone in the bed, Paige didn't have to be worried about trying not to disturb Elias, so she switched on the lamp on the nightstand and sat up.

"Hello?" she said as she picked up her phone and answered it.

"Paige, it's Melissa."

Melissa Buswick was her boss. Melissa had taken over after her last lieutenant, Belinda Jersey, had retired about a year ago. Belinda had been her boss for most of her career as a detective, and she still sometimes found herself expecting to hear Belinda's voice on the other end of the phone or when she walked into the precinct. The fact that Belinda had been unexpectedly murdered six months ago didn't help.

"What's up?" she asked, her gut tightening with expectation of bad news. A call from her boss at two in the morning couldn't mean anything good, and she was worried the bad news that was about to be delivered was that Ryan and Sofia had been best-case-scenario, attacked, or worst-case-scenario, murdered.

"A call came in reporting a body in the empty lot beside your house," Melissa replied.

She couldn't help but let out a sigh of relief.

It wasn't Ryan and Sofia.

Her relief was short lived.

Call her paranoid or cynical or pessimistic, but her mind immediately jumped to one thing.

A trap.

At the moment, Macey and Elle Staines were their primary suspects. Killing Amy, Tara, and Teagan had been relatively easy. They already had access and other than with Teagan they hadn't even been hands on with any of the kills. But trying to kill her would be a whole other ball game. She was a cop, she was armed. It made sense that the killer would use a ruse to try to increase their odds. There was a lot of construction work going on in her neighborhood, and the empty lot beside her house gave the killer perfect access to get to her.

"You want me to go and check it out?" she asked, exceedingly glad that she had decided the kids shouldn't be here until this case was closed so she didn't have to worry about what to do with them.

"Yes, there was a gang shootout on the other side of town and most of the available patrols are tied up there. But, Paige, be careful," Melissa warned. Apparently she wasn't the only paranoid one.

"I will," she assured her boss. Hayley, Arianna, and Elias were the most important things in her life, more important even than her own life, and she was always as careful as she could be to make sure she came home to them each night.

"ETA on backup is five to ten minutes," Melissa warned.

While that might not seem like a lot of time, if something went wrong and this was a setup, it would feel like an eternity. "Okay, I'll keep you updated."

She disconnected the call, climbed out of bed and threw on the nearest clothes—a pair of jeans shorts and a tank top—and slipped her cell into the back pocket of the shorts. Then she retrieved her gun from the lockbox on the top shelf of her closet, where it was safe from curious little hands, and headed downstairs.

Outside, everything was quiet and seemingly peaceful, but she wasn't fooled. The streetlight right in front of the neighboring block was out. It had been on earlier this evening; she specifically remembered because she had dropped her keys on the sidewalk while going for her jog after dinner.

Coincidence?

Possibly, but she preferred to err on the side of caution. If this was Macey or Elle making their attempt at eliminating her as a perceived threat, then taking out the streetlight certainly added to their advantage.

With her gun drawn, she slipped passed the construction fence and into the empty lot. It was fairly overgrown given that it had been sitting empty for the last eight months, and in just the last day or two, there had been deliveries of lumber and bricks which provided numerous places to hide.

Paige was about a third of the way down the lot when she spotted the body.

It lay partially covered by a blue tarp and obscured behind a lump of weeds. She wondered how anyone had spotted it. Of the five houses that bordered the lot, including the two that only touched at the two back corners, the family that lived on the other side of it were away. She knew because they had asked her to bring in their mail for them. And the house that backed onto the lot was owned by an elderly couple who were usually in bed before dark and slept late.

She supposed it could have been kids up to no good on a hot summer evening, or a jogger perhaps who somehow had exceptional eyesight. But it seemed much more likely that someone had reported the body because they *were* the body. Paige was fully expecting that as soon as she was in striking distance, the person under the tarp was going to jump up and try to attack her. She could only hope that they didn't have a gun.

Paige was still moving closer, only a dozen feet or so away from the body now. She was watching closely for any signs of movement, while still keeping an eye on her surroundings, aware that if this was Macey or Elle that the body could be a diversion and they could be hiding, watching her, and biding their time. The possibility that mother and daughter were working together was also still on the table.

The night was clear, and the moon gave off a reasonable amount of light, and she was about three feet from the body when she realized ...

It wasn't a body.

It was a mannequin.

It was a trick.

She was just spinning around when someone came flying at her.

Although she had been prepared for an attack coming from any direction, the person seemed to come out of nowhere, and they slammed into her with their entire body weight, sending them both sprawling to the ground.

Paige landed awkwardly on the arm that she had injured about a month ago tackling another suspect who thought killing cops was a legitimate way to stay out of prison. She had dislocated her shoulder, and although she had been religiously performing the strengthening exercises her physical therapist had given her, the joint was still weak.

When her attacker landed on top of her, the added weight was enough to pop the joint out once again, leaving her not only one arm down but without the use of her shooting arm.

She tried to switch the gun to her other hand—it wasn't her primary hand, but she was still a perfect shot with either—when her attacker made a grab for the weapon, knocking it from her hand. She could try to search for it, but it was dark, and she didn't really need a gun to overpower her attacker. She was strong; she'd gone through the police academy,; she worked out every day and taught self-defense classes weekly. She knew how to get out of pretty much any bad situation she might find herself in.

The person attacking her was too small to be a male and too clumsy to be very good. The woman was trying to swing fists at her, but even with a dislocated shoulder Paige was able to block almost all the blows.

Lifting her knee, Paige rammed it into the woman's stomach, hoping to wind her enough to get out from underneath her and then pin her down until help arrived.

The woman gagged and began to wheeze, and Paige was able to shove her off.

As her attacker staggered sideways, Paige saw something catch the moon's glow.

A knife.

Her attacker had a knife.

She tried to get to her feet, but the other woman was already swinging the knife toward her as she, too, tried to clamber to her feet.

The blade connected with her leg, slicing through flesh and muscle.

The pain was instantaneous and made her nauseous.

Paige ignored it and reached for the woman who was swinging the knife through the air, bringing it down to deliver another blow.

She was able to catch it, and although the blade cut into her palm, she was able to twist her attacker's wrist sideways, satisfied when she heard the other woman's grunt of pain.

Now that she'd lost her weapon, her attacker seemed to realize that she wasn't going to get what she wanted and come out of this on top, so she turned and ran.

Paige would have gone after her, but between her leg—which was already soaked in blood—and her dislocated shoulder, she wasn't sure she would get very far.

Instead, she sank down to lie on the ground and thanked God that she was still alive.

* * * * *

1:59 A.M.

Xavier felt bad about leaving Annabelle at home alone with their screaming four-month-old teething twins. JP and Katie were named after Annabelle's siblings—Julian, Paul, and Katherine—who had been murdered a decade ago. Since both he and Annabelle worked full time jobs, they shared all the duties of running the house and raising their children, so if the kids were up during the night, they were both up tending to them.

He hadn't gotten a full night's sleep since the twins had been born, and even before then with Annabelle's horrible morning sickness that had plagued her entire pregnancy, there had been a lot of sleepless nights. As tired as he was and as wonderful as lying in bed and getting a full eight hours sleep sounded, he was loving every second of being a father. It was a long time coming and he was going to cherish every moment, every tear, every smile, every little detail because he knew how quickly these years were going to fly by. He would blink and his babies would be grown up with babies of their own.

As bad as he had felt leaving Annabelle to try to calm down the twins enough to get them to go to sleep, his boss had called him to say that an anonymous caller had reported a body in the vacant lot beside Paige's house. Since they knew that she was in the sights of a killer, it was a reasonable conclusion that this reported body wasn't a body dump or a drunk or high teenager passed out, but a setup.

Annabelle had just gotten JP to sleep, so he'd taken the baby upstairs, so his sister didn't disturb him. They'd learned quickly that one of the hardest part of having twins, when one baby cried it set off the other. Then he'd kissed his wife and both his children, jumped in his car, and well and truly broken the speed limit to get to his friend's house.

Paige's house was only ten minutes away, but he was there in about six. Apparently there had been a gang shootout on the other side of the city and the response time was going to be slow, meaning Paige was on her own. This killer had proved to be persistent and determined, even tracking down their intended victim when they had moved away. Paige needed backup; for all they knew, Macey and Elle Staines were both involved, and even though she was a trained officer, two against one—the odds weren't in Paige's favor.

Even if it was only one killer, they'd obviously planned this out. Knowing Paige was a cop and killing her wasn't going to be as easy as killing their other victims, so they had no doubt worked out a plan that they thought was foolproof.

When he pulled to a stop outside Paige's house and got out of his car, the first thing he noticed was that it was quiet.

Too quiet.

If Paige had been able to find and restrain whoever was trying to set her up, or if it had been someone who genuinely needed help or a real dead body, then she would have called it in, or she would have called out to him when she heard him pull up.

Instead, there was nothing.

His gun was already in his hands and his cop instincts were on high alert, searching his surroundings for anything that seemed out of place.

There were no lights on in Paige's house, so he assumed she wasn't in there and headed for the lot.

Part of the fence had been knocked over and his adrenalin kicked up.

Something had happened.

He could feel it.

You weren't a cop for half your life and not develop trust in your gut.

Climbing around the fence, he ventured into the lot. It was badly overgrown and there were several piles of bricks and wood; it looked like building would soon resume here.

The moon gave off quite a lot of light, so it didn't take him long to spot the body.

He had known Paige for a decade now, and he immediately recognized her mess of brown curls.

"Paige?" he called out as he started to jog toward her, scanning every shadow in case the killer was still here. Just because he wasn't on the killer's list didn't mean that they wouldn't try to take him out if he became a threat.

"She's gone," Paige's weak voice floated through the dark.

She didn't sound good and she wasn't moving. She'd been injured. As much as he wanted to get to her and see how badly she was hurt, he had to be sure that the threat really was gone.

"Are you sure?"

"She ran when I got the knife."

Knife.

So Paige had been stabbed.

Holstering his gun, he pulled out his flashlight and ran the rest of the way to where Paige was lying. Her eyes were closed, and she didn't bother to open them when he dropped to his knees at her side.

Blood coated her right leg, and there was a long, jagged gash that looked like it was at least ten inches long.

"Paige, are you hurt anywhere else?" he asked, already shrugging out of his shirt.

"My hand, and my shoulder popped out," she answered.

Her shoulder would be painful, but it wasn't life threatening. The cut on her leg was gushing blood. He needed to deal with that first, then he'd check her hand. Xavier wrapped his shirt tightly around the wound, hoping it would stem enough of the blood flow that she wouldn't pass out before help arrived.

"Let me see your hand." She lifted it and he took it and examined it. The cut was deep, but it wasn't bleeding too much and didn't look particularly serious.

Before setting her hand back down, he pressed his fingers to the inside of her wrist and checked her pulse, which was weak. Her skin was cold and clammy, but he had nothing to cover her with and he was wary of picking her up and carrying her inside because he didn't want to make her leg bleed any more than it already was.

Wanting to try to keep her talking to keep her awake, Xavier pressed his hands against the wound to keep pressure on it and started questioning her. "Did you see who attacked you?"

"A woman, but I couldn't see her face."

"Did she say anything?"

"She just grunted when I twisted her wrist to get her to let go of the knife."

The killer was stupid to think that she could trick a cop and come out on top. "Is there anything that you can think of that would help us identify her?"

"I don't think so. I'm sorry; everything happened so quickly, and I was more concerned with getting the knife away from her." Paige shuddered beneath him. "I'm tired."

"I know you are, but you have to stay awake for me, okay?"

"Yeah, I'll try." Her voice was sounding weaker by the second.

"You'll do better than try," he told her. "Every time you think you can't do it, you think of Elias and the girls. They need you. Tell me everything that happened." He could see the mannequin and could figure out the rest, but he wanted to keep her talking.

Paige began to haltingly relay the events of the evening while he held his hands tightly against the cut on her leg. Blood had already soaked through his shirt, but he thought it was slowing a little. It didn't look like the knife had sliced through any major arteries; if it had, she would probably have bled out before he got here. Although she would lose a fair bit of blood, he didn't think her injuries were life threatening.

After what felt like a lifetime, sirens finally sounded in the distance.

Backup.

"Help's coming, Paige. You just have to hold on a little longer."

"I'm okay, don't worry, and when you call Elias and tell him, downplay things. I don't want him to worry about me."

That was his friend, always more worried about everyone else than she was about herself. "I'll call him as soon as help gets here. I don't want to let go of your leg; the bleeding is slowing down, I don't want it to start up again."

Flashing lights and headlights lit up the night, and car doors slammed.

"Over here," he called out.

"Xavier." Paige's eyes finally forced themselves open.

"Yeah?"

"I remembered something."

"What?" Paige was the only one who had come face-to-face with this killer and lived to tell about it. She was the only one who could give them something that would help them identify her. At least now they did know for sure that they were looking for a woman.

"She held the knife in her left hand; she was left-handed."

* * * * *

7:43 A.M.

She was tired, she was in pain, and yet she was so unbelievably happy.

Laura felt on top of the world.

This wasn't the first time she had come close to death. She had been there before, but this time it was different. Last time she had been a twenty-year-old kid. If she hadn't survived the assault that had changed her life, she wouldn't have been leaving behind a husband and two small children. This time if she had died, she would have left her husband a widower and her kids without a mother.

Yesterday after she had fallen asleep with her fingers entwined with Jack's, she had been out for hours, awakening to the most beautiful sight in the world.

Her kids.

Zach and Rosie had been playing Go Fish with Jack at the small table by the window.

At first, they hadn't noticed that she was awake, and she had just laid there and watched them.

It was such a beautiful sight.

Her son's serious little face, his blue eyes sparkling as they caught the sunlight streaming through the window. Her daughter's infectious giggles and long dark braids whipping about as she bounced all over the place, her boundless energy not allowing her to stay still for more than a minute or so at a time. Her husband's relaxed stance and ease with the kids; he was always so affectionate with them. It was one of the things she loved most about Jack. He could be bossy, but with the kids, he was always firm but kind. They wanted both their children to grow up knowing how important it was for a man to be sensitive and open with his emotions.

Her family.

They were her light at the end of a very long tunnel.

When she had been trapped in a prison of her own making, it had been Jack who had finally helped her escape. When she had still felt the bonds of that prison wrapped around her, pulling her back, it had been her children who had given her the strength to finally break the hold her bonds had on her once and for all. She had wanted to be the wife Jack needed and the mother her children deserved.

Without her family, she was nothing.

The joy on Zach and Rosie's faces when they had realized she was awake and had come rushing over to throw their arms around her was something she would never forget. Their hugs had jarred the gash in her side, but she hadn't cared. She would gladly suffer the most excruciating pain if it meant being able to hold her children in her arms.

After spending hours together talking and laughing, she finally succumbed to exhaustion and told Jack to take the kids home and go with them so they could all spend the night in their own beds. Although reluctant, he had agreed, and as soon as the door closed behind them, she had drifted back off to sleep.

Now it was morning and she knew that they would soon be back.

She couldn't wait.

When the door swung open, she turned toward it expectantly

but was surprised to see Macey Staines standing there and not her family. Jack had filled her in on everything that had been going on, so she knew that someone was killing off the people whom Deacon had held hostage and that Macey and her daughter Elle were the prime suspects. She also knew that Elle was suspected to have done something to her that caused her to go into cardiac arrest.

Despite all of that, she knew Macey and Elle and she couldn't see either of them killing anyone.

"Good morning, Macey." Laura smiled and tried to drag herself into a sitting position.

"Hello, Laura." Macey hovered near the door. "Is it okay that I'm here?"

"Of course. Come in," she said and pointed to the chair beside her bed. "Come and sit."

Macey complied but still looked nervously about. She looked so anxious that Laura began to wonder if maybe she had misread the woman and was about to hear a murder confession.

"Is there something you wanted to talk to me about?" she asked when Macey didn't make any move to start talking.

"I don't want to put pressure on you considering what you've been through."

"If you need to talk, Macey, then talk; I promise it's fine."

Macey hesitated a moment longer, then blurted out, "It's Elle."

"What's Elle?"

"I think it's her. I think she's the killer." Macey stood and began to pace up and down the small hospital room. "I am the worst mother in the world. How can I be thinking this way? She's my daughter. My little baby girl. I raised her; I know her; at least, I thought I did. But who else could it be? The cops said that someone had been poisoning Deacon. It was only the three of us in the house. It had to have been her. And now she's killing off anyone she thinks might be a threat to her. But I don't understand why? Why is she doing it? It doesn't make sense. She wasn't even in the room when her father was killed, so why does she feel like she had to kill everyone?"

"I don't know. But sometimes the simplest answer is the right one."

"What is the simplest answer?"

"That Elle hasn't killed anyone."

"But then, who is it?" Macey looked desperate for an answer.

"I don't know, Macey. All I know is that you have a beautiful, strong, kind, caring, empathetic daughter. You're right, you *do* know her. And you know that Elle isn't capable of cold-blooded murder."

Macey still looked conflicted. "I guess you're right. I should go. I'm sorry ... I shouldn't have come ... I shouldn't have bothered you while you're recovering."

Before Laura could assure her again that it was fine, Macey had run out the door.

Tired, she let her eyes fall closed. She was still very weak, and the smallest things left her feeling completely drained and empty. Maybe she would just have a little nap before Jack showed up with the kids.

She was just drifting off when the door swooshed open again.

Oh well; she could nap later. Nothing was going to rejuvenate her more than her family anyway.

Only when she opened her eyes again, it wasn't her family standing in the doorway. This time it was Elle Staines. Like mother like daughter, when they needed someone to talk to, it seemed they turned to her.

"Hello, Elle."

Unlike her mother, the teenager didn't hesitate but started talking immediately. "I didn't try to kill you, Laura. I didn't. I promise. I just needed to talk to you. I always talk to you. You're the only one I can talk to, and I didn't know where else to go. My dad is dead, and I think my mom is killing people."

Tears were brimming in Elle's eyes and Laura wanted to take

the girl's pain and fears away. Her assault had changed her forever in so many ways. Yes, in some ways, it had nearly destroyed her life, but in others, it had given her a gift she never would have had without it. It had taken her a long time to be okay with the fact that what she had been through enabled her to help others in a unique way that not many other psychiatrists or psychologists could.

"Why do you think your mom would kill anyone?" she asked. Since both mother and daughter were suspecting the other of the murders, she wanted to understand why.

"Who else could it be? Who else would want to kill the people that were there when my dad died?"

"So the only reason you think it's your mom is because you don't have another suspect in mind?" That appeared to be the only reason Macey thought it was Elle as well. If Macey thought her daughter was the killer, and Elle thought her mother was the killer, then it was unlikely that either of them was actually the killer. She needed to talk to Jack.

"I guess," Elle shrugged. "If it's not her, then who? I'm scared. I don't know what she's going to do next. What if she tries to kill me too? Or what if she tries to kidnap me and take me away and lock me up someplace?"

"Elle, look at me." She waited until the teenager looked at her. "I don't believe that your mother is a killer. I believe that you're safe with her. But if you feel unsafe with her, then it's okay to keep your distance until this is sorted out."

"Okay," Elle agreed, looking very young and vulnerable. The girl had gone through a lot in a short period of time. It would take her a while and it would be hard, but Elle would get back on her feet; she was a strong kid. "I'm going to go … I need some time to think."

"Be safe," she cautioned.

Alone again for the second time this morning, Laura once again closed her eyes and rested back against her pillows. She was already tired enough to probably sleep the day away, but she didn't want to be asleep when her family got here. They probably would have been here already, but she knew what Rosie was like in the morning. Her daughter was such a bundle of energy that she tried to do a million things at once and ended up getting nothing done.

When her door opened for time number three this morning, she saw her brother-in-law Mark standing there. She knew her face must have fallen in disappointment because Mark grinned.

"Don't worry, I'm not alone. The troops are with me."

A second later, her husband and children came bustling through the door, all laughs and chatter and life that she immediately felt stronger.

She was so grateful that she hadn't died alone out in the woods twenty years ago.

She was so grateful for Jack's stubborn determination to fight for her and their relationship when they first reconnected.

She was so grateful for her children's youthful innocence that had helped her learn to let go and have fun again.

She was so grateful for this second—or fifth—chance she had been given, and she was going to make the most of it and live her life to the fullest.

* * * * *

8:15 A.M.

"Are you working this case with me now?" Ryan asked as he and Xavier sat down at the conference table where everything they had on the Deacon Staines case was laid out.

"Melissa said yes. Paige will be out for at least a couple of days," Xavier replied.

His partner had needed almost a hundred stitches to close the gash on her leg that stretched from just above her knee to halfway down her calf. Her shoulder had been relocated, and the cut on her hand hadn't been deep enough to need stitches. When he had visited her at the hospital, she had been annoyed with herself for letting the killer get away, with the killer for trying to kill her, with the paramedics for making her go to the hospital, with Xavier for backing the paramedics up, with her husband for leaving work to go to the hospital to see her. Basically, she had been in pain and scared and annoyed with anyone and everyone.

Although she would be out for a few days, at least, and unable to do field work until she was off crutches and back on her feet, at least she was alive. But that wasn't what was going to be reported.

Outside of Paige's family and those actively working this case, everyone else was going to believe she'd been killed. What would be reported was that a police officer had been attacked and had bled out from her injuries before help could arrive.

They were hoping that if the killer thought that Paige was dead, there would be no need to try to go after her again. With another name crossed off their list, then the killer would move on. The only other people left who had been there when Deacon died were Macey Staines, Kimberly Ute, Sofia and himself. Hopefully, he and Sofia were next, then they could set a trap and end this.

"On my way here I heard Paige's death reported on the radio. I know she's alive, but it was still disconcerting," Xavier said.

Ryan had heard it, too, on the way from the hospital to the station. He hadn't bothered going back home in between; it wasn't like Sofia wanted to see him.

They were barely speaking.

Last night she had deliberately hung around at the center with Paige so she could get home as late as possible. That had terrified his daughter, and once their problems started affecting their kids, it was time to do something about it. He was hoping to make an arrest in this case today, and then he and Sofia were going to talk whether she liked it or not.

It was time to sort something out.

If she was leaving, then she was leaving. The sooner they could start making the transition for Sophie and Ned, the better.

"Laura told Jack that she had visits from both Macey and Elle this morning," he told Xavier.

"What did they want?"

"She said that Macey came to talk to her, worried that her daughter was the killer."

"Trying to shift the blame off herself, or do we believe her?" Xavier asked.

"I'm starting to believe her." Ryan wasn't sure why, but the more time went on, the less he believed that Macey was the killer they were looking for.

"Elle, then?"

"Well, Laura said that Elle was there to tell her that she didn't do anything to hurt her and that she wasn't responsible for Laura going into cardiac arrest. She was also terrified that her mother was the killer and was going to either kill her or kidnap her."

"She was worried about that the other day as well, right?"

"She was. She and Macey were both accusing each other of being the killer. Apparently, Sofia told Paige last night that she had stopped Elle from running away. Again, that could be interpreted as either fearing her mother or as an admission of guilt."

"So do we believe that Elle is genuinely afraid her mother is going to hurt her?" Xavier asked.

"Laura does, and I trust Laura's opinion. But I don't know where that leaves us. If the killer is Macey and she had been poisoning her husband and she was killing off the hostages because she was afraid that Deacon had said something that would tip us off, then why keep killing after we already knew about it? She knew we knew; if it was her, there was no reason for her to go after Paige."

"Unless she thought silencing you two would make the whole

thing go away," Xavier contradicted.

"Maybe," he acknowledged. "Macey had also said that Elle's behavior had changed around the same time as her father's. We took blood and ran a test to see if Elle was also being poisoned with mercury, but she was clean."

"Well, if it wasn't Macey and it wasn't Elle, then who poisoned Deacon?" Xavier asked. "There were only the three of them in the house. Who else could have done it?"

"Who else had something to gain?"

"You have an idea?"

"Just one. Elle's biological mother."

"Kimberly Ute. She was in the room when Deacon died which should put her on the killer's list, and yet the killer skipped her to go on to Paige. It would have made more sense for the killer to do Kimberly and then move on to you, Paige, and Sofia given that you and Paige are cops and Sofia is your wife."

Xavier was right. It made sense that the killer would have taken out all the easy targets before moving on to the tougher ones. "Laura also told Jack that Elle knew that Macey wasn't her biological mother, only Macey didn't know that."

"Which means she had to have found out some other way."

"I doubt Deacon told her. If he wanted both Macey and Elle back, then it doesn't make sense that he would have told his daughter that Macey wasn't her mother. Kimberly said that the first time she'd seen Macey and Elle since she gave Elle up fifteen years ago was at the hospital, but how did she know it was them? It had been fifteen years. Macey had been only eighteen back then; so was Kimberly. According to Kimberly, she was a drug addict and alcoholic who didn't want a baby. I doubt she paid much attention to what Macey looked like. Then Kimberly was quick to take them away from Deacon, and she hung around even after she got them someplace safe."

"You think that Kimberly tracked down Deacon, Macey, and Elle and told Elle that she was her biological mother?" Xavier asked.

"That or she told Deacon and Macey she wanted back in on her daughter's life, and it didn't go down well. Elle could have overheard. She didn't tell anyone but Laura that she knew the truth, so she wanted to make sure her parents didn't know that she knew. If Elle had wanted to cause trouble for Deacon and Macey, then all she had to do was tell them that she knew they'd been lying. She wouldn't have had to go to all this trouble."

"If Kimberly wanted Elle, the courts wouldn't have been on her side. She signed away her parental rights, and Deacon and Macey had been providing a stable, loving home for Elle since she was an infant. There was no way Kimberly would have gotten custody."

"Which could be why Kimberly decided to go to the extreme," Ryan said. "She decided to poison Deacon and alter his personality, probably hoping he'd become violent, and Macey would leave with Elle. She was a nurse, and she knew what mercury would do to him, and that eliminated the first obstacle. Then she ingratiates herself with Macey so she can spend time around Elle. Then all she had to do was lure Deacon here and set it up, so it looked like Macey was hiding something and killing people to keep it quiet."

"Deacon was still being poisoned, and it had been six months since Macey left with Elle," Xavier said. "Macey and Elle hadn't left the center in all that time, but Kimberly came and went. I don't know how she was doing it, but if she was the one giving Deacon the mercury, then she had the opportunity to do it."

"And Kimberly had been pressuring Macey to go out. If she knew that Deacon was stalking all the places Macey used to go to in the hopes of seeing her there, then she wanted him to find her. She wanted him to follow her. She wanted him to break in and get himself killed. She was probably hoping that we'd find out he'd been poisoned, assume Macey did it, arrest her, and then she would be free to swoop in and get Elle, who would have been left all alone with no one else to look after her."

"It all seems so extreme," Xavier said. "To go to those lengths just to try to get what she wanted."

"What lengths would you go to for your kids?" he asked, knowing that there wasn't anything he wouldn't do for Sophie and Ned.

Xavier nodded slowly. "Paige told me that the person who attacked her was left-handed. Macey and Elle are both right-handed."

"We need to find out everything we can about Kimberly Ute."

* * * * *

9:23 A.M.

"I miss having little babies," Sofia said as she cradled Annabelle and Xavier's four-month-old son JP in her arms.

"You miss the no sleep and the constant crying and the throwing up?" Annabelle stopped walking up and down the room, trying to rock Katie to sleep.

She remembered those days.

She had loved every second of them, and she knew Annabelle did too.

"You can't fool me; I know you're loving having these two terrors around." She smiled at her friend. "Cherish these days, Annabelle, because before you know it, they'll be talking back and arguing with you, and it's a battle to get them to do what you want."

As much as she loved watching her kids grow and learn new things and become more independent, she missed them being this small. She missed holding them in her arms and rocking them to sleep. She missed those beautiful baby laughs. She missed them being so sweet and innocent, and she missed being able to make their tears dry up just because she was Mom and she had near-magical powers.

Now Sophie was ten and Ned seven. Their friends were becoming more and more important to them with each passing year, and she and their dad less important. Now she couldn't just make everything better for them just by being there, and they were old enough to worry about things that she thought it would be years still until they had to even think of things like that.

It had shaken her to know that Sophie had been eavesdropping on adult conversations and learned about the killer. She didn't want her daughter afraid that someone was going to murder her mother. She wanted the biggest problem in Sophie's life to be negotiating to get the blue dress she wanted for the charity ball. She didn't want her kids to grow up so quickly. Some days she wanted to keep them little and living at home forever.

"I might complain sometimes," Annabelle said, coming to sit beside her on the sofa, "but I wouldn't change a thing. They're so perfect. Even when I'm exhausted and my head feels like it's going to explode from all the crying, I'm just in awe of them. How can you love something this much so quickly? I knew when Xavier and I met that I felt something for him; maybe even love at first sight, but it didn't feel like this."

"Nothing else feels like this." Sofia felt a smile cross her face as she reminisced. "I remember the first time Ryan put Sophie in my arms. I might not have given birth to her, but she's every bit as much my child as Ned is. I remember the day he was born. I remember every second of those thirty-six hours of labor. I remember the pain and the fear, but most of all, I remember holding him for the first time and crying a flood of happy tears. I remember bringing them home from the hospital; they were so tiny. I used to love letting their little fingers curl around mine."

"I love that," Annabelle agreed. "Some days I'm so overwhelmed that I'm scared to death I'm going to mess up. It's hard enough just juggling feeding and changing them and convincing them to sleep at the same time. What am I going to do when they're both walking and I'm trying to chase them around the house? Or when they both get older and have different interests and different activities that they do. How will I choose which one to go and watch? And what about when they're teenagers and they start dating … I don't know how I'm going to cope with that."

"I think you have some time before you have to worry about that." She laughed.

Annabelle giggled too. "I guess I can focus on just the feeding and changing for now."

"And bonus, they're both asleep," she said, nodding her head at Katie who had finally fallen asleep in her mother's arms.

"That is a relief." Annabelle sank back against the couch cushions. Sofia remembered those days of utter exhaustion, where you were so tired you weren't even sure what you were doing because it felt like you were walking around in a fog. One time when Sophie was a baby, she'd been tidying up and packed all of the toys into the laundry hamper and then spent a solid forty-eight hours trying to find them. One day when Ned was a baby, she'd spent nearly an hour getting the kids ready to go out to the grocery store, and it wasn't until she was driving home that she realized she had forgotten to get herself dressed and had walked around the market in her pajamas. At the time, she'd been mortified, but now she just looked back and laughed.

"Want to put them down in their cribs?" she asked.

"No, I don't want to risk waking them. As long as you don't mind holding JP."

"I don't mind at all," she said, snuggling the baby closer. She loved holding his warm little body and watching his little chest rise and fall in peaceful sleep. "Are you and Xavier planning on having any more kids?"

"I'd love a big family. Xavier and I both had a few siblings, so I'd love to make these guys a big brother and sister one day, and it has to get easier with each new baby, right?"

Sofia laughed. "Not easier, but different. That first year or so was hard, juggling a baby while also trying to entertain a three-year-old, but now its great. They always have someone to play with, and Sophie adores being a big sister and looking out for Ned. I hope they always stay close."

"Did you and Ryan ever talk about having another baby?"

She felt her face drop.

Ryan.

Even the mention of her husband's name made her stomach clench in nervous anticipation.

It didn't go unnoticed.

"What is going on with you two?" Annabelle asked.

Sofia shrugged. She wasn't even sure how to go about answering that.

She was so confused.

Last night she hadn't wanted to sleep in her bed with Sophie and Ryan, but it had been the only thing that was going to let her daughter fall asleep. Sophie needed to feel safe, and she wasn't so selfish that she was going to mess with her daughter's sense of security. Ryan had left early to go to the hospital when they heard about Paige being attacked so she hadn't had to face him yet today, but she'd made up her mind that tonight they were going to sit down and talk. Which was part of the reason she had come to visit Annabelle.

"What's wrong?" Annabelle's pretty face creased with concern.

"I'm not sure. Ever since I had to shoot Deacon, I just feel different. Weird. Even being in the same room as Ryan makes me feel odd. I don't know why."

"You know that you did the right thing though, right?"

"I know. Deacon started shooting. He would have killed everyone in that room including me and my husband if I hadn't."

"You sound like you're reciting something you were told rather than something you believe," Annabelle pointed out.

Maybe her friend was right.

Maybe she hadn't really accepted yet that she had done the right thing.

"I don't mean to pry, but …" Sofia trailed off, not sure she had the right to ask Annabelle to talk about this.

"But you want to know how I felt after I killed someone," Annabelle finished for her.

"Kind of. But you don't have to tell me if you don't want to," she added quickly.

"No, it's okay; it's been a long time now, so I don't think about it very often but those first few months I thought about it all the time, and I dreamed about it most nights. I was like you; I knew that I had done what I needed to, to protect myself, but that didn't change the facts. I had taken a life. Another human being's life. And no matter how justified it was, it just made me feel all mixed up inside. Like I thought one way but felt another."

"How did you cope with those feelings?" She was hoping to hear some magic cure for what she was going through.

"I wish I could give you some sort of quick fix, but I can't. Taking a life nearly destroyed what Xavier and I had. It made me feel stronger … empowered … to know that I had protected myself, that I hadn't needed someone to rush in and save me, and that felt good. But eventually, it made me feel like I needed to keep proving that I could be strong and independent, and that led me to make some decisions that I still to this day regret, and well, you know how they turned out. Can I give you one piece of advice?"

"Of course." She greatly welcomed any advice; she clearly wasn't doing very well handling this on her own.

"Don't let it come between you and Ryan. However you're feeling and whatever you're going through, find a way to deal with it. Don't let it consume you, and don't let it come between you. You love Ryan and he loves you. You two have an amazing life and an amazing family together. Don't let anything ruin that."

Annabelle was right.

The only problem was Sofia didn't know how to stop what she was feeling from ruining her marriage.

* * * * *

9:41 A.M.

This time Macey was going to sit perfectly still and wait for them to come and question her.

No pacing.

No fidgeting.

No fiddling.

No shaking.

No panicking.

She was just going to sit here and wait, and then when they came to ask her their questions, she was going to answer them as calmly and as confidently as she could manage.

"Relax, Macey," Ryan said as the door opened and he and Xavier Montague came and joined her in the drab, suffocatingly-small interview room. Their presence seemed to use up space that wasn't there, and Macey was swamped by a sudden rush of claustrophobia.

"Really, Macey, relax," Xavier echoed Ryan's words.

They made it sound so simple.

Relax.

Like she wasn't a suspect in a murder investigation.

Like she wasn't terrified beyond words that her daughter might have committed four murders.

Like her world wasn't crumbling around her.

Calm and confident out the window, she looked up at them, broadcasting the fear inside her. "Do you really think I did it? Do you really think I poisoned my husband and killed Amy, Tara, Teagan, and Paige?" she asked. That Paige was dead still hadn't sunk in. She wished she hadn't been so afraid when she came to

236

the center and had gotten to know the cop better.

Ryan and Xavier exchanged glances.

Her paranoia racketed up a few notches.

Something was wrong.

What did they think she had done now?

How much worse could things get?

"Paige isn't dead," Ryan announced.

Her mouth fell open in shock.

Had she heard that right?

"Wh-what?"

"Paige was attacked last night," Xavier explained. "Someone called in to report a body in the vacant lot beside her house. We thought it might be a setup so I headed straight there. When I got there, she was bleeding badly from a deep cut on her leg, but she survived. She's fine, driving her husband crazy because she can't get up and around like she wants to. We reported her dead because we didn't want the killer coming back after her again."

Macey's face fell.

They meant her.

"You can relax. We *don't* think that you're the killer," Ryan told her.

That should make her relax.

But it didn't.

If they thought she was innocent, then that meant they thought Elle was guilty.

Where had she gone wrong?

She had always thought that she was a good mother.

Yes, she had doubts—as all parents did—about whether or not she was doing a good job. She worried about the mistakes she had made and wondered about what she could be doing better.

But obviously, she had been a terrible mother.

Her daughter was a killer.

A murderer.

She hated the sound of those words in the same sentence as

her child.

"I'm sorry, it's my fault." She couldn't stop the tears from flowing. "I'm Elle's mother; it's my fault. If I'd done a better job raising her, she wouldn't have killed anyone. I'm sorry. Please, punish me ... not my little girl."

"Is Elle left-handed?" Ryan asked calmly, like he knew the answer but was wanting to prove something to her—exactly what, she had no idea.

"N-no," she replied.

"Are you?"

"No."

"Then neither of you is the killer. The woman who attacked Paige was left-handed."

This time relief washed over her.

Not because she was finally cleared as a suspect but because her little girl was still the sweet, kind, compassionate girl she had always known.

How had she ever doubted Elle?

The last few days had been so stressful and overwhelming that they had messed with her head and caused her to lose her common sense.

Of course, her baby girl would never hurt anyone.

So, if she and Elle were no longer suspects, who did the cops think it was?

"Is Kimberly Ute left-handed?" Xavier asked.

Kimberly.

Elle's biological mother.

Like someone had flipped a switch, everything fell into place.

Macey could feel the blood drain from her face.

It must have been noticeable because Xavier reached across the table and rested a hand over hers. "Are you okay?"

"Kimberly is left-handed," she said in a small voice.

"We need to know everything that you know about her," Ryan said.

She nodded, but her mind had gone blank.

All she could think about was that a woman she had allowed to spend time around her child, whom she had trusted to be near Elle, was not just a killer but had actually tried to set her up so that she could get her claws into her daughter.

"Macey," Xavier still held her hands and he squeezed gently. "We need to know *every*thing that you can tell us about her."

"Okay, okay." She had to focus; she could do this. Her and Elle's safety depended on it.

"Kimberly wanted Elle back, didn't she?" Ryan asked.

"Yes," Macey tearfully confirmed. "And it wasn't the first time."

"When was the first time?" Xavier asked.

"She came back when Elle was eight—out of the blue. We hadn't heard from her since she dropped Elle off with Deacon and split. She said she made a mistake giving her daughter up and that she wanted her back. She said that she would agree to share custody with us, but she was still on drugs. We told her that if she wanted any part of Elle's life that she was going to have to get clean first; otherwise, she was a threat to her daughter's safety. We didn't think she'd do it. We didn't think she could complete rehab and get clean."

"But she did," Ryan said.

Macey nodded. "She came back two years later when Elle was ten and said that she was clean and offered to take a drug test to prove it. She asked for visitation so she could get to know Elle before we finalized a joint custody arrangement."

"You refused her visitation."

"We did." Maybe it had been selfish, but she hadn't wanted to share her beautiful daughter with anyone else. And Kimberly had signed away her parental rights. She hadn't wanted Elle, and she had no legal claim on the girl. "We told her that she had to get a job, prove that she could be a stable influence in Elle's life before we let her near her."

"She became a nurse," Xavier said.

"She came back when Elle was twelve, but Elle had just gone through a long battle with pneumonia. She had been in and out of the hospital over a four-month period. She would get better, and then she'd nosedive again. She had missed a lot of school. She was feeling left out and lonely because she was no longer close with her friends. We told Kimberly that it wasn't a good time to be disrupting her life further."

"How did Kimberly take that?" Ryan asked.

"She was upset and angry, but we reminded her that she had no legal claim over Elle and that any visitation or joint custody would be at our discretion."

"When did she come back next?" Xavier asked.

"Last year. But Elle had been having trouble with a boy in her class, and again, it just wasn't a good time to be messing with her life. Once more, Kimberly didn't like it, but we were the ones in control, and we had to exert that control to do what was best for our daughter." Elle was theirs. They had raised her and she and Deacon had wanted to keep their daughter, their family.

"Were you ever going to let her into Elle's life?" Ryan asked.

"Honestly, probably not. We probably would have kept putting her off indefinitely. Elle was ours. Kimberly gave her up, she didn't want her, but we did and we gave her a good home, a loving home. Until …"

"Until someone started poisoning Deacon and your whole world changed," Ryan finished for her.

"Could Kimberly have gotten access to Deacon to poison him?" Xavier asked.

"Maybe. She knew where we lived, and we didn't have a security system, so I guess she could have gotten in and out of our house if she wanted to."

"If you knew that Kimberly wanted Elle, why did you let her help you?" Xavier asked.

"I didn't know what else to do. Kimberly saw us at the

hospital, and she said she wouldn't push the issue of visitation or joint custody again, that she just wanted us to be safe. Do you think her plan all along was to get me and Deacon out of the picture so she could get Elle?" What did this woman have planned for her daughter?

"Yes," Xavier answered honestly. "We believe that she was going to try to kill Ryan and Sofia, then you, and then grab Elle and run. But we want to try to get ahead of her. We want to try to use you to trap her, if you think you're up to it."

"Of course," she replied without hesitation. She would do anything to keep Elle safe. "I'll do anything you want me to do; you just tell me what it is, and I'll do it."

"Macey, there's one more thing you should know," Xavier said. "We're not sure how she found out, but Elle told Laura that she knows that you aren't her biological mother."

The bottom fell out of her world.

* * * * *

11:18 A.M.

Macey was going to pay for what she had done.

Kimberly hated the other woman.

Hated her.

How dare the woman think that it was acceptable to steal her daughter. Elle was *hers*. *She* had given birth to her. Elle had lived inside *her* body for nine months, and it was her blood that ran through Elle's body. It was her DNA that had created the amazing young woman Elle had grown to be.

She had done every single thing that Macey and Deacon had asked.

Every.

Single.

Thing.

And what did they do every time?

They reneged.

They acted like whether or not she got to see her daughter was up to them just because she had signed away her parental rights.

Well, guess what?

She changed her mind.

There was nothing wrong with that. When she was eighteen, she'd been in no place to raise a child, so she had done right by her baby and given it to people who would be able to love and care for it.

Why should she be punished for doing the right thing?

Would they have preferred she had kept Elle and the child had grown up surrounded by drugs and alcohol?

No, they wouldn't.

So, she had done what any decent person would have done and made sure her baby was safe. Then when she was in a place where she was ready to be a mother, she had returned for her child. She'd had so many dreams of what it would be like to get her daughter back. She imagined the little girl coming running into her arms, hugging her and crying, so thrilled to be reunited. She imagined taking her home and playing with her every day, doing her hair and picking out cute outfits to wear. It would all have been so perfect, but Deacon and Macey had ruined it with their holier-than-thou attitudes.

What made them think they would be better parents than her?

She would be a fabulous mother. She and Elle would have so much fun together. They would get their nails and hair done, go shopping together, and talk about boys. It would all be so perfect.

Kimberly was going to make it happen.

Nothing was going to stop her.

After all, she was only going to reclaim what was hers anyway.

And her daughter belonged to her.

The idea to poison Deacon had been a stroke of genius, and from that very first step, everything had gone according to plan. It was like she had written the whole thing out and hired people to act it out.

Sneaking in and out of the house had been risky, but she had been careful and any time she went to lace Deacon's favorite drinks with mercury, no one had ever spotted her. Deacon turning abusive had been just what she had hoped would happen, and she hoped that every time he hit Macey the woman realized what a mistake it had been to steal her daughter.

She hadn't expected Deacon to hit Elle though, and when she realized it was getting out of hand, she had stepped in and convinced Macey to leave, which had been easier than she had anticipated.

It had taken longer to convince Macey to leave the center than she had thought it would and she had almost lost her patience and started looking for another way to lure Deacon here. She hadn't been sure exactly what he would do when he got there, but she had hoped it would be something crazy that would get him killed, and she couldn't have thought up anything better than what had happened. Deacon acting all insane and ranting on and on about how he never laid a hand on his wife had been perfect. Kimberly believed that he honestly believed that.

With Deacon out of the way, she just had to set up Macey, then there'd be no more obstacles standing between her and her daughter. Ever since they arrived at the center, she had been dropping little hints, planting little seeds in people's minds, that maybe Macey wasn't one of them. That maybe she wasn't a victim of domestic violence. She assumed that sooner or later the cops would find out about the mercury, and since the other hostages were being killed off, they would believe that Macey was trying to cover her tracks by killing anyone who might possibly know anything that could incriminate her.

It had worked.

All it took was killing Amy Frankstone to get that doubt building.

Add in Tara May's death and then Teagan Vonce's, and the cops started seriously looking into Macey as a suspect.

Killing Paige Hood had been harder, and she hadn't been entirely sure that she'd been successful because the woman had kept fighting back. However, she had heard on the news this morning that a cop had been attacked and passed away at the scene from her injuries, so she knew that she had achieved her goal.

That only left Ryan and Sofia Xander.

And then Macey.

Macey, she was saving until last.

Everyone else she had just killed because she had to. She wanted to set up Macey, and she had been worried that Deacon's crazy ramblings might end up turning the cops in her direction, so killing those who had been in the room served two purposes. One, it turned the heat up on Macey; and two, it made sure that there was no one who might figure out the truth.

She wouldn't allow anything to derail her plan.

That was unacceptable.

She *would* get her daughter back.

She wasn't going to fail when she was this close. Not after all the time and effort she'd put into this plan. She had been working on it ever since she came back last year only to find out that Elle was having trouble with some boy at her school and Deacon and Macey had told her that the timing was wrong, and she couldn't disrupt Elle's life further by dropping the bomb of her maternity on her.

Kimberly really didn't see that it was such a bomb.

Surely Elle knew that she wasn't really Macey's daughter. She didn't look anything like Macey.

Finding out that she was her mother was going to be wonderful for both her and Elle.

They would be fine together.

Just fine.

And soon it would be just the two of them.

All her dreams would come true.

But before they could, she had to figure out a way to kill Ryan and Sofia. That was going to be a tricky one. A fire at their house, maybe? Tampering with the brakes of their car? She wasn't sure yet; she didn't want to do anything that would hurt Ryan and Sofia's children. Sophie and Ned hadn't done anything to her, and they weren't a part of this.

She wasn't a monster, after all.

She was just a woman who had been kept from her child and was trying to get her back.

She didn't enjoy killing people. Once she had her daughter back, she wasn't going to keep on murdering.

There would be no reason to.

All she had to do was find the perfect way to kill Ryan and Sofia. She was sure she could figure something out. She had come up with the whole Deacon mercury idea, after all. She was good at this.

Something would come to her.

And once it did, she would kill Macey and then she and Elle would ride off into the sunset together. Or maybe she would bring Macey with her. That could turn out to be a lot of fun. Making Macey watch someone else being a mother to Elle would let her know just how Kimberly had been feeling all these years. Then, when she grew tired of that, she would kill Macey in some long-drawn-out way befitting a thief and a liar. Maybe she'd lock her up in a room and leave her to starve to death.

That sounded like the perfect idea.

Her stomach was swirling in delightful anticipation. She was so close. Soon, she would be holding her daughter in her arms. They were going to have the perfect life together. Just the two of them.

Despite what Macey and Deacon seemed to think, she loved her daughter—loved her so much that it hurt. Being away from her for so many years made all of those years seem like a waste.

She had missed so much.

Elle's first smile, her first laugh, her first word, her first step, her first day of school, her first date, her first kiss.

She hadn't been there when Elle was sick or scared, when she had nightmares and was afraid to go back to sleep. She hadn't attended dance recitals or baseball games or parent teacher conferences. She hadn't been there to make her daughter laugh when she was sad or make all the bad things in the world disappear. She hadn't supported her.

Kimberly knew she had a lot to make up for.

A *lot*.

But there was still time.

Elle was only fifteen; they still had the rest of their lives to be together. She had missed a lot, but she wasn't going to miss another second of her daughter's life. She was going to be there when Elle graduated. She was going to help her pick which college she wanted to attend. She was going to be there for her daughter's wedding and be by her side when she went into labor and gave birth to a child of her own. Then Elle would be by her side taking care of her when she grew old.

It was going to be wonderful.

Perfect.

Mother and daughter together again as they always should have been.

* * * * *

12:10 P.M.

Sofia hung up the phone and debated heading home.

Her daughter wasn't coping well.

She had never seen Sophie so stressed and worried. Usually her daughter was a little bundle of energy and confidence who bustled about zipping from one thing to the next with barely a pause in between.

Although she could be loud and boisterous, Sophie was a very empathetic child. She was always looking out for anyone who was lonely or sad or being bullied or mistreated, and then she stepped in to do something about it. Five years ago when Paige and Elias had adopted Hayley and Arianna, Sophie had made it her mission to help Hayley adjust and learn how to be a normal kid.

Sophie was strong, but seeing Deacon holding people hostage, and then finding out that someone was killing off the people who had been in the room at the time, had really knocked the equilibrium out of her world.

And Sofia didn't know how to help her get it back.

One thing she did know, though, was that the tension between her and Ryan wasn't helping. Sophie had already picked up on it and asked several times if something was wrong. Sofia kept telling her that everything was fine, but Sophie was smart and intuitive. Ten years old now—not a baby—she knew that something was going on. The only way to convince her that everything was okay was to find a way to make everything okay, or at least as okay as they could be, given the circumstances.

She sighed. She was really doing a good job of messing things up—and messing up her family was the last thing she wanted to do.

Sofia glanced at her watch—it was a little after midday. She had a mountain of work to get through because she hadn't been able to concentrate the last few days, so she was behind in everything. She also wanted to check in on Elle Staines and make sure the teenager wasn't still thinking of running away. Maybe she could do that and then go and have lunch at her in-laws; they were looking after Sophie and Ned today since Sophie hadn't wanted to come back here.

Her mind made up, she stood and stretched, then pushed her desk chair back in—for some reason, she couldn't leave her office if the chair wasn't pushed in to touch the edge of the desk.

Elle and Macey were staying in different rooms, and Macey had been at the police station for the last couple of hours, so she had no idea what Elle was up to other than the teenager hadn't left her room all day.

Nodding to the officer who was stationed outside Elle's room, she knocked as she opened the door. "Elle, it's Sofia," she called out as she stepped inside.

Elle's eyes darted toward her and she dropped something that made a small clink as it landed on the floorboards.

From the look on the teenager's face, Sofia knew something was wrong. "Elle?"

The girl turned to flee, and as she was moving, Sofia saw a flash of red on the girl's white arm.

Blood.

She looked down at what had fallen from Elle's hand and saw a small razor blade.

"Elle, stop." She hurried forward and grabbed the girl's arm, holding her in place. "Were you cutting yourself?" She lifted Elle's arm and saw not just three small fresh cuts, but several others all in various stages of healing and some completely scarred over. Elle had obviously been doing this for a while. "Come and sit down."

Sofia guided Elle over to the sofa, and although the girl didn't fight her, she clearly wanted to be anywhere but here.

"Are you sure you want to be around me? I'm a murder suspect," Elle said. Since she said it without attitude and without any heat, Sofia knew the girl was more sad than angry about what was going on.

"I don't think you killed anyone," she said, allowing the girl to take a few moments to procrastinate and put off the inevitable conversation they needed to have about her cutting herself.

"Then you think it was my mom." Elle refused to look at her and kept her gaze fixed firmly on the floor.

"No, I don't think your mother is a killer."

Elle chanced a quick glance at her. "Then who *do* you think it is?"

"I don't know, but I trust my husband to figure it out." That was true. Regardless of the unusual feelings she was having about being around Ryan since shooting Deacon, Sofia knew that he was good at his job and trusted him to find the killer before the killer came after her.

"I wish I did," Elle muttered.

They had procrastinated long enough. "How long, Elle?"

"How long, what?"

She played along because she didn't really know what else to do to get the girl talking. Laura was the one who was good at this sort of thing. She was the business side of things at the center. She was too blunt, which might work with her friends and family but wasn't so good when dealing with traumatized and abused women and children. "How long have you been cutting yourself?"

"I ... I ... I ... about a year and a half," Elle finally answered with a sigh.

"What made you start?" Sofia felt completely out of her element, but she wasn't going to back out. She could do this. If it were her daughter, she'd just want the person talking to her to make her know that she was loved and cared about, that she mattered.

Elle still wouldn't look at her, but she did start talking. "A boy at my school wanted me to have sex with him but I wouldn't. I didn't want to; I wasn't ready yet. But he didn't like that, so he started making up lies about me and spreading them around our school. He would make kissing sounds at me whenever we passed in the halls and wiggle his hips at me. It kept going on and on. My mom found out and she went to the school, the boy's parents, and eventually the cops. He stopped, but ..." she trailed off.

"But the damage was already done?"

"Mm-hmm. I started feeling really bad about myself, and I didn't know what to do about it. I'd always been pretty confident around boys, but after that, I wasn't. I had all these feelings and emotions inside me." Elle finally looked up and met her eye directly. "I didn't know what to do with them. Then one day I accidentally scratched my arm on a nail sticking out of the side of the shed while I was taking out the trash. I can't explain it, I just felt … better."

"So you kept going."

Elle nodded. "I couldn't stop. I felt like it was my fault that that boy started targeting me. I should have just said yes when he asked for sex. And then I felt bad that my mom had to step in and fix everything. I was fourteen, old enough to fix my own problems. Every time I cut myself, I felt like I was punishing myself for my mistakes, and those feelings inside me that felt like they were choking me, went away, at least for a little while."

Was she doing the same thing?

Was that why she kept shoving Ryan away and rejecting his attempts at supporting her?

Was she metaphorically hurting herself as punishment for taking a life?

Sofia knew that she had done the right thing. She'd heard it repeatedly from her friends and family and from herself. But she couldn't shake the horror that she had killed someone.

She had put a bullet through his brain.

She had ended Deacon's life.

She had killed him.

Killed him.

And no one seemed to care.

The cops weren't interested because they had deemed it a justifiable homicide. Her family and friends cared only about the impact the shooting had on her. Macey and Elle were distracted by the murders.

But Deacon was dead.

Dead.

Someone should have to pay for that.

And that person should be her.

She was the one who had pulled the trigger.

If no one else was going to punish her then she had to punish herself.

Everything was so clear now.

She finally understood why she hadn't been able to be around Ryan without feeling so uneasy and wrong. She just prayed that he was able to forgive her and be patient with her while she worked through her feelings.

Right now, though, she had to do what she could for Elle. "Does Laura know?"

"Yes. I told her not long after my mom and I came here. She was helping me, I was doing well, I hadn't cut myself in almost three months, but then today ..." Elle trailed off again, then squared her shoulders and straightened her back. "Today, I kind of had a relapse, but Laura said that I would. She said not to be too hard on myself when it happened."

"Laura's pretty smart, you know." She smiled at the girl.

"Yeah, she is," Elle agreed.

"You're pretty smart, too, Elle. You know that you did the right thing saying no to having sex too young when you weren't ready. Sometimes we doubt ourselves; sometimes we lose faith in ourselves, and sometimes we even lose faith in the people who love us. But when we feel lost, when we feel like we don't know which way is up, there's only one thing left—and that's love."

Elle gave her a half smile that made her look much older than her fifteen years. "Are you talking to me or yourself?"

"See ... pretty smart." She smiled back. "And both of us. I was talking to both of us. Sometimes we all need a reminder of how important love is."

* * * * *

1:31 P.M.

Sofia was right.

About being smart.

About doubting yourself.

About losing faith, not just in yourself, but in others too.

About how important love was.

About everything.

She had to see her mom. She had to apologize to her. How could she have ever thought that her mother was capable of killing anyone?

Elle knew without a shadow of a doubt that her mother was not a killer. She hated that she'd thought it was possible, even for a second. When she saw her mother, she was going to hug her and tell her how much she loved her.

Where was Mom?

It was one-thirty in the afternoon and she hadn't heard from her all day.

That was not like her mother.

As much as she adored her mom, she had always been one of those very hands-on, over involved moms who was always all up in her kid's business. Although Elle usually pretended that she hated it and wished her mother would stop being so overbearing, in truth, she loved it. She loved it because she knew it meant her mom cared. And that was what everyone wanted to know, that someone cared about them. As much as it drove her crazy, she wouldn't change one single thing about her mom.

If it was into the early afternoon and her mother hadn't made any move to contact her, then something was wrong.

Had the killer tried to kill her?

She was one of the people in the room when Dad died, so she could be the next victim.

Or had she been arrested?

It seemed like the cops believed that she was guilty. Maybe they had hauled her down to the police station and thrown her in jail.

Maybe she should go down to the police station and see if her mother was there. If she wasn't, then she could report her missing.

Elle looked around for her purse. She had her learner's permit, but she couldn't drive on her own. And even if she could, they didn't have a car. Maybe she could walk to the bus stop. Or she could see if there was someone here who could drive her. Sofia probably would or maybe even Annabelle.

It might be better not to involve anyone else in case they tried to stop her. Taking the bus was probably the better option.

She threw open the door and was surprised to see Kimberly Ute standing there, her hand poised and ready to knock.

Kimberly was the last person she wanted to see right now.

"I was just heading out," she said, trying to brush past.

"Oh." Kimberly looked disappointed. "I had hoped to talk to you. Just for a moment."

Maybe it would be quicker just to get it over with, see what Kimberly wanted, then she could go and check on Mom.

"Everything okay, Miss Staines?" the cop at her door moved closer.

"Fine," she said. She didn't like Kimberly, but what could the woman do while there was a cop on her door.

She stepped back into her apartment and closed the door behind Kimberly when she stepped through.

"I hate to be the one to tell you this, but your mom is at the police station. She's been charged with the murders," Kimberly informed her.

Arrested.

Her mother.

For murder.

This was a nightmare.

She had to go down there, convince the cops that they were wrong.

If her mom was arrested, what would happen to her? She had no one else. Her dad was dead; there weren't any other relatives to take her in. Would she be thrown in foster care? Could she stay here at the center until this was sorted out and her mother was cleared?

What if her mother was found guilty?

Four murders. They would sentence her to life, and she would never get out.

She had to find a way to fix this.

If she talked to the cops, she was sure she could convince them that they were wrong, that this was just a mistake, that her mother would never hurt anyone.

"Don't be scared." Kimberly took a step forward. Elle took a step back. She didn't like Kimberly, and she didn't want to get close to her. She should have told the cop to make Kimberly go away.

"I need to go," she said.

"Wait, Elle. I mean it … you don't have to be scared. Until things get sorted out with your mother, I was thinking you could stay with me."

Stay with Kimberly?

That was not going to happen.

"I don't think so," she said. She would rather be on the street than live with Kimberly Ute.

"Look, Elle, there's something I have to tell you. Something that your parents should have told you a long time ago." Kimberly tried to look sympathetic and concerned and like she cared, but Elle knew it was an act. Kimberly only cared about herself.

"I really have to go." She didn't want to hear anything that Kimberly had to say about her parents.

"Elle, I'm your mother," Kimberly announced.

"I know."

Elle had known for months—for over a year. A few months before her dad had changed, she had gotten home from school early one day, before anyone else got home. She had been up in her room, texting with a couple of her friends when she'd heard loud voices.

She'd wondered if it was her parents fighting. They rarely fought, and when they did, it usually didn't last long. But when she had crept to the top of the stairs, she'd heard a third voice.

Kimberly's voice.

She had heard everything.

That Kimberly had given birth to her but hadn't wanted her, so she had given her to her dad and his new girlfriend. Apparently, Kimberly had come back for her several times, but her mom and dad wouldn't let Kimberly have her.

She had been shocked.

Confused.

Angry.

Hurt.

But despite all of that, she had understood.

Kimberly hadn't wanted her. Mom and Dad had.

In the end, it was as simple as that.

The woman standing before her wasn't her mother. She was nothing more than the egg donor.

"You don't have to worry about who will look after you with Macey in prison. I'm your mother; I'll take care of you." Kimberly gave her another one of those smiles that sent shivers up and down her spine.

"You are *not* my mother," she said firmly.

"Elle, dear, I know this is a shock, but I am your mother. I gave birth to you."

"And that's all you did. I might have come from your body but that doesn't make you my mother. A mother is someone who cares about you, who is always there for you, who goes to bat for you, who gets all up in your business and drives you crazy because they love you. All you did was give birth to me."

Like a flip had been switched, Kimberly's face darkened. Gone was the false smile; in its place was a vicious scowl. "I wanted to be your mother, but Deacon and Macey wouldn't let me."

"That is not true."

"It is. Whatever else they told you is lies."

"They didn't tell me anything. I *heard* everything. The last time you came to my house, I was upstairs."

"They stole you from me."

"*You* gave me away."

"I changed my mind. I wanted you back, but they said no. They tricked me. They kept asking me to do things if I wanted to see you, but they were never going to let me have you."

"Because they loved me." Anyone with eyes could see that Kimberly wasn't cut out to be a parent. But she had been lucky. Her dad had wanted her and he'd given her the best mother in the world.

"Well, they aren't here anymore," Kimberly said, her voice gone snarky and her scowl turned into a smug smile.

Kimberly was the killer.

It was written all over her face.

She had done this.

All of it.

She had set this whole thing in motion. She had done something to her dad to make him become violent. Then she had purposefully made sure that she saw them at the hospital that time so she could tell them about this place. That's why she had hung around all these months, because she was waiting for a chance to set up her mom. Then with both of her parents out of the picture, she probably thought she could swoop in and play mommy.

Well, Elle already had a mother, and she wanted her back.

Kimberly was insane. She belonged in prison.

Elle didn't know what Kimberly had planned next, but whatever it was, she wasn't getting mixed up in.

The cop was still outside her door. All she had to do was call out and help would come.

She was just opening her mouth to scream when Kimberly pulled out a gun.

"Don't make a sound."

* * * * *

2:12 P.M.

She was feeling much better.

After checking in with Elle, Sofia had picked up Sophie and taken her to the hospital to visit with Laura, and the three of them had lunch together; rather, she and Sophie had eaten, but Laura wasn't up to eating much yet. They had laughed and talked and just enjoyed being together again. Laura had fought so hard to get back to her husband, it seemed almost disrespectful—not to mention stupid—for her to throw away her marriage because she subconsciously wanted to punish herself for shooting a dangerous man to protect a roomful of people.

After lunch, she'd dropped Sophie back off at her grandparents' house and come back to work. She wanted to see how Elle was doing after their talk. She hoped that after some time to think, Elle would realize that she was a smart, strong young woman who didn't need to punish herself for anything. Sofia was sure that Laura had given Elle the tools she needed to deal with her compulsion to cut herself; she just needed to remind herself that she was capable of using them.

Her steps slowed as she approached Elle's room.

The cop was gone.

There was no way that Ryan would have recalled the order to have a cop stationed on Elle at all times. Not while the killer was still out there.

So where was he?

Uneasy now, she had to decide what to do. Go and call Ryan and see if the cop had been called back or go and check on Elle?

A couple of days ago she would have thought, what were the chances of anyone breaking in here. They had a state-of-the-art security system and an armed guard, but none of that had done them any good when Deacon broke in. Neither had it stopped someone from killing Amy and Tara. She might not think that Macey or Elle was the killer, but someone was, and that someone could be here right now, trying to go after Elle.

Sofia was going to do the sensible thing and go and call in and find out what was going on when she heard what sounded like a muffled scream.

Cursing herself for leaving her phone in her office, she ran toward Elle's room, thankful that there was no one else staying in any of the other rooms in this area. At least if something was going down, the chances of anyone else getting mixed up in this was slim.

"Elle?" she called out as she threw open the door.

She had been expecting to find Elle and possibly the killer. What she found was Elle standing in the middle of the room looking terrified, and on the floor of the apartment, the cop who had been stationed at her door. There was blood on his shirt from what looked like a gunshot wound. There had been no reports of shots fired, so maybe the killer had used a silencer. While that didn't actually make the gunshot silent, it might have muffled it enough that no one else had heard it.

"What happened?" she demanded. For a split second she wondered if she had been wrong all along and Elle Staines really was the one who had killed Amy, Tara, and Teagan, and tried to kill Paige.

The teenager just stood there. She didn't have a gun in her hands, she wasn't doing anything to help the bleeding cop, she wasn't doing anything.

She was just standing there, her gaze fixed on the still open door.

Sofia realized a moment too late what Elle was looking at.

She was just turning around as something slammed into the side of her head.

The blow didn't knock her out, but it did knock her down.

Sofia staggered and then dropped down onto all fours, the world spinning in a series of sickeningly quick revolutions. She gagged and nearly threw up but managed to keep her lunch down.

"Thank you; you saved me a trip," a voice said above her.

It took Sofia a moment to place the voice. It was familiar but with her head spinning a million miles a minute she couldn't figure out who it belonged to.

Then it clicked.

Kimberly Ute.

The nurse who had come to work here six months ago.

The woman who had brought Macey and Elle here.

The woman who had gone out of her way to harass Macey into not staying cooped up here at the center.

The woman who spent most of her time hanging around Macey and Elle.

Kimberly had been in the room when Deacon was holding them all hostage.

Kimberly lived here so she would have had access to Amy and Tara. She also would have had the opportunity to follow Teagan when she left to find out which motel she was staying at.

Kimberly could easily have found out Paige's home address. All she would have had to do was look it up in the office or follow her home one night.

Kimberly was the killer.

She must have come to get Elle. She must have deemed the girl a threat to her; the cop had probably just been collateral damage.

She was already on the killer's list and now she'd made it that much easier for Kimberly to murder her. She had practically offered herself up on a silver platter.

There was no point in begging for her life. Kimberly was in

full-on self-preservation mode; she wasn't thinking logically; in fact, she wasn't thinking at all. All she cared about was eliminating everyone she perceived as a threat.

"Get up," Kimberly ordered, kicking her in the ribs.

Kicking someone who you had already hit over the head wasn't a good way to get them to do what you wanted.

"I said, get up." Kimberly jabbed her in the side with the barrel of the gun.

Why didn't Kimberly just shoot her and be done with it?

As if reading her mind, Kimberly said, "I think I'll take you with me. That way I can lure your husband in and kill both of you … you'll be the perfect bait."

She didn't want to be bait.

If she was going to be killed, then so be it, but she certainly didn't want to be the one to lure her husband to his death.

"Let's go, Elle." Kimberly obviously decided she was still too woozy to get up and walk so she wrapped a hand around her arm and dragged her to her feet.

"No, Elle, run," Sofia said as she staggered to her feet. If she could distract Kimberly long enough to let the teenager run, then she would do it. She was a dead man walking anyway.

"Don't even think about it," Kimberly warned. "You do not want to make your mother angry."

Mother?

Kimberly was Elle's mother?

Was that why she was doing this? She wanted to get her daughter back?

"We are going to walk out of here like nothing is wrong," Kimberly ordered. "We're going to go down the back stairs and out the back door, heading straight for my car."

"At least call for help for the cop, please," Sofia said as Kimberly started to walk her to the door. "He has nothing to do with this."

"He doesn't, but he's sacrificing his life so I can get back the daughter who was stolen from me. Don't worry; he's dying a noble death. Elle, help me with Sofia."

"I'm sorry," Elle whispered in her ear as they walked out the door.

"Not your fault," she whispered back. Her head was clearing by the second and she was biding her time before making her move. She wouldn't go down without a fight.

"Hurry up," Kimberly hissed, jamming the gun into her back.

Sofia hoped that no one accidentally stumbled upon them. As unstable as Kimberly was right now, she wouldn't hesitate to shoot anyone who got in her way.

They made it all the way outside without seeing anyone, and before Sofia had a chance to think up anything she could do that wasn't going to get her killed instantly, they were at Kimberly's car.

"Get in the trunk." Kimberly popped it open.

Every cell in her body wanted to protest, to argue, to downright refuse, but the gun was still shoved against her spine.

Reluctantly, she climbed into the trunk.

Even open, it was stiflingly hot in there. If Kimberly wanted to use her to trap Ryan then she was going to have to do it quickly because Sofia didn't think she would live long trapped inside there.

Kimberly pulled out some zip ties and bound her wrists and ankles. Then she pulled out a silk scarf. "Don't want you screaming for help until I'm ready for you." She smirked gleefully as she gagged her. Kimberly was enjoying this. She might not have started out as a killer, but she had gotten surprisingly good as it in such a short period of time.

With a last smile, Kimberly slammed the trunk shut, leaving her trapped in this stifling heat.

Sofia didn't hold out much hope that she was walking out of this alive, but she prayed that Ryan would.

EIGHT

* * * * *

2:45 P.M.

Playing bait was a lot harder than it sounded.

It was the waiting.

Macey was trying to keep busy by cleaning up the mess Deacon had left behind. His mania was evident in the house that used to be her home. Even if she made it through this alive, she wasn't sure that she and Elle could come back and live here. Too much had happened; too much had changed. It just wouldn't be the same here now.

Although she knew that Deacon was still the man she'd fallen in love with all those years ago, and that he wasn't to blame for all those times that he'd hit her, what Kimberly had done had ruined her home.

This place used to be her safe place.

Her sanctuary.

Now being in here just reminded her of the woman who had set out to destroy her family and her life—and succeeded.

Deacon was dead. Elle hated her, and there was a chance that she would be dead by nightfall.

Macey wished that Kimberly would just hurry up and come for her. She didn't want to wait any longer. She just wanted this to be over then see if there was any chance that she could rebuild her relationship with her daughter.

If Elle wanted to.

But why would she?

Now she knew that they weren't really mother and daughter, she would surely see her differently. They had lied to her Elle's entire life. Kept the truth from her. Kept her from her biological mother. Made decisions for her based on what they believed was the right thing to do. Maybe Elle wished that they had given her back to Kimberly.

If she could go back and do things over, would she do them any differently?

Macey didn't think that she would.

She knew that Deacon would gladly have given his life to protect his daughter, as would she. As much as she wanted to keep Elle to herself, she had always felt that something was off with Kimberly Ute. Had she thought the woman was a deranged killer? No. But she had known something wasn't right and that was why she'd kept putting off letting the woman into her daughter's life.

There wasn't anything she wouldn't do to keep Elle safe, even if that meant keeping her maternity a secret.

Even if it meant sacrificing herself.

Even if it meant taking a life.

She knew that the cops were watching the house and that they were ready to swoop in and take care of Kimberly as soon as they had what they needed to put her away for the rest of her life, but if Kimberly came at her, she wouldn't hesitate to do whatever she needed to, to protect herself.

Macey almost hoped Kimberly *would* come at her.

She wanted the woman to suffer for everything she had put her family through.

Kimberly was the one who hadn't wanted Elle. She and Deacon hadn't manipulated her into giving up her baby or stolen Elle from her. The only decent thing Kimberly had ever done was giving away her child. They had given Elle everything she couldn't.

Kimberly should be grateful, not vengeful.

It might be too late for Deacon, but Macey would make sure that his death wasn't in vain. She would make sure that Kimberly *never* got near Elle again.

With a nervous sigh, she continued cleaning up the kitchen. Deacon had made such a mess out of it. There were plates and utensils in the freezer, food stored in piles all over the floor and the counters. There was a sleeping bag in the pantry, and Deacon had smeared peanut butter all over the walls. Why, she had absolutely no idea, but the impact the mercury poisoning had had on him was written throughout this room and the rest of the house.

She was halfway through scrubbing down the walls when she heard the back door swing open.

Finally.

It was time.

Macey straightened but didn't turn around. She wanted to wait and see what Kimberly had planned before she decided what she should do.

"It didn't have to end this way, Macey," Kimberly said. She sounded sincere but Macey knew she would never have been satisfied until she had Elle all to herself, and that was never going to happen. She, Deacon, and Elle were a family and that family didn't include Kimberly. But in Kimberly's mind, she and Elle were the family, and Deacon and Macey were definitely not included.

They couldn't both be right.

And since she and Deacon would never give up their daughter and let her spend time around an unstable person, it had been inevitable that something like this would happen.

Macey just wished that Kimberly hadn't dragged innocent people into this mess.

"All this has done is prove that we were right," she said quietly, turning to face Kimberly, her eyes growing wide in horror when she saw Elle standing there, a gun held to her head.

Automatically, she moved toward her daughter to pull her away from the danger.

"Uh, uh, uh." Kimberly smiled and shoved the gun into Elle's temple.

Her daughter cried out and Macey froze, unsure what her best move would be.

If she stayed where she was, her daughter was in danger, but if she moved closer, Kimberly could shoot Elle just to prove a point. As much as Kimberly obviously wanted Elle back, Macey wouldn't put it past her to take on an "if I can't have her then no one can" mentality.

Every move she made would drastically affect how this turned out.

Hadn't Ryan and Xavier and the other cops watching the house seen Macey walk in here with Elle? Her daughter was only fifteen. How could they let her walk in here knowing she was in danger?

Macey would never have agreed to play bait if she'd known that Elle was going to get mixed up in this. She had thought her daughter was safe at the center. There had been a cop on Elle's door. Her daughter should have been okay. How had Kimberly gotten to her?

"You think you were right to keep a child from her mother?" Kimberly looked and sounded outraged at the very notion.

"You *aren't* her mother," Macey said. "You have to try to accept that. You signed away your parental rights. I am Elle's mother."

"No!" Kimberly screamed.

"Yes!" she screamed back. Macey didn't know what was wrong with her. Kimberly had a gun; she shouldn't be antagonizing her, and yet, she couldn't stop. It was just like when Deacon had held a gun to her head at the center a few days ago. She had kept arguing with him about what he'd done even though she knew he could blow her brains out at any second.

"Stop saying that. I am going to make you sorry that you ever stole my daughter. I did everything you wanted me to do. I got clean. I trained to be a nurse. A *nurse*. I help people every day of my life and yet you still thought I wasn't fit to raise my own flesh and blood. But every time I came to get her you had some excuse about why it wasn't a good time. Well, guess what? Now *is* the time. Now we're working on *my* timetable."

"You think you can just kill me and walk away with my daughter?" Macey couldn't help but laugh. This was all so stupid. Kimberly was crazy. "Do you really think Elle is going to love you just because you tell her that you're her biological mother? Do you really think she's going to love you after you poisoned her father? After you killed four people, including a cop?" All she needed to do was get Kimberly to admit out loud what she had done and then the cops would come storming in here and it would all be over.

"I did what I had to do," Kimberly shouted. "Deacon was willing to keep our child and not share her; he got what he deserved. And the others had to die. It wasn't like I got any pleasure from killing them, but I was doing what I had to do for my daughter, just like any good mother would."

Macey felt herself sag in relief.

She had done what the cops asked her to do.

It was over.

Any second now, Ryan and Xavier and the others would come rushing in.

Kimberly would be hauled off to prison.

And she and Elle could go home.

A shot rang out.

At first she thought it was the cops.

But then pain exploded in her chest.

Macey looked down and was surprised to see red on her mint green tank top.

Blood?

Was it blood?

Someone was screaming but she wasn't sure who.

The world was shimmering in and out of focus in front of her.

There were lots of noises now.

Loud noises.

Then she was falling.

Landing with a crash.

Her last conscious thought was a prayer that she had done enough to save her daughter.

* * * * *

3:03 P.M.

"That was very satisfying," Kimberly said as she lowered the gun. She had been planning on keeping Macey alive for a while and bringing her along, but five minutes in the woman's company and she knew she couldn't. The woman drove her insane. Macey thought she was so perfect, like she had never made mistakes.

That was the only thing she had done wrong; she had made a mistake in trusting Deacon and Macey with her child.

"Mom," Elle screamed when Macey dropped to the floor.

"What?" She turned to her daughter.

"Not you," Elle glared at her. "You are not my mother."

"Don't make me punish you on our first day together," she warned. She was not in the mood for sass from a teenager. She still had to take Sofia Xander and use her to lure her husband then kill them both before she and Elle could leave.

"You can't punish me. What about this are you not getting? You are not my mother."

Deacon and Macey might like to talk up their parenting skills, but they had clearly let Elle get away with too much if she thought it was acceptable behavior to speak to her mother that way.

Well, she would learn.

She would teach her daughter proper manners and etiquette.

"Let's go. We'll talk about your behavior and what an appropriate punishment will be once we get home."

"I'm not going anywhere with you." Elle tried to wriggle out of her grasp.

Elle was working her last nerve right about now.

"Let's go," she ordered.

"You're not going anywhere, Kimberly."

She spun around.

She was surrounded.

Ryan Xander, Xavier Montague, and a bunch of other cops she didn't know filled the house.

They were everywhere.

This was a setup.

Macey had set her up.

As if the woman hadn't done enough to mess up her life. She had stolen her daughter and the life that could have been hers with Deacon and their child. And now she had led her straight into a trap. The cops had known that she would track Macey down. They had sent her here to the house Macey had shared with Deacon and Elle, so they could lie here in wait for her.

The absolute audacity of the woman was astounding.

Macey was scum.

Worse than scum.

She was the lowest of the low.

She was rotten to the core.

At least she was dead now.

If she was going down, at least she had taken Macey down with her.

"Put the gun down, Kimberly," Ryan ordered.

No chance in hell.

She wasn't setting her weapon down, not for anything.

The gun was the only thing stopping her from being shot or arrested.

Macey was dead, but she still had Elle. She wasn't above using her daughter as a human shield. Elle belonged to her. She was her property and she was free to do with her whatever she wanted.

She wasn't sure what, but maybe there was a way to walk out of here having achieved everything she wanted.

She had a Glock 17. It could hold seventeen rounds; it had

been fully loaded when she came to the house. She'd fired one bullet at Macey, hitting her in the chest. That meant she had sixteen rounds left. Depending on how many cops were here, it was possible she could use Elle as a human shield and shoot them all, then run with Elle before reports of shots fired could bring more cops running.

"Put the gun down," Ryan repeated.

She ignored him.

She had no time for him right now.

She had to figure out how many cops were here if she was going to have any chance of getting away.

Drawing her daughter up tightly against her chest, she unobtrusively tried to scan the room and do a head count.

"Come on, Kimberly. You have to know you aren't going to walk out of here," Xavier said.

"My mom," Elle sobbed. "Is she dead?"

Xavier moved to check on Macey, but she wasn't having anyone moving. She couldn't keep track of everyone if they were moving about.

"Nobody move," she shouted, jamming the gun into Elle's head for emphasis.

Everybody froze.

At least these cops knew how to follow instructions unlike that stupid Macey.

"But my mom, she needs help." Elle struggled in her grasp.

"She is not your mother," Kimberly screamed. How many times was she going to tell Elle that before the kid believed it? It was like Deacon and Macey had brainwashed her.

"You love Elle, right?" Ryan asked.

"Of course." What kind of stupid question was that? What kind of mother would she be if she didn't?

"Right now, she's scared. I know that you're her mother, that you gave birth to her, but this has been a lot for her to take in, in a very short space of time. I'm sure she's not trying to upset you on purpose, right, Elle?"

"R-right," Elle said.

"You're going to cut her some slack, right, Kimberly? I mean, that's what we do for our kids, isn't it?"

"I guess," Kimberly agreed. She had the feeling he was just trying to trick her, distract her, make her feel like he understood so that she would let her guard down, and then he was going to make his move.

Well, it wouldn't work.

She wasn't stupid.

"Why don't you let us check on Macey, then I'm sure Elle will be much more willing to listen to you."

"I was raised by parents who didn't coddle their children," she retorted. "The parents are in charge. It's the children's jobs to listen and obey without complaint. I intend to raise my daughter the same way."

"I teach my kids to respect me as well. But I also want them to grow into responsible adults who are capable of making their own decisions and choices without me there telling them what to do," Ryan said.

Was he questioning her parenting?

How dare he.

She was so sick of people meddling in her relationship with her daughter.

It wasn't happening anymore.

She wasn't doing this again.

Deacon was dead; Macey was dead; she had come so far to get what she wanted, and she wasn't going to lose it when she was this close to finishing. This wasn't going to fail. She had worked too long and too hard. She had been patient; she had been meticulous; she had been dedicated; she hadn't hesitated to eliminate every threat that presented itself, and she had done every single thing needed to make this happen.

No one was stopping her.

No one was getting in her way.

She hadn't been able to count all the cops, so she was just going to have to start shooting and hope that she had enough bullets to take them all out.

Then she was taking Elle home and locking her in her room until she learned some respect.

Kimberly said a silent prayer for forgiveness for taking the lives of the innocents, just like she had before killing Amy Frankstone, Tara May, Teagan Vonce, Detective Paige Hood, and the cop who had been on Elle's door back at the center. They were dying an honorable death helping a mother be reunited with her daughter. Unlike Macey and Deacon, they didn't deserve to die, but she didn't have a choice. If she wanted to get her daughter back, then she had to do what she had to do.

She wrapped an arm tightly around Elle's neck and then lifted the gun, ready to start firing it.

Just as she did, a hand clamped around her wrist, twisting her hand to the side.

She fired off a shot, but it went wide and missed everyone, plowing into the wall instead.

The hand around her wrist twisted it again and pain shot up through her arm, causing her to drop her weapon to the floor.

As soon as she was disarmed, she was swarmed by cops.

They dragged Elle from her arms.

They tackled her to the floor.

They yanked her arms behind her back and slapped on handcuffs.

They began to read her her Miranda Rights.

They pulled her to her feet and toward the door.

"Elle?" she yelled over her shoulder, searching the room for her daughter. "I love you. Everything I did was for you. For us. Because I love you. Because I wanted us to be together. Like we were supposed to be. I love you, Elle. I'll always love you. One day I'll find a way to get us back together. I'll never give up on us.

I love you. I love you!"

* * * * *

3:19 P.M.

It was so hot.

Too hot.

So hot, Sofia could hardly breathe.

She had been sweating so much at first that it was dripping off her, drenching her ankle length white skirt and ice blue tank top.

But now she was drying up.

The sweat had gotten under the zip ties binding her wrists and ankles, the plastic rubbed against her wet skin, cutting through another layer with every single move she made.

It was dark in the trunk, and between that and the heat exhaustion she knew she was suffering from, she was starting to get sleepy.

Maybe she should just let her eyes fall closed and go to sleep.

It had to be better than roasting all cramped up in this tight space.

Closing her eyes might actually help with the dizziness and the headache.

It might help with the nausea too.

Several times now, she'd had to choke down some bile. She still had the gag in, and with her wrists tied behind her back, she couldn't remove it. If she threw up with it in her mouth, she would choke on the vomit and suffocate.

Thinking about that didn't really help.

Sofia had a major phobia about vomit.

When the kids were sick with stomach bugs, it was always Ryan who tended to them.

That putrid smell, the way it was all sloppy and mushy with chunks of half-digested food, it was disgusting. Even the thought of it was enough to get her stomach churning.

But Ryan just took it in his stride.

He cleaned it up like it was spilled orange juice.

That wasn't the only thing he was good at cleaning up.

He had helped her clean up the mess her life had become after her family's murders.

He had been there for her every step of the way. He'd taken care of her while she'd been recovering from her injuries. He had held her when her sleep had been plagued by nightmares; he had helped her rebuild her confidence in herself.

She loved him.

She *really* loved him.

The kind of love that could last a lifetime. The kind of love that could climb mountains and cross raging rivers and delve the depths of the deepest parts of the ocean.

How could she have even considered throwing that away?

She was an idiot.

Now she couldn't even apologize for pushing Ryan away and basically telling him that he wasn't good enough.

But he was.

He was perfect.

He was everything that she needed.

When she was down he didn't just lift her up, he told her that she was strong enough to lift herself up. When she was scared, he wasn't just her light in the dark, he reminded her that she could shine just as brightly on her own. When life got to be too much and she didn't know which way to turn, he showed her that she was already facing the right direction.

Ryan was the best thing that had ever happened to her, and she didn't want to lose him.

One minute.

That was all she needed.

One minute and she could have apologized; she could have made amends; she could have fixed things.

Now it could be too late.

She didn't know how much longer she could survive in here, or what Kimberly's plans were, but it had been ages since she had stopped the car and left.

A loud bang pierced through the haze she was descending into.

Gunshots.

Was it Ryan?

Had Kimberly enacted whatever plan she had cooked up and told Ryan that she was locked in the trunk of a car, then shot him as he came to rescue her?

It was too late.

Ryan was dead; she would soon be dead too.

The sense of loss was crushing.

Stifling her more than the relentless heat.

Her heart ached worse than any other pain she'd ever felt in her life.

* * * * *

3:32 P.M.

As Xavier tackled Kimberly Ute to the ground, Ryan ran to Macey Staines. She hadn't moved since they had come storming in here.

As soon as Macey had gotten Kimberly to admit that she had not only poisoned Deacon but murdered Amy, Tara, and Teagan, and attempted to kill Paige, they had started to move in, but unfortunately, they hadn't gotten here quickly enough to stop Kimberly from shooting Macey.

"Macey?" he called out as he dropped to his knees beside her. She was drenched in blood that had pooled out around her body. She didn't look good.

Macey's mouth moved but no sound came out, her eyelashes fluttered on her pale cheeks, but her eyes didn't open.

"Mom?" Elle dropped down beside him. "Is my mom going to be okay?"

Ryan put his fingers to Macey's neck and detected a pulse. It was weak but there. He had no doubt that someone had called an ambulance. The best thing they could do for her was try to stem the flow of blood until help arrived.

"We're going to do everything we can to make sure that she will be," he assured Elle.

Someone shoved a towel into his hands, and he pressed it to Macey's chest. They might have been too late to save Amy, Tara, and Teagan, but Paige had survived, and he and Sofia were safe, as was Elle. They just had to pray that Macey survived too.

"Kimberly took Sofia," Elle cried. "She's in the trunk of the car. She was going to use her to lure you and then kill you both."

Sofia was trapped in the trunk of a car?

It was over a hundred degrees outside.

In the trunk of a car, it would be …

He had to get to her.

"Go." Xavier knelt beside him and took over keeping pressure on Macey's wound.

They had watched Kimberly drive up, so he knew which car to go to.

Outside, he went straight to the driver's door, yanked it open and popped the trunk.

Sofia moaned when he opened it and the bright sunlight hit her eyes.

The sound was the best he had ever heard in his life.

She was still alive.

She was bound and gagged. He saw blood, but she was alive.

"Just hold on," he said as he scooped her up and carried her inside out of the heat of the sun. "I need cold cloths and cold water. Now," he screamed as he lay Sofia down in the living room.

Sofia mumbled and tried to say something but all that came

out was an indecipherable groan.

"Don't try to talk, sweetheart." He stroked her tangled hair. She was burning up and drenched in sweat. Which was a good thing. It meant she hadn't progressed to the heat stroke phase.

"Here." Xavier handed him a cold cloth.

Ryan blotted Sofia's face then pressed it to her neck to try to cool her down as Xavier poured cold bottled water over Sofia's body.

"Honey, can you hear me?" he asked, as he ripped off the gag.

"Mmm," she murmured, but she nodded her head.

Resting the cold cloth on her neck, he turned his attentions to the plastic zip ties that had bit into the tender flesh of her wrists and ankles. Pulling out the Swiss Army knife he had on his key ring, he leaned down and cut through the plastic at her ankles, flinching as Sofia winced. Then he carefully rolled her to her side so he could get to the zip ties at her wrists.

There was blood streaking the side of her head, and he took hold of her chin and tilted her face so he could see the gash better. It didn't look deep and he didn't think it would need stitches. Kimberly must have tried to knock her out so that she could kidnap her and use her to try to lure him to his death.

Kimberly Ute would spend the rest of her life in prison.

He would make sure of it.

"Ryan?" Sofia asked, her hands reaching up to clutch at his shirt the second he rolled her back down onto the floor.

"Just rest, sweetheart, an ambulance is coming." He leaned down to kiss her forehead.

Sofia shook her head and her eyes struggled open, seeking his. "I'm sorry. For the last few days," she said. Her voice was faint, but she was clearly lucid. "It was Deacon's death. No one seemed to care. It was my fault. I needed to be punished."

"Deacon's death was unfortunate, but the only person to blame is Kimberly," he assured her.

"I shouldn't have shut you out. I shouldn't have thought about

moving out."

He hated that the idea had ever entered her head. But it was what it was. He understood that taking a life had affected her in ways she had never even realized. The important thing was that she was alive and that they could put the last few days behind them.

"Don't worry about it, baby," he said, sitting beside her and sliding her head into his lap. "Don't worry about it."

Xavier brought more cold cloths and they positioned them on Sofia's groin, under her armpits and on her neck. Her body temperature was too high, but they should be able to start getting it down even before the paramedics showed up. It had been a close call, but Sofia would be fine. If Elle hadn't told him Kimberly's plans, then she might not have been. Kimberly had been so close to getting what she wanted.

So many people dead all because of an unwanted teenage pregnancy.

Fifteen years ago he doubted anyone could have predicted that this was how things would turn out.

Deacon and Macey had thought that they were doing the right thing, giving a home to a baby that Kimberly hadn't wanted. Ryan doubted that they would have done anything differently even if they had known this was how it would turn out. They did what they thought was best for their daughter, and that was what you did when you were a parent.

He thought of Sophie.

She was growing up practically right before his very eyes.

Soon they were going to have to sit her down and explain her own biological parentage to her.

He just prayed that she took it well.

Whatever happened, he knew he had his wife at his side. He and Sofia were better as a team than they were on their own. That's what marriage was. It was being with the person who didn't change you; they just made you a better version of the you

you'd be without them.

Cradling his wife's head, he leaned down and lightly whispered his lips across hers. "I love you."

A small smile curled her lips up. "I love you, too."

* * * * *

6:46 P.M.

As bad as she hurt and as bad as she felt, the only thing Macey was worried about right now was seeing her daughter.

It was all she had been thinking about ever since she had woken up from surgery.

If she had ruined her relationship with Elle by lying to her, then it would have been better for Kimberly's bullet to kill her.

What was the point in living without her daughter?

She had already lost so much.

Deacon was gone now, and if she had lost Elle as well, then she would be all alone in the world.

So much had happened over the last few days that she hadn't even grieved her husband. That made her feel like the worst wife in the world. The whole situation did. She should have known that something was wrong, that the man she married would never have turned violent and started hitting her and their daughter for no reason. Maybe if she'd had more faith in Deacon, then she would have taken him to a doctor when he first started exhibiting behavioral changes instead of hiding because she was scared and embarrassed about staying with a man who hit her.

If she had done that, then none of this would have happened.

Kimberly's plan would have been found out before it ever even really started. Then Deacon, the security guard, Amy, Tara, and Teagan would all still be alive. Paige and Sofia wouldn't have been hurt, she wouldn't be lying in a hospital bed, and her daughter wouldn't have been traumatized.

Macey would gladly take a million bullets if it meant she could spare Elle even a portion of the pain she must be feeling right now.

In her mind, she was already preparing for what she would do when Elle rejected her. She didn't have any family nor did she have any close friends, but maybe Sofia would be happy to have Elle continue to live at the center. Maybe if she stayed there, too, one day they could find a way to reconnect. But was it fair to stay at the center when she wasn't really an abused wife? Deacon's abusive behavior hadn't been his fault, so it felt wrong to stay at a place that was supposed to be for victims.

She didn't feel like a victim.

Just like a fool.

She and Deacon shouldn't have led Kimberly on. They had never intended to allow her to have any part of Elle's life; at least, so long as Elle was a minor and in their care. After that, there wasn't anything they could do to stop it from happening. If they had just said no the first time Kimberly came asking to have her daughter back, then maybe she would have been able to move on and found happiness and a family of her own.

The door to her hospital room opened and Macey didn't even have to look to see who was there.

She already knew.

She could always sense her daughter.

They shared a bond that she had hoped nothing could ever break.

Hesitantly, she turned her head toward Elle. She wasn't sure she wanted to see the anger and resentment and betrayal that she was sure would be in her daughter's face.

Slowly, her eyes met Elle's.

She didn't say anything.

Neither did her daughter.

She couldn't move even if she'd wanted to.

Elle didn't move either.

Macey didn't know what to say and Elle clearly didn't want to say anything at all. Maybe someone had forced her to come here; it was pretty clear she didn't want to be anywhere near this room.

She opened her mouth, wished she had some soothing words of wisdom that would heal this rift, realized she didn't and snapped her mouth closed again.

Then Elle's face crumpled, and tears rushed down her cheeks.

"Mommy." Elle ran the few steps across the room from the door to the bed then froze inches away. "I want to hug you, but I don't want to hurt you."

"I don't care, baby." Knowing her daughter wasn't angry with her was exactly the medicine she needed right now.

Elle threw herself into her arms, just like she had when she was a little girl. Pain knifed through her chest, but it was a small price to pay.

"I'm so sorry, sweetheart," she cried as she held her daughter.

"Why?" Elle asked.

"For lying to you. We should have told you, but your father and I just loved you so much, and we knew that Kimberly wasn't the right person to take care of you." She wanted to make Elle understand the choices they had made.

"I'm not angry with you. I don't care why you and Daddy didn't tell me. You were the best parents. I was so lucky to have you. I miss Dad, but we still have each other."

All her fears floated away.

Elle was right; they did still have each other. Deacon was dead, but Kimberly was in prison. She couldn't hurt them again. They could rebuild their lives. Their family might have changed, but it was still a family.

Despite everything that had happened, Macey knew she had done the right thing. She and Deacon had raised a daughter who was smart and sweet, compassionate, strong, and understanding. Kimberly hadn't been able to poison the woman Elle was becoming.

"Come and lie on the bed with me." She moved over a bit to make room for Elle. Her daughter climbed on and rested her head on her shoulder. When Elle was little they used to lie on the bed together on cold, rainy days and Macey would make up stories about princes and princesses and dragons and faraway castles. She had loved those times together.

Apparently, Elle was thinking of the same thing because her daughter began, "Once upon a time …"

* * * * *

7:53 P.M.

They were all together.

His family.

Ryan hadn't been able to wipe the smile off his face since he knew Sofia was going to be okay.

They were all going to be okay.

Laura was getting stronger, Paige was itching to get back on her feet and back to work, and Sofia had already been discharged. Kimberly was behind bars where she belonged, and the threat hovering over his family was gone.

It was crowded in here. The entire family had gathered in Laura's hospital room and they were one, loud, talking, laughing army. His parents were here, and Laura's parents, her sister and her family, both his brothers, Paige and Elias, Xavier and Annabelle, and all the kids. They'd eaten pizza for dinner, followed by ice cream, and then cotton candy, and enough soda to stock a small supermarket. It was safe to say the kids were hopped up on sugar and extremely hyper.

The kids were getting a little too rowdy and he thought it was time to start quieting them down. This was a hospital, after all, and it was almost eight at night. There were patients here who were no doubt not feeling well and wanting to go to sleep.

Ryan was just about to tell them to keep it down when the door swung open and Daisy stepped into the crowded room with a tall blond teenager.

The room fell silent.

Which in and of itself was a bit of a miracle. His family was large and boisterous and there were never silences when they were all together like this.

All eyes were on the teenager, and he shrank back, drawing closer to Daisy.

Daisy looked around at them nervously, like she wasn't sure how they were going to react. Ryan understood her uneasiness. The young man was her nephew who had been involved in the black-market baby business that Daisy's family had started several decades ago. Blaze had been raised by his father, Daisy's brother, completely isolated from the outside world. He knew nothing but the world of luring teenage runaways, caged girls in the basement, and ripping babies from their mother's arms to sell them.

"Everyone, this is Blaze; Blaze, this is everyone," Daisy said, a tight smile on her face. "Blaze is going to be coming to live with us."

Ryan hadn't been expecting to hear that.

His brother and sister-in-law had four kids, who were still coming to terms with what had happened seven months ago, and had to balance their family life with busy jobs, taking on a teenager who had lived through what Blaze had was going to be a lot of work.

From the silence in the room, it seemed like he wasn't the only one wondering how this was all going to work out. He had expected that Daisy and Mark would get to know the boy while he lived in foster care, and then maybe a few months from now, once Blaze had gotten some help and started to adjust, maybe have him move in.

After an uncomfortable ten seconds or so of silence—that felt much longer—it wasn't one of the adults who broke the ice.

No, it was Sophie.

His daughter who had an innate ability to seek out anyone who needed love and support and immediately offer it to them.

"Hi, I'm Sophie. Do you play baseball? I'm thinking of trying out for Little League for the fall, but I need someone to help me with my fast balls."

Blaze stood still for a moment, probably overwhelmed by the sheer number of people standing there staring at him. Together, they were kind of an intimidating bunch—especially like this with all thirty of them together.

But Sophie's warm sincerity did the trick, just like it always did, and Blaze gave her a shy smile. "My dad and I used to play baseball all the time."

"Cool," Sophie beamed. Blaze didn't know it, but with that answer, he'd just won a friend for life.

Ryan leaned back against the wall and watched as his family burst back to life. Sofia was right beside him, close enough that their bodies were touching, and he slid his arm around her waist.

Families.

They were complicated and difficult, a little nutty and crazy, often full of problems. Sometimes they could be a little malicious, taking out the hurt and anger inside them on one another, often dysfunctional, and occasionally even borderline psychotic. But they were also love and strength. They understood you even when you didn't understand yourself. They were your everything, your world, they were forever.

And he may be biased, but Ryan thought his was possibly the best family in the world.

Jane has loved reading and writing since she can remember. She writes dark and disturbing crime/mystery/suspense with some romance thrown in because, well, who doesn't love romance?! She has several series including the complete Detective Parker Bell series, the Count to Ten series, the Christmas Romantic Suspense series, and the Flashes of Fate series of novelettes.

When she's not writing Jane loves to read, bake, go to the beach, ski, horse ride, and watch Disney movies. She has a black belt in Taekwondo, a 200+ collection of teddy bears, and her favorite color is pink. She has the world's two most sweet and pretty Dalmatians, Ivory and Pearl. Oh, and she also enjoys spending time with family and friends!

To connect and keep up to date please visit any of the following

Amazon – http://www.amazon.com/author/janeblythe
BookBub – https://www.bookbub.com/authors/jane-blythe
Email – mailto:janeblytheauthor@gmail.com
Facebook – http://www.facebook.com/janeblytheauthor
Goodreads – http://www.goodreads.com/author/show/6574160.Jane_Blythe
Instagram – http://www.instagram.com/jane_blythe_author
Reader Group – http://www.facebook.com/groups/janeskillersweethearts
Twitter – http://www.twitter.com/jblytheauthor
Website – http://www.janeblythe.com.au

sic enim dilexit Deus mundum ut Filium suum unigenitum daret ut omnis qui credit in eum habeat vitam aeternam